Searching for Steely Dan

Searching for Steely Dan

Rick Goeld

Searching for Steely Dan

All Rights Reserved
Copyright © 2006 by GGFC Properties, LLC

No part of this book may be reproduced or transmitted in any form or by any means, graphic, electronic, or mechanical, including photocopying, recording, taping, or by any information storage retrieval system, without the written permission of the publisher.

No part of this book may be used in preparation of a derivative work without the written permission of the publisher.

This is a work of fiction. Other than "Steely Dan," "Donald Fagen," and "Walter Becker," all names and characters appearing in the book are the product of the author's imagination. Any resemblance to real persons, living or dead, is entirely coincidental.

ISBN: 1-4116-7682-3

First Printing: February, 2006
Second Printing: March, 2006
Third Printing, June 2006

This book is dedicated to Donald Fagen and Walter Becker.
They have kept the music and the mystique alive for more than 30 years.

This book is also dedicated to all of the musicians, technical people, and support people who have worked with Fagen and Becker over the years.

And, this book is dedicated to all the fans of Fagen, Becker, and Steely Dan.

> Eric (Rick) Goeld
> Scottsdale, Arizona
> January, 2006

Prologue

Sunday, April 11, 1993

Spring has sprung, and those breasts are about to spring right out of that dress.

Eddie Zittner eyed his wife-to-be from across the room and contemplated his good fortune. Alison was beautiful, and she loved him, and all was right with his world. He leaned against the wall, arms folded across his chest, and savored the aroma of beef and onions cooking downstairs. His younger brother, Mark, would get an eyeful of Alison's cleavage with his pot roast and mashed potatoes.

"That outfit sure looks good on you." He was getting aroused.

Alison turned and smiled. "That's three times you've said that today."

Sunlight picked up the blond highlights in her hair, and Eddie was reminded of the "Madonna Look" that Alison was trying to cultivate. He watched as she continued to wander. This was the first time she'd been upstairs in the Zittner home.

"The room is so bare, Eddie. Where is everything?"

"At my apartment, Alison."

"No stereo, no CDs, no nothing."

"They're all at the apartment. You've seen them. You've been there a hundred times."

During his years at Rutgers, first in a dorm and later in an apartment, he had moved most of his "essential stuff" out of this room, this bedroom—the room where he'd spent his teenage years. But he had left some memorabilia, mainly posters on the walls celebrating past glories of the Mets and Knicks.

He watched Alison as she moved to the dresser and nodded at two scruffy-looking men captured smiling in a picture frame. "Who are these guys?"

"Fagen and Becker. You know, Steely Dan?"

"That's it? Just these two guys? You never told me it was just two guys."

He moved across the room and grabbed her from behind, wrapping his arms around her belly as he pushed himself gently against her. He peered over her shoulder at the picture. "It was just those two guys, and whoever they hired to record with them." He felt himself getting harder.

Alison took his hands in hers, turned around, and began to grind her hips against his. "I'm beginning to feel your Steely Dan." She rubbed her husband-to-be through his khakis. A minute later, his pants and underwear were around his ankles, and she was down on her knees, kissing him.

"Let's do it," he said, predictably enough.

She looked up. "Here? In your bedroom?"

He leaned against the dresser, breathing hard. "Yeah. We have time."

"Your family is downstairs!"

"So what? Dinner won't be for another hour." He glanced at his watch. "Thirty minutes, anyway." He pulled her up by her shoulders and maneuvered himself onto the bed, pulling her down on top of him.

"Eddie," she whispered, "they'll hear us."

"No, they won't. Anyway, they know we're sleeping together. Christ, Alison, we're getting married in June." He watched as she leaned back and contemplated his penis, which was pointing due north. She leaned over and kissed it, then tweaked it with her tongue. He groaned as it twitched uncontrollably.

"Get on top of me."

"Wait a minute, Eddie. I've got to pee. Where's the bathroom?"

"Down the hall."

She kissed him one more time, prompting another series of twitches. "I'll be right back."

"Just hurry, please, Alison?" He watched as she eased off the bed, tiptoed to the door, opened it, slipped into the hallway, and closed the door behind her.

He lay there, penis throbbing, staring at the ceiling. He looked forward to being married to "the love of his life," marital bliss, and the regular sex that went with it. In fact, he wished they hadn't waited; they could have been married months ago. But her parents—both sets of parents, actually—had insisted they wait until after graduation. *So be it.*

He and Alison had been seeing each other for more than a year. They would graduate from Rutgers in June, both with bachelor's degrees, his in journalism and hers in marketing. A week later they'd be married—*finally!*—right here in Saddle River, at the synagogue where he'd had his bar mitzvah almost ten years ago. They would start out in near poverty, not that it mattered that much to him. They had already signed the lease on a starter apartment in Somerset, a town just down the road from Rutgers. The Kendall Commons was a huge complex of brown buildings, concrete driveways, and telephone poles. *Not very exciting, but cheap enough.*

He looked down at his penis. A few drops of liquid had formed on its tip. He felt like he was about to explode. *Where was she?*

Then he heard the bedroom door open, and he watched, stunned, as his mother stuck her head in and sang out, "Dinner is ready."

"Mom!" He quickly flipped onto his stomach, flinging droplets of semen against the second-story window.

Elaine Zittner blushed, eyes round as saucers, but she recovered quickly, and smiled knowingly. "It looks like someone is ready for dessert."

1

Tuesday, February 29, 2000

The man is a giant, with the brain of a reptile . . .

Eddie's thoughts trailed off, then rebounded with renewed frustration. *I can't believe this is happening. I should find the manager and make a big stink about this.*

But he wasn't the type to find the manager and make a big stink. And he knew it. His wife and mother had both told him to be more assertive, more times than he'd care to remember, and he was getting better at it. But outright confrontation was something he avoided.

"I'm sorry," the man repeated, leaning toward him from behind the counter.

At just under six feet tall and maybe 175 pounds on a good day, Eddie knew he wasn't a physically imposing person. He thought of himself as average. And the man across the counter, Reuben, had him by at least three inches and fifty pounds. Eddie knew he was no he-man, but he was no weakling, either. He stood as tall as he could. He would not be intimidated. Not this time.

"Reuben. You know me, Reuben. How could you do this to me?" He held his voice steady as he spoke. He remembered Reuben's name from that day two weeks ago when he'd reserved a copy of the CD. Not that anyone could miss the nametag pinned to Reuben's shirt, with letters that were, what, maybe two inches high?

Reuben looked puzzled. "How do I know you?"

"You took my reservation for the CD. Right here at this counter. See?" He held up the yellow copy of the reservation slip. "Your name is right here."

Reuben straightened and took a half step back, as if to avoid the truth. "Hey, I write up a lot of reservations. This is a busy store. Look around you."

He glanced at the line of people, just a few feet away, waiting to check out. Wearing bulky winter jackets, they looked like a herd of animals—buffalo, perhaps—swaying back and forth, threatening to encroach on his space. He would be trapped and crushed under their hooves, or squashed against the wall. *The key word is survival . . .*

The store was an oversized shoebox, he thought, a grey concrete turd of a building plopped down in the middle of a shopping center parking lot. No, you couldn't even call it a shopping center; it was just an overgrown strip mall. Everyone was funneled up to the front of the store and jammed into the one checkout line that was open. *This had to be the crummiest building ever constructed.*

"If you're so busy, why don't you have more registers open?"

"Well, partly because I'm standing here talking to you."

"Reuben, we're talking about *Two Against Nature*. Now what am I gonna do all week? Talk to my wife?"

"Why are you so hot on this particular CD?"

"It's Steely Dan, Reuben, Steely Dan. It's their first CD in twenty years."

"Who is Steely Dan, anyway?"

"You don't know who Steely Dan is?"

"I'm sorry. Never heard of them." Reuben forced a smile, dimly recalling his training in customer service. "When were they popular?"

"In the seventies and eighties; the early eighties, anyway. And now, of course; they made a huge comeback in the early nineties. How old are you, anyway?"

"I'm twenty-four," Reuben replied, staring at his tormentor with a mixture of disdain and amusement.

"Twenty-four. I would think that at your age, you might take an interest in the stuff you're selling. If you don't know anything about music, then why work in a music store?"

"Uh, I work here because of the big money they pay me. Can't you tell?" Reuben was more than a little perturbed. "And how old are you?"

"Twenty-nine."

"Hey, if you're twenty-nine, you must've been born in, what, 1970 or 1971? So how come you like this old Steely Dan stuff?"

How do you explain to someone why you like one rock group and not another?

He had discovered "The Dan" as a teenager. He remembered the exact moment, sitting in his room doing homework, when he heard "Deacon Blues" on the radio. It had mesmerized him. He bought the album, *Aja*, the next day, and began playing "Deacon Blues" over and over. His parents, driven half crazy, bought him a set of earphones to preserve what remained of their sanity. It must have been the spring of 1984, he thought, just before his father had gone into the hospital, and his mother had gone a little crazy. And just before he had started to play keyboard. He had immersed himself in Steely Dan's music.

Patience pretty much gone, Reuben continued, looking for a way to end the conversation: "Look. Like I told you before, we got ten copies of the CD in this morning's delivery. We were sold out in an hour, before we had a chance to check the reservations." He held the white copy of the reservation slip in his hand.

"I guess those CDs just jumped off the shelves."

"I said I was sorry. Look, we'll get another shipment on Thursday. I'll do the best I can for you, Mister . . ." Reuben glanced at the piece of paper. "Mister Zittner. Come back Thursday."

Eddie dropped his head and sighed, a gesture intended to gain a little more sympathy that only succeeded in making him look pathetic. But, in any case, it was too late. Reuben had already turned, and was stuffing the reservation slip into his shirt pocket as he moved behind the counter, heading toward one of the idle registers. He watched as Reuben stopped, squared his shoulders, took a deep breath, and switched on the overhead light. A half dozen people broke free of the first checkout line and formed a new one in front of him.

Eddie pushed through both lines and walked out the door, scanning the parking lot for his car. It was a rotten day, typical of late winter in northern New Jersey, and he frowned as he walked through the freezing rain. *Fuck work, I'm going home.*

2

For Alison Zittner, it had been "one of those days" at the office. The boss—the president of Jacobs Advertising Agency—had called one of his rare communication meetings. All hands were to be in the conference room by eight-thirty sharp. Helga, his Hitler-like executive assistant, had sent out an email imploring everyone to be on-time so the boss could make his eleven o'clock flight. No doubt heading for his cabin in Vail, Alison thought, or, maybe, this time, a quiet getaway on some tropical island. *The man had it rough.*

The meeting had started with a few interesting slides about the Tri-State media market. That had been followed by an avalanche of useless drivel: introduction of new employees, birth and birthday announcements—thank God there were no death announcements—and the inevitable warning about pilferage of office supplies. The meeting had mercifully ended just before ten.

She'd spent the next two hours polishing the latest revision of her Account Penetration Plan. Then, over lunch—your choice of ham, turkey, or roast beef sandwiches—the actual presentations. As the newest account executive, she'd been asked to present first. Her presentation, which over a period of weeks she'd worked and reworked and reworked until she was sick of it, had gone well. At least she thought it had gone well. But her boss had punched a hole in her ego with his well-worn phrase, silently mouthed by her colleagues as he verbalized it: "You're forecast isn't aggressive enough." She got the usual action item: revise your plan and have it ready for next week's torture session.

She'd snuck out at four, navigated through the early stages of rush hour traffic, and dragged herself into the apartment at a quarter to five. Once home, she dropped her handbag, briefcase and overcoat, made her way into the master bathroom, stripped off her clothes, and stepped into a spray of steaming hot water.

Ten minutes later, a revitalized Alison Zittner stepped out of the shower, grabbed a towel, and quickly dried herself off. *What to do with my hair?* Let it hang, she decided; she'd blow dry it later.

She turned to look at herself in the full-length mirror. Twenty-nine years old—just months from The Big Three-Oh—and still attractive, she thought. She struck a few poses, and poked at her hair with her fingertips. *I need a touch-up . . . the blond highlights are fading fast.* She ran her hands over her breasts—*still firm*—and belly—*still firm*—and finally around her hips and butt—*which, admittedly, needed work.* She made a mental note to get out and run this weekend. She glanced at the clock: five-fifteen. Eddie would be home in a couple of hours.

They'd been at each other's throats for weeks. What was it? Was she losing patience with him? Or was he just wallowing in self-pity? Was he depressed, or was it lack of ambition? He'd been a knight in shining armor, that first day they'd met at Rutgers. Tall, thin—well, not really thin, he was pretty well-built; "wiry" would be a more accurate description—with deep brown eyes, and long black hair that curled around his ears. He reminded her of Russell Crowe in *L.A. Confidential*: handsome in a rugged kind of way. Not too polished. Rough around the edges. But, in seven years of marriage, she'd come to realize that her husband was no Russell Crowe.

*****

Eddie Zittner guided his car through the maze of buildings and parking lots at the Georgetown Woods, the large complex he and Alison had moved to three years ago. Parking near their apartment, he noted for the umpteenth time that there were no woods anywhere in sight, just a few threadbare trees scattered around. *What ever happened to truth in advertising?* Georgetown Woods was nicer than Kendall Commons, he thought, but not by much. He unlocked the front door and stomped into the tiny entryway, scattering mud over the throw rug.

He heard his wife shout: "Eddie, is that you?"

"Yeah," he said as he walked into the kitchen. Alison, in sweater, jeans, and sneakers, was sipping wine while stirring a pot of last night's marinara sauce. He spotted a box of linguini on the counter, next to a half-empty bottle of merlot. "Why, expecting someone else?"

*****

She picked up on the attitude, but decided to let it go for the moment. "What are you doing home so early?" Eddie's shift at the drugstore ended at seven. He normally arrived home at about seven-fifteen.

"I went over to pick up that new Steely Dan CD and they didn't have it. They didn't hold a copy for me."

The end of the world is at hand. She knew that he had reserved a copy, and had talked about how great it was going to be having a new Steely Dan CD to listen to, which would have made this one boring week for her. She didn't know whether to be relieved or sympathetic or what. She put down the glass of wine and stared at her husband, arms crossed over her chest.

"What does that have to do with work?" she asked.

"I had a run-in with the guy at the music store, so I just said 'the hell with it' and came home."

"Oh, fine. I'm sure your boss will understand." She turned back to the marinara sauce.

"Do you know what's wrong with this country?"

I'm sure you're about to tell me. "No, what?"

"It's the incompetence of the working people."

"Do tell."

"Yeah . . . incompetence."

She could see that he was working up a head of steam. "Could you be more specific?"

"Yeah. It's the clerical help. They've got their heads up their asses."

She decided not to mention the fact that Eddie himself was clerical help, albeit a lead sales associate. "Go on," she said.

"Specifically, clerical help in music stores, and more specifically, a fat piece of shit by the name of Reuben who didn't hold a copy of that CD for me."

Correct that: a boring week with an unhappy husband. "Are you going to sue the bastards?" She raised her eyebrows, and thought about tapping the ashes off an imaginary cigar a la Groucho.

He scrunched his face. "Funny," he replied.

"Eddie, why didn't you just go to another store?"

"What makes you think other stores will have it?"

"Oh, yeah, excuse me, all the Steely Dan fans have already rushed right out and snapped up every copy in town. What was I thinking?" She watched as he sat down at the table. "Are you going to call your boss?"

"What for?"

"Uh, maybe to keep your job? Which is where you're supposed to be, right now?"

Eddie muttered a few words to himself. To her, it sounded like "fuck it," which she'd heard way too many times in the last few weeks. She put the spoon down, turned off the gas burner, walked over to the kitchen table and leaned over the chair opposite him.

She spoke softly. "Eddie, this is bullshit. You've got to stop with this obsession about Steely Dan. All the time, Steely Dan, Steely Dan, Steely Dan. I can't stand listening to that music anymore. I want you to call your boss, right now, and tell him you got sick and had to go home."

*****

He just sat there, head down, tapping the silverware with his fingers, staring at a pattern of yellow flowers on the placemat.

His wife raised her voice. "Eddie. Do it."

"Alison . . . I don't think I'm going back."

"Eddie. Another job you're going to walk away from? How many is that now?" He continued to tap on the silverware. His wife sat down opposite him.

She spoke softly again. "Eddie, you know I love you."

He looked up and smiled, trying not to look like a whipped dog. "I love you, too," he replied.

"But Eddie," she continued, "love is not getting us anywhere. What's happened to you? You used to be interested in writing. I haven't seen you sit down and write for months now. All you do is listen to that music, or fool around on your keyboard."

His head dropped, and he went back to staring at the flowers.

"Eddie. Why don't you try to get a job at a newspaper? Or a magazine? You have a degree in journalism, for Christ sake."

They had had this discussion—argument, really—many times. Why wasn't he using his degree? Or, why had he gotten a degree in journalism anyway? And then the inevitable: why not take some evening classes and learn how to do something else?

She leaned toward him. "Or why don't you go back to work at the bookstore?" He could tell she was trying hard to control her voice, but an edge had crept in. "Jerry's the manager now, isn't he? Call Jerry and get your old job back."

Jerry was his best friend, and had been promoted to store manager a few months ago. Alison liked Jerry. They had even gone out a few times together, he and Alison with Jerry and whoever he was seeing at the time. Jerry was a fun guy—"the life of the party," Alison liked to call him—and she thought he had a serious side to him, too. Career oriented, she thought. *He was manager of a fucking bookstore, for Christ sake.*

He snuck a peek at her. Her cheeks were bright pink, on their way to cherry red. She was about to come unglued.

"Eddie." Her voice rose. "What about the bookstore? What about writing? Or are you just going to sit around here and vegetate all day?"

He looked up at her. "Vegetation sounds good. I could probably be good at that."

She stood and moved away from the table. "Eddie, why don't you get out?" Her eyes flashed with anger. "Why don't you just *get the hell out*?"

"Maybe I will," he said, and regretted it immediately. He heard her mumble something that sounded like "I don't care anymore" as she turned and walked out of the kitchen. Uncharacteristically, she kept on walking. A few seconds later, he heard the front door slam, and then a car starting, backing up, and roaring away.

He had fucked up, and he knew it. A wave of fear shivered through him. It wasn't like Alison to get so angry. For a fleeting moment, he wondered what his life would be like without her. Then, pushing the negative thoughts from his mind, he got up, walked over to the stove, and turned the gas burner back on. At least he would have something to eat before he left.

3

After eating a bowl of linguini with marinara sauce—washed down with the rest of the merlot—Eddie packed an overnight bag, locked the apartment, and headed north toward his parent's home in Saddle River. He decided to take the direct route, right up the Garden State Parkway, and loaded The Dan's *The Royal Scam* into the car's CD player to keep him company. It was an hour's drive in normal traffic, but at nine on a Tuesday evening he could do it in forty minutes, still plenty of time to think about his situation.

He loved Alison—"the love of his life"—but he realized all too well that their relationship had deteriorated. He thought it had something to do with her career. In December, she had been promoted to account executive at the advertising agency, and she wasn't cooped up in the office anymore. She was out there drumming up business, pitching ideas, and meeting clients. *Meeting new people.*

And he had just been kicking around since college. After graduation and a June wedding, he had gone to work at a bookstore, a job he thought would be a good starting point for a career in writing. He wouldn't get bogged down, he thought. He could just do his job, come home, and work on his writing projects. And he had liked the bookstore. He had even done well there. After a year, he was in charge of the fiction department, and a couple of years later, a shift manager—no small accomplishment, he thought. But then came problems: clashes with a new boss, a matronly woman who insisted that he get to work on time, every single day, without fail.

After the bookstore had come a succession of jobs: a year selling furniture—good money, more than at the bookstore, until the boredom had finally overwhelmed him—and then sales positions at a home improvement store, and now a drugstore.

Since graduation, he had written a number of short stories, jumping from one genre to another, trying his hand at science fiction, mysteries, and even a literary attempt or two. He had even tried to write a novel. He wrote sporadically, when the mood was right, and when he felt inspired, which hadn't been very often in the last few months. He would compare his short stories to those he read in *New Yorker*, *Ellery Queen*, and numerous other magazines. When he thought he had something really good—after weeks of editing and revising and fine-tuning and word-smithing so that each sentence was "just right"—he would make his copies, write his cover letters, and send them off, sometimes fifteen or twenty submissions at a time. And then the rejection slips trickled in, one after another. He saved every one of them. He'd read somewhere that keeping your rejection slips was a good way to stay inspired. So far, it hadn't worked.

He parked in front of his parent's house, a two-story red-brick monster on Gabriel Way, and began walking up the gentle slope. He stayed on the granite walkway, which wound through beds of dead groundcover and rotting flowers, victims of the harsh winter. In another month or two, he thought, all these flower-beds would be completely replanted—by the gardeners, of course. He rang the bell, and immediately heard shouting inside, first by his mother: "Can you get that?" and then his father: "No, I can't, I'm busy," and then his mother again: "I'm busy, too," and then his father again: "So, we're both busy. You get it." It was like listening to the back-and-forth of a tennis match. He heard his mother again: "Harry, I'm upstairs," and finally, his father's concession: "All right, already." A few seconds later his father peeked through the entry window and then opened the door.

"Hey, Easy. What brings you to this part of the world?"

"Hey, Dad." Harry Zittner was a heavyset man with stick legs, and was wearing a Mets T-shirt, baggy shorts, and slippers—his normal attire for an evening in front of the television—but covered tonight with a heavy robe in deference to the weather. He had run his own accounting firm for more than twenty years, a one-man shop specializing in financial advice and preparation of tax returns. He'd finally sold out to H & R Block, and now managed an office for them in Teaneck.

He saw the overnight bag in his son's hand. "What's wrong?" he said as he beckoned him to come inside.

"Problems at home," Eddie replied as he walked in. His father closed the door and he followed him into the living room. This was the house his family had moved into, what, fifteen years ago, he thought, when he and his brother were in their early teens. The furnishings were contemporary Italian, dotted with artwork and lamps his parents had purchased on a number of trips to Europe.

"What kind of problems?" his father asked as he sat on the sofa, and then shouted in the direction of the stairs, "Ellie. It's Eddie."

Eddie glanced at the screen—his father was watching *Law and Order*—and sat down on the adjacent love seat. Seconds later he heard his mother's muffled reply: "I'm coming down."

His father picked up the remote and switched off the television. "So, you gonna tell me what's going on?"

Eddie looked up from the empty screen. "Let's wait for Ma, and I'll tell you both together."

They didn't have to wait long. A few seconds later Elaine Zittner glided down the stairs and made her entrance, wearing a silk robe and slippers. "Ellie the Shark" as she was known in the local real estate community had been a top-producing salesperson for as long as Eddie could remember. His mother had been very attractive as a young woman, and still worked hard at the gym to keep her figure. Her blond hair streaked with grey was a more accurate indication of her age; Eddie's parents were in their late fifties. He stood as his mother walked toward him. She smiled and gave him a hug.

"So, what's wrong?" she asked, the suspicious gleam in her eyes tempered by the concern on the rest of her face.

"Problems at home. Alison threw me out. Can I crash here tonight?"

"Sure," his father said. "What happened?"

"I was a jerk. I said the wrong thing."

"What?" his mother jumped in with a smirk. "Did you criticize her cooking?"

"I told her I was quitting my job, and she told me to get out, so I said 'maybe I will.'"

His father grimaced. "Eddie, we know Alison. She's pretty even tempered. What else is going on?"

His mother seized the opportunity: "Is it sex?" She grinned, displaying the mouthful of teeth that were yet another reason for her nickname. "What, you're asking for it too much? She's not giving it to you?"

"Ma, give me a break, will ya?"

"She's not good enough for you, anyway. Remember what I told you before you got married? She's too quiet for you. She's got no personality. You need someone with a little more life to her."

Like you, Ma?

"And she's not even a real Jew."

"Ellie!" his father said, indignant. Harry Zittner was always a voice of reason and tolerance. "She's a real Jew, just like us. She's a Reformed Jew."

His wife made a face. "That's not a real Jew in my book." She took pride in being a member of a Conservative congregation. She even went to services every now and then. And if she nagged him enough, she could get her husband to go with her—once in a blue moon. The temple was where she made most of her real estate contacts, but she was not averse to dealing with Reformed Jews. Or non-Jews.

But yet another thought had popped into her head. "I'll bet it's that crazy music you're always listening to. What is it you call it, steal something?"

"Steely Dan, Ma."

"Eddie," she said, serious now, intense, "You've gotta stop this craziness about that music, and find yourself a real job. Look at you. You're almost thirty years old, no career, no home, nothing. Look at your brother, Mark, with a good job and a nice apartment in Manhattan. And he's younger than you!"

"Ellie," his father said, "take it easy."

"Easy nothing, Harry. Mark has a nice career going, Alison has a nice career going, and Eddie's got nothing. That's probably why she threw him out."

"Ma, Dad, hold on. It's a lot of things with me and Alison. The job thing is just part of it."

"Stop with the craziness about the music, too. Why can't you listen to Celine Dion like a normal person?"

Eddie quickly suppressed a gag reflex. "Yeah, Ma, you're right. That's part of it. I'm probably driving her crazy with Steely Dan. It's just something I'm interested in, you know?"

"No, I do not know," his mother said, shaking her head like a bulldog tearing meat off a bone. "Grow up. Make something of yourself."

"Ellie—" His father jumped in, but it was too late. Elaine Zittner was already on her feet and moving across the room. Her husband and son watched as she disappeared up the stairs.

"Dad, listen, I'm just going to crash here tonight. Okay? I'll call Mark tomorrow. Maybe he'll let me crash at his place for a while. Maybe I can find a small apartment near his place."

"What, you're going to move to Manhattan now?"

"Yeah." He thought about it for a long moment. "Yeah, maybe I will."

*****

Over the objections of his father, who implored him to sleep in one of the guest rooms—his old bedroom, in fact—Eddie decided to sleep in the basement.

The basement was divided into two rooms: a large one paneled in wood, and a smaller, unfinished utility room that was dominated by the oil furnace. Eddie stretched out on an old sofa, the only piece of furniture left in what had been the family game-room. Moonlight filtered intermittently through long rectangular windows as clouds rolled across the sky. *Another storm coming . . .* He gazed at framed photographs that still hung on the walls, photographs that recorded family vacations in the Poconos and Adirondacks, and fishing trips to the New Jersey shore. He spotted a couple of old fishing rods leaning in a far corner, and a cardboard box overflowing with baseball bats and gloves. The billiard and ping pong tables and easy chairs were long gone, likely hauled away, he guessed, by a charity—tax deductions his father wasn't about to miss.

But fond memories of his childhood were soon displaced by worries about Alison. He tossed and turned, tangling himself in the sheets and blankets. Frustrated, he got up and took his CD player and earphones out of his overnight bag. He lay back down listening to *Gaucho. The end of a perfect day.* He drifted off to sleep.

4

Wednesday, March 1, 2000

Eddie woke early as sunlight flooded the room. After putting on a sweatshirt, jeans, and sneakers, he climbed up the stairs into the kitchen, where his father was making coffee, something his mother usually did.

"Morning, Dad."

"Hey, Easy, good morning," his father replied, fumbling with a coffee filter. And then his father looked up, and smiled, and his eyes danced, and Eddie remembered the face that had delighted and comforted him a thousand times as a child. "How was it sleeping in the basement?"

"Okay. It was fine, Dad." He plopped down on a chair. "Where's Mom?"

"Uh ... I don't know. She went out early."

Eddie glanced at his watch: just after seven. "What, a meeting?"

"I don't know," his father replied. "I didn't see her. Maybe she had a breakfast meeting, you know, or maybe she went to work out."

Or maybe she didn't want to see me.

Breakfast was a bowl of fiber-fortified cereal. Like many people of their generation, his parents were obsessed with calories and roughage and the like, and Eddie's father had had a number of health problems over the years. There was no other cereal in the house. Eddie sprinkled some Equal over it—no sugar in the house, either—and threw in a handful of raisins.

As they ate, his father asked him about the money situation: Did he understand how expensive it was to live in Manhattan? Did he need some help getting by? No, he replied, he was in good shape. He and Alison had socked away some money, and he didn't think Alison was nasty enough to keep him from having access to it. Anyway, we were talking about a few weeks, or maybe a month or two. He would find a job, a temporary job, in Manhattan. And he could always sell his car, he thought, if it came to that. He wouldn't need a car in Manhattan. His Honda Accord, three years old and completely paid off, should be worth something like ten grand. But he would need a car when he moved back to Somerset.

Then, in his own subtle way, his father steered the conversation back to those same points that a few hours earlier had been bludgeoned into Eddie's head by his mother. They talked about Eddie's career, his father making many of the same points, quietly and rationally, that Alison and his mother had made, and then advise, predictably, to focus a little more on his career and his marriage, and a little less on music. The soft sell, Eddie thought—as smooth as the opening riff of "Babylon Sisters." He nodded absently as his father spoke, and shoveled more cereal into his mouth.

After breakfast, his father went upstairs to finish dressing, and Eddie sat down to make some phone calls. The first one, to his boss at the drugstore, would be easy, he knew, because his boss didn't get in until noon. He left an apologetic voicemail, quitting for personal reasons—a family emergency, if you will—compelling him to take care of matters in another state. He planned to find the time to pick up his personal stuff "one of these days."

The second call, to his friend Jerry, was a little tougher. After a short discussion, he convinced Jerry to pick him up that afternoon at the apartment in Somerset and give him a ride to Manhattan. A pain in the ass, Jerry had complained, and he had countered that having a car in Manhattan was an even bigger pain in the ass, which was the reason why he wasn't driving himself. And anyway, Jerry was the store manager now, wasn't he? Couldn't he give himself a few hours off? Before Jerry could answer, Eddie had promised to explain that afternoon in the car. *Case closed.*

The third call, to his brother, Mark, was the tough one.

They had been close as children—two boys raising the usual kinds of hell in the neighborhood—but had grown apart in their early teens. Eddie had always been an avid reader, starting with comic books and progressing to adventure stories, mysteries, and science fiction. He still had stacks of comic books, and paperbacks, and a few years worth of *Mad* magazines stored somewhere in his parent's house. Mark had shared Eddie's love of comic books, but by his early teens had gotten interested in business, and making money, thus endearing himself to his father. Mark was the kid with the newspaper route; the kid selling magazines door-to-door. He learned how to use spreadsheets. He saved his money, and wanted to invest it in the stock market.

An interest in music was something else that the brothers had shared, initially with great reluctance, and then eagerly, but along diverging paths. Their parents, wanting to expose the boys to "culture," schlepped them to numerous plays and children's concerts. Elaine Zittner insisted that both boys take music lessons, and bought a baby grand piano specifically for that purpose, and to insure in-house compliance. After struggling through months of lessons, Eddie had begun to like it, surprising both himself and his parents. At fifteen, he was playing keyboard in a pick-up band that fooled around with rock and blues—anything they could play at school functions that might improve their chances of attracting girls. Mark had gone in another direction, taking to classical music, opera, and show tunes, yet another thing he had in common with his father. There were times Mark and his father would sit in the den, both doing their "math homework," listening to Brahms, or Mozart, or Leonard Bernstein. But Mark had also caught the downside of the gene pool, having begun to lose his hair in his late teens.

Eddie glanced at his watch: eight thirty. His brother was probably on his way to work. He dialed Mark's cell phone.

A few seconds later, Mark picked up: "Mark Zittner, may I help you?"

Formal, aren't we? "Mark, it's Eddie."

"Hey, Eddie. How are you?"

He sounds surprised that I called. How long has it been? "I'm fine, Mark. Uh, where are you? I figured you must be on your way to work."

"I'm already at work. Been here for an hour."

"You must be busy."

"No. We always start at eight."

How early did Mark wake up?

"So, Eddie," Mark continued, "what's up?"

"I need a place to stay for a few days. Do you mind if I crash at your place for a while?"

Silence on the line. Eddie knew Mark was quickly calculating his options. He figured his brother would weigh the benefits—*what benefits?*—against the risks—*loss of privacy? What else?* Mark must think I'm desperate, Eddie thought, to ask him for a favor.

Mark broke the silence. "Eddie . . . what's going on?"

"Alison threw me out."

"Oh."

"Look, I'll explain it to you later, you know, tonight, when I get there. I'll buy dinner." *Trying to close the deal . . .*

Mark hesitated, then replied. "How could I refuse an offer like that?"

Eddie sensed his brother's uncertainty. He took a deep breath. "Thanks, Mark. I really do appreciate it."

"Uh, what time are you coming?"

"What time do you usually get back to your place?"

"Around seven. You remember where it is?"

"I have it written down somewhere. On Third Avenue, right?"

"Good memory. The Future Condominiums, on the southeast corner of 32nd and Third.

"Got it. And Mark, thanks again. I really mean it."

"No problem." Mark said.

Eddie again heard the uncertainty in his brother's voice.

<u>5</u>

Eddie sat at the kitchen table, staring into his coffee, thinking about his next move. Call Alison? Stop by her office? No, too much anger and frustration, on both sides, to try that now. He could leave her a note at the apartment. He made a mental note to call Jerry again and ask him to come by at five-thirty. Then he gathered up his toiletries, repacked his bag, locked up, and headed south.

It was a cold, bright day. Last night's storm had cleared the haze that usually hung over the city, and had left a dusting of snow on the ground. Having decided to take Interstate 287, which was the long way but avoided the dense city traffic, Eddie first headed west on Route 17, stopping at a Dunkin' Donuts for a mid-morning sugar fix. This state gets a bad rap, he thought, as he chewed on a glazed donut. *Once you get away from the cities, it's a beautiful place.* He drove west and then south, through rolling hills interrupted by small towns and housing developments. He and Alison had driven out here many times, looking for a place where they might someday settle down, and even have a baby or two. He listened to *Can't Buy A Thrill* as he drove. Traffic was light and he made it to Somerset in just over an hour.

He pulled into the apartment complex wondering if Alison might be working from home, but her car was nowhere in sight. He went inside, tossed his bag on the sofa, and spotted a handwritten note sitting dead center on the coffee table. Alison had cleared off everything else: the wicker basket filled with assorted junk, the stack of magazines, the crystal bowl he had bought for her birthday a year ago; all of it had been moved to the mantle over the tiny fireplace. The only thing missing was a flashing neon sign that said: "READ THIS!!!" He sat down and picked up the note.

Eddie,

I think it best that we don't see each other for a while. We need some time apart. Don't you agree? Call me in a couple of weeks—perhaps we could talk then.

- A

He leaned back and closed his eyes. *Perhaps we could talk then.* He turned the phrase over in his mind. *Perhaps . . . what did that mean?* After thinking about it for a minute, he concluded that she was probably right, that they did need some time away from each other. He thought some more, then leaned forward and wrote below her note:

> *Am I that predictable? Were you sure I would come back today???*
>
> *-E*

After further thought, he decided to scratch that, and wrote instead:

> *I agree...Eddie*

A minute later, he picked up the note, crumpled it, and put it in his pocket.

*****

Jerry pulled up in front of the apartment at a quarter to six and honked the horn a few times, waking Eddie from a sound sleep on the sofa. A minute later, he was out the door, wearing one winter coat, carrying another, shouldering a large duffle bag, and pushing a huge roller-boy suitcase in front of him. The suitcase was filled with jeans, slacks, shirts, sweatsuits, and a variety of shoes—most of his wardrobe. The duffel bag contained his CD collection, CD player, keyboard, earphones, laptop computer, back-up floppies containing every short story he had ever written, and various other items, all packed in t-shirts, underwear, and socks. He had also packed his Steely Dan memorabilia: baseball caps and programs from the 90s tours, and a framed photo of Fagen and Becker taken in the late 1970s. That was it. There wasn't much memorabilia out there.

"Haitian Divorce," from The Dan's *The Royal Scam*, was blaring from Jerry's stereo. He turned down the volume, popped the rear door of his black Ford Explorer, and stuck his grinning head out the window.

"Hey, Zit."

"Hey, Jerome. Is there gas in the car?"

Jerry was momentarily confused, but then remembered the classic line from "Kid Charlemagne." "Yeah, there's gas in the car," he replied.

Eddie moved toward the back of the Explorer. "Jer, skip to the next track, will ya?" Nice that Jerry was playing The Dan—he was a fan, too—but he really didn't want to hear that particular track. Not today.

"Oh, yeah, sorry, man," Jerry said as he turned and punched a button on the dashboard. The first notes of "Everything You Did" began, just as Eddie knew they would. He had all the Steely Dan CDs, all except the latest one that is, and knew all the track sequences by heart. He loaded the suitcase, duffle bag, and spare jacket into the cargo space, slammed the rear door, and climbed into the passenger seat. The Explorer started rolling through the parking lot.

"You must have everything you own in those bags." Jerry had known Eddie for almost six years. He knew Eddie wasn't big on owning a wide variety of clothing—or anything that smacked of "fashionable." Eddie was a meat-and-potatoes dresser.

"Pretty much everything," Eddie replied.

"You don't have that many clothes."

"Hey, I don't know how long I'll be gone."

"So why Manhattan, man? You've got plenty of places to go."

But not your place, right, Jerry? That would cramp your style. Realistically, he hadn't expected Jerry to offer him the spare room at his place, a two-bedroom apartment in New Brunswick. Jerry usually had a steady girlfriend. He did pretty well with the grad students at Rutgers. But it was more than that: in the last few months, it seemed to him that Jerry had better things to do than hang out. It was almost like his best friend was avoiding him.

Jerry continued, "What about your parents' house?"

"You've met my mother. Enough said."

"Is she really that bad?"

"Yes. She'd drive me crazy from day one."

Jerry thought for a minute. "Hey, you could stay at my place for a couple of days."

What? Maybe old Jer wasn't doing so well between the sheets.

"You know," Jerry continued, "until you get your own place. My girlfriend is out of town this week."

That explains it. "Thanks, Jerry, but I really think I need to get out of town. You know what I mean?"

"But why Manhattan? You hate Manhattan."

"I don't hate Manhattan."

"Come on, Easy. Too many people and too much pollution: your own words."

"My brother, Mark, offered me a place to crash for a while." Jerry had never met Mark.

"Hey. I know why you're going."

"Why?"

"Remember that night we got drunk? You're going to see the man: the Dan Man."

Eddie was surprised that Jerry had remembered, as wasted as both of them had been that night, what, six months ago? The man—the Dan Man—was Donald Fagen, who lived in Manhattan and was one of the two founders of the band. Fagen played keyboard, and was thought to be the jazzier side of The Dan. Not that he had anything against Walter Becker, the other half of The Dan. Walter was very smooth, very cool on bass and lead guitar, and was thought to be more the rock and roll influence on the band. But who really knew? Little was known about the band and how their music was created.

Eddie looked east over the wasteland that was Elizabeth, New Jersey, with Staten Island a smudge in the background. They were driving north on the New Jersey Turnpike, heading right up the industrial gut of the state. Fields of railroad tracks and stacked metal containers spread out as far as he could see. Through the cloud cover he spotted the World Trade Center dominating the Manhattan skyline. Newark Airport was coming up on the left. The stereo was playing "Black Friday" from The Dan's *Katy Lied*. "Bad Sneakers" would come next.

That night we got drunk. It seemed like only yesterday. It had been a night when Alison was off somewhere, shopping, carrying on, or whatever it was she and her friends did together. After work, yet another day escorting browsers around the furniture store, he had picked up a pizza and a couple of six-packs and gone straight to Jerry's apartment. After eating the pizza and drinking most of the beer, they had gotten to talking about The Dan, and how sad it was that Fagen and Becker were so publicity shy—almost reclusive. Steely Dan had never been a mainstream band, not like Aerosmith or Journey, in large part because they had never toured when they were at the peak of their popularity. Except for some brief touring they did in the early seventies, they were a so-called "studio band." After a long quiet period, Fagen and Becker had come out again in the early nineties, first as participants in shows around New York City, and then with full fledged Steely Dan tours in 1993, 1994 and 1996. But Fagen and Becker were still reclusive. Since the 1996 tour, they hadn't been seen very often in public.

So Eddie had gotten pissed off—pissed off that good, loyal fans like the two of them couldn't see their heroes on television, couldn't see them flogging new CDs on Letterman and Leno, couldn't even see a candid photo, captured by paparazzi on the street. Couldn't get an autograph! Eddie had made a vow, right then and there, after consuming another couple of beers, that he would find Fagen and Becker, track them down, and meet them, shake their hands, congratulate them, get their autographs, and then, maybe, buy them a beer—or a cup of coffee, if they preferred. Or whatever.

Before, Eddie had been a fan, an avid fan, but now he really started to dig, doing research with a vengeance, trying to find out what made those guys tick. He went to bookstores and libraries and pored over reference books. He re-read the liner notes on all his Steely Dan CDs, and searched the web for any shred of information that might give him a clue as to their whereabouts. But there was very little; next to nothing. Those guys were invisible. Who were they? Where did they live? What the hell did they do all day? And slowly, like a newborn turtle crawling toward the ocean, the idea hatched in Eddie's mind: he would find out where they lived, the reclusive Fagen and Becker, and seek them out.

After what he thought was a prodigious effort in a noble cause (and what his wife thought was a colossal waste of time), he determined that Fagen had been spotted at a few jazz clubs in Manhattan. From this, and other evidence, he concluded that Fagen lived in Manhattan, most likely in the Upper East Side, at least part of the time. Becker was easier to find: the liner notes of a couple of CDs indicated that he lived in Hawaii, on the island of Maui. Eddie had never been to Maui, had never been to Hawaii for that matter, but he figured, hell, how big was Maui, anyway? How difficult would it be to find one person?

But Fagen was closer, so he'd start there, looking for him, probably camped in a nice, quiet, secluded, whatever-kind-of-place-he-lived-in, right across the Hudson River. There were, however, a few minor details. The first, and, perhaps, the biggest: Fagen's exact address, a closely guarded secret. And, once he had that, there would likely be security people who would discourage his quest. Obstacles to overcome, sure, but were there not obstacles in every noble endeavor? Wasn't this worth doing?

An even bigger problem: he wasn't all that comfortable in Manhattan. Jerry had been right: Eddie didn't like the crowded streets and the pollution. Not that northeastern New Jersey was the Garden of Eden, but Manhattan was definitely worse, with lots of cars, trucks, and people, some of whom were pretty unsavory. And aggressive. People who, perhaps, wouldn't take kindly to someone loitering on the sidewalk.

Alison hadn't understood at all, hadn't understood why her husband would be interested in meeting a couple of aging rock stars. Hero worship was for teenagers, she had said. After a couple of attempts, he had stopped trying to explain it to her. But it would have been hard for him to explain it to Jerry, who was a friend and a Dan Fan. He had trouble stating precisely what it was he was feeling to anyone. His life was on a downward spiral—going to shit, really—and he couldn't seem to get it back on track. Meeting

The Dan was something that might somehow inspire him, might somehow give him some new ideas. It might even get him writing again.

    Eddie gazed out over a tangle of iron bridges, steel towers, and smokestacks that seemed to fade into the gloom. As they approached the entrance to the Holland Tunnel, "Any World (That I'm Welcome To)" was playing on the stereo. He glanced over at Jerry. Not only does he not have a care in the world, Eddie thought, he's probably getting laid a lot more often than I am.

6

Thirty minutes later, Eddie dragged his suitcase and duffle bag through the revolving glass doors of The Future, a high-rise condominium in the Murray Hill section of Manhattan. *What happened to the heat?* And the lobby's stark grey marble interior only added to the chill. He spotted an older man, perhaps sixty, wearing what passed for a guard's uniform, sitting behind the podium reading *The New York Times*. A portable heater blasted hot air over the man's shoes. Eddie identified himself, and the guard, not looking up, buzzed him into the elevator lobby. *Great security!* Two minutes later, he was on the twenty-eighth floor, shoving his luggage through the elevator doors.

Having heard the doors chime open, Mark came out of his apartment, turned toward Eddie, and, inexplicably, raised his left arm as if hailing a cab on the street. "Hey, Eddie," he said.

Eddie, struggling with his luggage, looked up and replied, "Hey, Mark, can you give me a hand?"

What happened next was one of those awkward moments when people who know each other well, but have drifted apart, perhaps more than a little apart, come together and attempt to greet each other. Mark, caught unaware by his brother's request for help, at first hesitated, and then took a faltering step forward. Seconds later, Eddie arrived at the apartment door, dropped his luggage, and extended his right hand. Mark, however, had reached down with his right hand and grabbed the duffle bag's strap. Noticing his brother's hand extended toward him, he offered his left hand, palm turned outward, in an awkward attempt to reciprocate. Thus began a clumsy handshake, with Eddie's right hand grasping Mark's reversed left. Both realizing the awkwardness, they released their grips, grinned, and proceeded to the next stage: a brotherly hug while leaning over two large pieces of luggage. Disengaging, the brothers finally worked their way around the luggage and consummated the hug, complete with a few slaps on the back and mumbled greetings of "long time no see," and "good to see you, too."

Five minutes later, having stowed the luggage in the spare bedroom, and Eddie having duly noted and admired the remarkable view overlooking the East River and the boroughs of Brooklyn and Queens, the brothers were back on the sidewalk, heading in the direction of Ming's, a good Chinese restaurant that Mark knew. It was near freezing, and a salty grit crunched under their shoes as they walked. Eddie remembered the smell, the unique smell of commercial Manhattan: a mixture of diesel exhaust and spilled garbage and cheap food and who-knew-what-else.

In short order they were in the restaurant, sitting at a booth by the window, drinking beer, and waiting for the food to arrive. It seemed to be a decent place, Eddie thought, as he scanned the crowd. He spotted a few Asian families, and considered that a good sign.

Neither brother had yet broached a serious subject. Mark, whose philosophy was that the best defense is a good offense, made the first probe, the tentative jab of a boxer trying to get the feel of his opponent.

"So, Eddie, what's going on with you and Alison?"

Right to the point. At least he remembered her name. "Well, Mark, it's been coming for quite a while now. I just think we need some time apart." As he said the words "time apart," Eddie thought he detected a flash of concern on his brother's face. Careful, he thought, I don't want to scare him before I even unpack.

"What do you mean, it's been coming for quite a while now?"

"Well, you know," Eddie replied, "we both have our own interests, and, you know, we're both pursuing our careers, so . . ."

His brother continued to probe: "So?"

He fumbled for the right words, "So, it's just gotten pretty tense in the last few months."

"I'm sorry to hear it," Mark said, leaning back in his seat.

"Yeah." Eddie sighed, took a deep breath, and plunged on. "But, you know, deep down, we love each other, and, well, I think . . . I hope we'll be together again, soon."

"What's Alison doing now?" Mark asked. "Still at the ad agency?"

"Yeah, she's still there, five years now."

"Five years. She must be running the place."

"No," he parried as he finished his beer and signaled to the waiter for two more. "No, not quite yet. She's a junior account executive." *Emphasis on the junior.*

The food arrived, and the waitress arranged the platters and bowls in the center of the table. The sizzling black pepper shrimp was still sizzling, but the egg foo yung just sat there like malignant pancakes coated with congealed maple syrup. Eddie dug into the shrimp, while Mark grabbed a couple of barbequed ribs.

"Mmm," Eddie said, chewing on a shrimp, "that is so good."

"Chinese food," Mark smiled, "medicine for the blues."

Eddie popped another shrimp into his mouth. "Mark, do you mind if I ask you kind of a personal question?"

His brother sampled the egg foo yung, made a face, and dropped it back onto his plate. "Go ahead."

"How can you afford that apartment?"

"It's a condo. I know the owner from work. He's been in London for a year, opening a new office. I'm doing him a favor by looking after it."

"Some favor. What's it cost you, if you don't mind my asking."

"I pay him two thousand a month, and I'm responsible for the utilities." Mark smiled. "Shit, I couldn't afford to own a place like that."

Eddie whistled softly. "When does the owner come back?"

"In a couple of years."

"Nice." Eddie helped himself to a spare rib, and more shrimp. "So, Mark, what else is going on with you?"

"What else?" Mark pondered the question. "Well, things are going well at work."

"What are you doing these days?" Eddie knew very well what his brother did for a living. His mother reminded him every chance she got.

"I'm still in investment banking," Mark replied, as if that answer was sufficient for someone like Eddie, who didn't understand the world of finance and big business.

"I still don't understand what it is you do there," Eddie continued, perhaps subconsciously playing for time.

"I analyze deals."

"What kind of deals?"

"All kinds. You know, real estate, mergers and acquisitions, stuff like that."

"Sounds interesting."

"I'm just doing analysis, verifying facts, running the numbers, doing on-site evaluations; that kind of thing. It gets really interesting when you get into the negotiations."

"On-site? Does that mean you travel?"

"Some . . . once or twice a month."

Eddie decided to change directions. "So, how's your love life?"

Mark put down his chopsticks and wiped his mouth.

"Pretty good, I guess. Slow at times."

"You dating anyone in particular?"

"No. Not really." Mark attempted to reclaim the initiative. "So, Eddie, where are you working now?"

I should have seen that one coming. "Uh," he hesitated, "after this thing happened with Alison, I had to quit my job." *No way I'd commute from Manhattan to Somerset every day!* "I'm just going to find something around here. You know, something temporary."

"Do you need some help?" Mark asked, reflexively leaning forward and extending his hand toward his back pocket as if reaching for his wallet. "You know, just to tide you over?"

"Thanks, Mark, but I'm okay."

The conversation drifted into less troubled waters. When the check came, Eddie grabbed it, as he had promised he would.

7

Thursday, March 2, 2000

Eddie woke, sat up in bed, and looked around the spare bedroom. It was small but well organized, with desk, dresser, leather chair, and bed fitting snugly around the room's perimeter. The desk and dresser had a deep mahogany finish, and the leather chair, piled high with pillows and bed spread, was a rich shade of tan. Eddie's suitcase and duffle bag sat in the middle of the room, right where he'd dropped them last night. He got out of bed and walked to the window, which faced south. The view was completely blocked by an office building. *Can't have everything.* He put on a flannel shirt and corduroy pants—the same clothes he wore yesterday—straightened the sheet and blankets, and strolled into the kitchen.

Eddie didn't know what to expect, but the smell of bacon and coffee put a smile on his face. He found Mark humming something from *West Side Story* as he scrambled eggs in a porcelain bowl. Over breakfast, the brothers talked, not jabbing away at each other as they had done the night before, but instead talking about the ongoing battles between Mayor Guiliani and Hillary Clinton, the local sports teams, and, of course, their parents. After breakfast, they moved into the living room and quickly scanned through the *Times* as clouds rolled across windows overlooking the East River. Minutes later, the sky cleared, and the boroughs of Brooklyn and Queens spread out before them, backlit by the morning sun.

Mark asked Eddie if he wanted to join him at his fitness club, which was a few blocks away. After they worked out, he would take a cab to work and Eddie could come back to the apartment. But Eddie declined, explaining that he needed to get out and start looking for a job and a place to stay, a good cover story for hitting a few music stores. He appreciated his brother's hospitality, but didn't want to get quite that comfortable in Mark's world.

After showering and dressing, Eddie locked the apartment and took the elevator down to street level. No guard on duty, he noted, and the lobby was still freezing. He hopped on a northbound bus, and by early afternoon had purchased a copy of *Two Against Nature* at a Tower Records store in Midtown. Back out on the sidewalk, he loaded the CD into his Walkman, adjusted the earphones, and began listening as he walked south. It was bright and sunny, but the wind had picked up, and he was blasted with dust and dirt at every intersection. The streets were jammed with shoppers, hawkers, and drifters, more than he expected on a Thursday afternoon, and there were times he had to weave through the crowds.

By the fourth track, "Janie Runaway," he was frowning. The CD was, he thought, a bit of a disappointment. Yeah, sure, it was Steely Dan, but it was somehow different. Some of the old riffs were there. Some of the music was vaguely familiar, reminiscent of the great old stuff, but it was mostly too new, too "jazzy," and, even, in a strange way, alien. By the time he reached 40th Street he was shivering, and he flagged down a taxi. *No point freezing to death.*

Minutes later he was back in the apartment. He decided to give the CD another shot. After all, it was The Dan, and sometimes you had to listen to music a few times to get the feel of it. So he stretched out on the bed, turned on the Walkman, plugged the earphones into his ears, and began listening. The music was a little more familiar, sure, but still, well, strange. *Yet another reason to track down Fagen and Becker.* By the end of the third track, he was asleep.

*****

Mark banged the door open and flipped on the overhead light, waking Eddie from a sound sleep.

"Hey . . ." Eddie said, momentarily disoriented. He squinted up at Mark, who was a blurry silhouette in front of the window. "Hey, Mark. What time is it?"

"It's almost seven, Eddie. I thought you might want to get up." Mark was wearing a maroon turtleneck under a charcoal-grey suit that looked like money, Eddie thought, and he had a black overcoat folded over one arm.

"Yeah," Eddie said, "thanks. Where are you going?"

"I've got a date."

"Oh . . . good. With who?"

"One of the girls at the office."

"Oh. Where are you going?"

"Just dinner. Look, I've got to run. You've got the whole place to yourself tonight."

"Okay . . . good."

"I'll see you later. Don't wait up, I might be late," Mark said, going out the door.

"Okay, Mark. Have a good time."

A few seconds later, he heard the apartment door close. He rolled out of bed and stretched, and then went into the bathroom to take a leak and splash cold water on his face.

He was starving, and there was nothing interesting in the refrigerator. Scrounging around in the kitchen cabinets, he found a pile of take-out menus, including one from Ming's. He grabbed the phone, dialed the number, and was soon ordering the sizzling black pepper shrimp and vegetable fried rice. An hour later, he was eating while listening to the CD again, this time on the Bose stereo system in the living room. Still strange, he thought, as he finished off the shrimp.

He spent the next hour planning what he needed to accomplish in the next few days. Find a job and an apartment; those had to be items one and two on his "things to do" list. What else? Track down Fagen's address, that was item three. He could do some more web searching and try to narrow it down to at least a neighborhood. And call Alison. Try to re-establish communication. Or maybe an email would be better. Or maybe he should just wait. He'd have to think about that for a while. He spent the rest of the evening reading Richard Russo's *Nobody's Fool*. Russo was special, he thought, an author who told great stories using beautiful prose. Finishing the book, he speculated on where his brother might be. *Probably out painting the town.* Eddie went to bed at the stroke of midnight.

8

Friday, March 3, 2000

    Eddie smiled as he arranged placemats, dishes, silverware and napkins on the kitchen counter. He was making progress, at least on some fronts. This morning he had started looking for work, and had lucked into a pretty good job at the brand new Borders on Second Avenue, just a long city block from his brother's apartment. The manager, a "take charge" guy who reminded Eddie of his mother, had asked him to browse around the store while he checked out Eddie's references. Twenty minutes later, after verifying his credit history and phoning Mark and Jerry, the manager had hired him on the spot, guaranteeing twenty-five hours a week, with more possible if he was willing to work. He had worked four hours this afternoon, quickly learning the ropes, and would work a ten-to-six shift tomorrow.

    He'd also spent some time surfing the web, researching Fagen's address. There were plenty of places to look: an official Steely Dan website, purportedly run in cooperation with Fagen and Becker—no way of telling how true that was—and literally dozens of sites run by fans that contained guest books, obscure lyrics, and just about any kind of trivia one could imagine. But there were damned few clues about Fagen's address. There were the names of a number of New York based recording studios that The Dan had used, and he looked up those addresses in the telephone directory, or on-line. He did find a few candid photos: one of Fagen on the sidewalk somewhere in Greenwich Village, another of Fagen coming out of Iridium, a jazz club on the Upper West Side, and a third of Fagen walking near the Guggenheim Museum. Eddie knew that musicians like Fagen had money, and lived in upscale neighborhoods. Perhaps near the Guggenheim.

    Thinking about nice neighborhoods, and not-so-nice neighborhoods, Eddie remembered his father's comments earlier in the week about the cost of living in Manhattan. He had looked at one tiny studio apartment in SoHo, which was barely within his ability to pay, even for a few weeks. A sublease anywhere in Manhattan would pretty much eat up his take-home pay, and he still felt obligated to help Alison pay the rent on their apartment, not that he'd spoken to her about that or anything else. And then there was the cost of the subway, and bus fares, and other details, like eating every day. He looked out the window and wondered what it would cost to live across the river.

    A minute later, his brother unlocked the front door and walked into the kitchen, a brown paper bag hanging from each hand. "Hey," Mark said, placing the bags carefully on the counter.

"Hey. How was work?" Eddie asked.

"Good. I got a lot of things done. It was pretty quiet today."

Eddie picked up the aroma of garlic and oregano. "Italian food?" He rubbed his hands together in anticipation.

"Yeah, from La Pizzaria, across the street. We're Zittner's, remember? We eat Italian at least once a week." Mark's voice boomed as if he were about to break into operatic song; then he started to unload plastic containers. "Let's see, two giant servings of lasagna in this one, and garlic bread in this one." He loaded the lasagna into the microwave and started the warming cycle. "Eddie, can you get the salad? It's in the other bag. And grab a bottle of red wine?"

"Will do," Eddie replied, unloading a container filled with lettuce, cherry tomatoes, sliced onions, and peppers. Minutes later, the brothers were sitting side-by-side at the kitchen counter, savoring beefy lasagna covered with a rich tomato sauce.

Mark was in a good mood, Eddie thought, the happiest he'd seen him since, well, yesterday, over breakfast. But, having spent the last few years separated by more than just the Hudson River, his brother was a bit of a mystery to him. In high school, Mark had been a serious student, and hadn't dated much. Then he'd attended Northwestern University in Chicago; not that far from New Jersey, but far enough to create more distance between them. Now, his brother seemed to be a workaholic, focusing on his job, but, surprisingly, he'd gone out last night, a week-night, coming home well after Eddie had gone to bed. Mark hadn't said anything about who he was dating, other than identifying her as a girl from work, perhaps implying that more than one was in-play. Eddie realized that, other than that first dinner, and yesterday morning, they'd hardly seen each other. At least they were getting along, if not completely comfortable around each other.

"So," Mark asked, "did you get that job at Borders?"

Eddie remembered that the store manager had called Mark. "Yeah. I even worked four hours this afternoon. I guess I have a special talent for working in bookstores."

"Well, great," his brother replied, biting into a piece of garlic bread, "at least you found something. Did you look at that sublet you saw in the paper?"

"Yeah, I took a look at it."

"And?"

"Well, it was small, a studio, you know, but it was nice enough. Expensive, though." He picked at the lasagna with his fork. "With my finances being what they are, it'll have to be a place like that, or some flea-bag hotel, I guess."

Mark put down the garlic bread and took a sip of wine, then swiveled to face his brother. "Eddie, look, I've been thinking, why don't you just stay in the spare bedroom?"

"Mark, I couldn't put you out like that."

"It wouldn't be putting me out. Not really. Hell, we hardly see each other."

Eddie, embarrassed, dropped his eyes and took a large gulp of wine. Yeah, he thought, we're like two ships passing in the night. Then he thought Mark might be talking about more than just the last couple of days.

His brother continued, "I mean, look at my schedule, and yours, now that you'll be working. We'll probably cross paths what, once or twice a day, tops? And I'll be traveling some of the time."

"Mark, I really don't want to impose. That wasn't my intention."

"You wouldn't be imposing. Brothers, remember?" Now Mark looked away, perhaps worried that he was getting too close. But then he turned back toward Eddie with a grin, "Anyway, we're talking about a few weeks, right?"

"A few weeks . . . hopefully."

"It's no big deal, Eddie."

"Hey," Eddie said, punching his little brother lightly on the shoulder, "you're going to embarrass me. See?" he said, pointing at his face. "Tears."

"You always were a crybaby," Mark snorted as he grabbed the last piece of garlic bread.

Eddie smiled. *Memories rush over me. We called each other "crybaby" when we were kids.*

9

Saturday, March 4, 2000

A persistent buzzing, like flies caught in a screen window, woke Eddie out of a sound sleep. He glanced at the clock radio—just after seven—reached under the bed, and picked up his cell phone.

"Hey," he mumbled.

"Zit, it's me, Jerry."

Eddie yawned. "Jer. Why you calling so early?"

"Did you see The Dan on Letterman last night?"

"What?" He sat up.

"Steely Dan. They were on Letterman last night. Didn't you get my message?"

Eddie turned on a lamp and held the phone under it. The message indicator was blinking away. "Shit no, I never got your message. I must've crashed after dinner. When did you call?"

"Right before they came on. After midnight. I turned it on just by chance. It was just dumb luck, my friend."

"No shit."

"No shit. The Dan on Letterman. It was unreal. They were hyping that new CD they just released."

"*Two Against Nature.*"

"Yeah. They played something from it."

"What? What did they play?"

"I don't remember . . . but I taped it for you. Right over *The Sopranos.*"

"Shit. I don't believe I missed it."

"You missed it, Zit."

"Shit."

"Zit, I've got to go. I'm opening the store today."

"Okay. Hold on to that tape for me."

"I will. Hey, Zit, you know what this means?"

"What?"

"Fagen and Becker. They're both in the city. In Manhattan."

10

From: EZEddie32@nyc.rr.com

To: HeyNineteeen@dandom.com, AlbertW500@nyc.rr.com, GGrimme8@cornell.edu, RSF6729@aol.com, MarKau55@nyc.rr.com, KBalla42@earthlink.net, Fuzzy77@yahoo.com, CoolK567@bellsouth.net

Subject: REQUEST FOR HELP

    I am a big fan of Steely Dan. I got your email addresses by searching the web. You guys all maintain SD related websites, or refer to SD on your website, or are mentioned as "knowledgeable fans." You might be able to help me out.
    I have not been able to find much SD memorabilia. There is almost nothing worth buying on eBay or any of the other sites that sell memorabilia. I've checked some stores in Manhattan and also struck out. By the way, I'm from New Jersey but living in Manhattan temporarily. Any of you living in the City?
    So anyway, I figured, maybe I can at least get an autograph at one of Fagen or Becker's "infrequent" appearances in Manhattan. I know they're in the City since they appeared on Letterman this week. Do any of you know where they hang out? I thought about hanging around Fagen's neighborhood (the best address I could come up with is 1675 Madison Avenue) and see if I could spot him, and maybe get his autograph. Or, maybe I would have better luck hanging around their recording studio (River Sound at 312 East 95th Street).
    Any suggestions or help would be greatly appreciated.
    Thanks in advance…
    EZEddie

****

To: EZEddie32@nyc.rr.com

From: KBalla42@earthlink.net

Subject: FUCK OFF, PSYCHO

    Hey, psycho, if you know anything about the Dan, you would know that they value their privacy. Real fans know enough to leave them alone. So go back to your hole in New Jersey.

****

To: EZEddie32@nyc.rr.com

From: Fuzzy77@yahoo.com

Subject: Re: REQUEST FOR HELP

  Thanks for your email!! It's always good to hear from another Dan Fan!!
  Anyway, I live in Seattle and run the SD Fan Club out here. We have over 100 people on our mailing list!!! I've never been to New York, and have no idea how to reach Fagen and Becker. Hey, you know Becker lives in Hawaii, right? Most of the memory-belia I've seen out here is from the tours the Dan did in the 90s. I'm not much for memory-bilia myself. I just groove to the sounds!!
  Have you listened to *Two Against Nature* yet? (assume you have if you are a Dan Fan) It is unbelievable!!!!!!!!
  Have a nice life!! Give me a shout if you are ever in Seattle!!
  Fuzzy

****

To: Fuzzy77@yahoo.com

From: EZEddie32@nyc.rr.com

Subject: Thanks

  Hey, thanks. Yeah, I know Walter lives in Hawaii. I forgot to mention it in my first email.
  …EZ

****

To: EZEddie32@nyc.rr.com

From: AlbertW500@nyc.rr.com

Subject: SD

  EZEddie, I get all the SD newsletters and monitor all the websites. Fagen and Becker are nearly invisible. Of course, Becker lives in Hawaii, but he hangs in New York quite a bit, if you believe the newsletters. Sometimes Fagen sits in at one of the jazz clubs in Manhattan. You might try asking around at Iridium or the Blue Note.
  Albert

****

To: EZEddie32@nyc.rr.com

From: MarKau55@nyc.rr.com

Subject: You've got the wrong address

    EZEddie, your search must have picked up the reference I have on my personal website. (Steely Dan Rules!) I don't know how you came up with 1675 Madison, but that's not it. I have it on good authority (I'm not saying how I found out) that Fagen lives at 59 East 88th Street. You're right on with River Sound, but that's no big secret, you can probably find it in the telephone book.
    Hope this helps
    MarKau

****

To: MarKau55@nyc.rr.com

From: EZEddie32@nyc.rr.com

Subject: Thanks

    MarKau55, thanks for the info, it helps a lot. I see we have the same domain. We can IM each other. Where are you located?
    EZEddie

****

MarKau55: I live in the East Village, and work at Zabar's on 80th and Broadway. Have you ever heard of it? We have the best smoked fish in the city…MK
EZEddie32: I've heard of it, but never been there. Hey, as a way of thanking you for your help, can I buy you lunch? How about tomorrow (Tuesday)? I don't have to be at work until two…EZ
MarKau55: Why not? We both have to eat, right? I'll do you one better, I'll bring the food (you can pay me back). How about nova, sable carp, bagels and cream cheese, etc? I can meet you at noon, right in front of Zabar's . . . Okay? If it's not too cold, we can eat on one of the park benches…MK
EZEddie32: Sounds good. I love nova, but never tried sable carp. How will I know you? EZ
MarKau55: I'll be wearing my SD hat from the 1994 tour. Sable carp is just another kind of smoked fish. See you tomorrow…MK

11

Tuesday, March 7, 2000

Standing on the corner of 80th and Broadway, Eddie scanned the sidewalk, looking for a Steely Dan hat. Zabar's had five doors facing Broadway, each under its own archway, with each archway sporting a bright orange "Zabar's" sign. *A bit redundant . . .* He wore his own hat from The Dan's 1994 tour, figuring if he didn't spot MarKau, at least MarKau would have a shot at spotting him.

It was another one of those cold, beautiful days in March: bright and sunny, with no wind. Perhaps forty degrees, Eddie thought. Trucks and busses lumbered by, spewing exhaust in his direction, and every so often he felt the rumble of the subway beneath his feet. The sidewalks were relatively clean, but still crowded with shoppers and delivery men.

He walked north, noting that the first door was the entrance to Zabar's coffee shop, the second was an entrance to the store itself, and both the third and fourth doors were exits. There was still no sign of MarKau as he approached the last door.

"Hey, Easy Eddie," someone shouted from behind him.

He turned and spotted a Steely Dan hat sitting on the head of a pretty young woman carrying a shopping bag. He waved and walked in her direction.

"You must be MarKau," he said, hiding his surprise as he approached. She was wearing a black leather jacket, a red sweater, jeans, and sneakers. He offered his hand, and she took it.

"Marcie Kaufman," she replied.

Nice smile. "I'm Easy Eddie . . . Zittner," he stammered, then managed to blurt out: "Eddie Zittner. Nice to meet you."

"Nice to meet you, Eddie."

"Uh, you're not what I expected," he replied, then immediately added, "I mean, I don't know what I expected . . ."

"What did you expect?" she said, frowning, adding to his embarrassment.

""Uh, I'm sorry. I didn't mean anything. I just—"

"You expected a guy, huh?"

"Yeah . . . I guess so."

"The Dan has a lot of female fans, you know."

"What can I say . . .?" *I'm blowing it.*

"Look, do you still want to have lunch?"

"Yeah, sure, why not? Always happy to meet another Dan fan."

"Well, it's too cold to eat outside."

"Agreed."

"We can eat in the coffee shop. You've never been to Zabar's, right?"

"Right."

"Follow me. I'll give you the nickel tour." Marcie turned and pushed through the last door. He followed as she worked her way through the store, first squeezing past waist-high barrels of fragrant coffee beans, and then turning left into baked goods, where he was overwhelmed by the smell of warm onion rolls. Continuing on, Marcie introduced him to Sal and Morey, the two guys that ran the smoked fish counter. They finally exited through the cheese department, another olfactory delight. A minute later, they were in the coffee shop. Marcie put the bag of food on the table, and then took off her jacket and swung it over the back of a chair.

"This is it. Nothing fancy, but it is warm." She smiled, her eyelids fluttering over blue eyes that reminded him of Liv Tyler. Finally, she took off the hat and shook her head—just a little, just enough to free up her auburn hair—and sat down. *Very nice*. He swung his jacket across the chair opposite hers. After standing for a few seconds, looking like a nebbish, he sat down and tried to think of something intelligent to say.

"Oh, this is great." He grinned. "They won't hassle us about bringing food in here?"

"No. It's all the same food. Anyway, I work here, remember?"

"Right. What kind of work?"

"Oh, this and that. Mostly I work behind the counters. Sometimes I do check-out."

"Well, thanks again. This is great." She had a nice smile, he thought; cute, with a dimple on her left cheek. She had those little stickpin-style earrings: two on the left, and two on the right. He didn't know if that was significant, not being up-to-date on the latest trends in ear fashion. He hadn't seen much of her body, but she looked slim and athletic. He guessed she was in her mid-twenties.

As he watched, Marcie busied herself unpacking the food. First she laid out the nova and sable on the paper it had been wrapped in, which was stained with grease. Then she took out four bagels, already sliced, and laid them across a couple of paper napkins. Good selection, he noted, spotting a sesame, a plain, an onion, and one with what looked like everything on it. Then she took out two containers of cream cheese, one plain and one with chives. Finally she laid out napkins, plastic knives and forks, and two bottles of water.

"Do you want coffee?" she asked.

"Uh, later would be fine," he replied as he spread chive cream cheese over half a sesame bagel. Then he laid a generous piece of nova on top. "This is great."

"You've already said that."

"But it is . . . great."

"That's four times now."

"Okay, I'll stop." he said, and, attempting to sound at least semi-intelligent, continued with "So, how long have you worked here?"

"I've been here for a couple of years," she said, carefully chewing a mouthful of sable and onion bagel. "I'm working my way through law school: N.Y.U."

Law school. He re-assessed the young woman sitting opposite him. "When do you finish?"

"December 16th." He started to respond, but she interrupted: "No need to say 'great' again."

"Okay, I won't."

They grinned at each other. Marcie continued, "So what do you do?"

"I'm just living in Manhattan, you know, temporarily. Working at a bookstore."

"No kidding. I guess you just pick up girls on the internet as, what, a hobby?"

"Uh . . ." He stammered again, glancing down at the wedding band still on his left hand, "yeah . . . I mean, no. Hey, I didn't know you were a woman."

"True. I'll give you that."

"And, uh, I'm separated from my wife. She left me," he quickly added.

"She back in New Jersey?"

"Yeah. How did you know?"

"You said you were from Jersey in your email."

Time to re-assess again . . . a lawyer-to-be, and sharp as a tack. He finished his half bagel and reached for another.

"Why don't you try the sable this time?"

"Okay. What's good with it?"

"Try it on the onion bagel, or the everything. No cream cheese."

"No cream cheese?"

"Well, that's how I like it, but it's up to you."

He picked up half of an everything bagel, forked a couple of slices of sable over it, took a bite, and chewed thoughtfully for a few seconds.

"Good?" she asked.

"Yeah, not bad at all. Moist. A little salty. Different."

"Subtle flavor, right?"

"Subtle would be a good way to describe it. I like it."

"What's not to like?" Smiling, Marcie decided to try the nova, layering it over chive cream cheese on the remaining half of the sesame bagel. "So, being a Dan Fan, I assume you've listened to *Two Against Nature*?"

"Yeah," he replied. "It's pretty good." He had listened to it numerous times, and had grudgingly conceded that it was quality stuff. When played on the stereo system at his brother's place, some of it was outstanding.

"I think it's a little too jazzy," Marcie said. "I guess I like the old stuff better."

"Yeah, I can see your point." He took a huge bite of his sandwich.

"I really like 'Jack of Speed,' though. You know, track six?"

"Mmm . . ." He nodded agreement as he wiped his mouth. "Yeah, you're right, that's one of the better ones." He was relaxed now, and feeling more comfortable. "So, how did you know Fagen's address?"

"Oh, I never give away my sources," she replied.

"Come on, at least give me a clue . . ."

"A friend of a friend knows him. Or, rather, lives in the same building."

"No kidding?"

"No kidding. And," she continued, "I really had second thoughts about sending you that address, privacy laws being what they are."

But you can't very well retrieve an email once it's sent.

The conversation rambled over less weighty subjects. They were washing down their third half bagels with cups of coffee when Marcie came back to the subject of Fagen's address:

"So, what are you planning to do? Walk right in and knock on his door? Ask for his autograph?"

"Uh, I don't know yet. I haven't figured out that part of it."

"I doubt that would work."

In fact, he had thought about it. He knew very well that the wrong kind of approach would get him tossed on the sidewalk, or perhaps worse. "Why?" he replied.

"Security. You wouldn't get close."

"Well, then, I might just hang around outside and wait for him to come out. Maybe carry a sign on my shoulder."

"What, march up and down the street? Like a parade?"

"Yeah. Like a parade." He hadn't pictured it that way, but there was something to the idea. *A parade . . . maybe he could recruit some followers.*

Marcie thought about it for a moment. "Might work," she concluded, "although, in that neighborhood, people don't take kindly to that sort of thing."

"What people?"

"The people that live there. And security. Doormen. Cops."

"What about free speech? Or the right to walk up and down the street?"

"Yeah, there is that."

"Hey, if I get arrested, will you defend me?" He grinned, and she grinned back at him. He continued, "Suppose I were to hang out—parade, as you said—on the sidewalk and wait for him to come out. Would you hang out with me? You know, strength in numbers?"

"Uh, I don't think so."

"What's the matter? No guts?"

"I just don't think hanging around on the street is a good idea. Too suspicious-looking."

"I'm harmless. I just want an autograph."

"This is New York City, remember?" she said, glancing at her watch. "Hey, almost one o'clock. I've got to get back to work."

"Well, thanks, Marcie. It was great . . . I mean, very nice to meet you."

"Same here."

"Hey, I'll send you an email if I have any success. Maybe we can stay in touch, you know? I'm new to Manhattan."

She weighed the pros and cons. "Yeah, send me an email. I'd like that."

They stood.

"What about the mess?" he said.

"I'll clean it up."

"Well, good-bye then. I'll send you that email."

"Eddie. Aren't you forgetting something?"

"What?"

"You owe me fifteen bucks for the lunch."

*****

He was euphoric as he walked south on Broadway. She was pretty, and smart. What if things didn't work out with Alison? Then, reaching the bus stop, he felt a strong surge of guilt. Yeah, 1675 Madison was a real address, and a real condo, a fancy one at that, but he had no idea whether or not Fagen lived there. He had "gone fishing" on the internet to see if someone would take the bait. Hadn't that been his intention? And it had worked. He had bluffed someone—Marcie—into disclosing Fagen's address. On the other hand, he hadn't coerced her or anything, had he?

12

Four hours later, Eddie Zittner was sitting at a table at the Café Indulge, stuffing his face with apple pie, washing it down with coffee, and staring out the window. Waves of students and mothers pushing baby carriages moved along the sidewalk. Across Second Avenue, people were lined up around the block, waiting to get into the Loews movie theater complex, which was adjacent to the Borders where he worked. He looked around for the waitress with the Russian accent, the one who reminded him of Julie Christie in *Doctor Zhivago*, but she was nowhere in sight. Sighing, he pulled out his cell phone, flipped it open, and punched in Jerry's number. Jerry picked up on the third ring:

"Brunswick Books, Jerry speaking."

"Jerry, it's Eddie."

"Easy, my main man, long time no hear from."

Long time? "Jer, you called me, what, Saturday? Remember? About the Letterman show?"

"Yeah, I guess that's right. Hey, hold on a minute."

Eddie heard voices in the background—people arguing?—and then Jerry's voice, telling them—ordering them—to hold it down. Seconds later, Jerry was back on the line.

"So," Eddie asked, "what's up?"

"Not much. Same old, same old."

Eddie heard more voices in the background. More arguing.

"Hold on another minute, will ya?" Jerry said, sounding a bit frustrated. "Let me get rid of these idiots." Eddie listened as Jerry gave his troops directions on the right way to stack books on shelves. "Okay," Jerry breathed a sigh of relief, "I'm back."

"Jer, what have you got going Thursday?"

"That's what, the day after tomorrow? I'll probably be in the store for a few hours. Why?"

"Why don't you come to Manhattan and help me smoke out The Dan?"

"What? You've already tracked them down?"

"Not exactly. I've got a line on Fagen's address." Silence on the line. *I've surprised him.* "You still there?"

"Yeah, man," Jerry finally replied. "How'd you get it?"

"I got it from another fan."

"Amazing. I guess it wasn't such a big secret after all."

"I think it is a big secret, Jer. I just happened to find someone who knew someone who, well, you know what I mean."

"That's great. So, what do you mean, smoke him out?"

"Jer, I've got it all worked out. We're gonna parade up and down the sidewalk, you know, with posters, and try to get his attention. He'll come out. Eventually."

"Zit, how'd you come up with that idea?"

"Well, we can't very well just knock on his door, can we?"

"Uh, no. But what makes you think Fagen will even know you're there?"

"I assume he looks out his window every so often."

"Yeah. Maybe." Jerry said. "And what if he doesn't?"

"Well, I assume there are people going in and out of the building all the time. Don't you think someone will tell him there's a parade in his honor, out on the sidewalk?"

"Yeah. Maybe. Zit, you're actually going to parade up and down the sidewalk?"

"Yeah."

"What about the cops?"

"What about them?"

"Won't they stop you?"

"I don't see why." He popped the last piece of pie crust into his mouth, and downed the last of his coffee. Spotting the Russian waitress, he held up his cup and gestured for a refill.

"You might want to check that out," Jerry said. "You know, before you go out there?"

"Jerry. We're talking a few people, with signs, walking up and down the sidewalk. We're not gonna disturb anything."

"Well, look, Zit, I don't think I can make it."

"Oh, come on, Jer." *My hypothetical friend.*

"Zit, it's a long drive to Manhattan."

"Jer. Buddy."

"Buddy nothing. And it's gonna be fucking cold out there."

"It's not that bad. Shit, the newspapers all say it's been a mild winter."

"Mild winter my ass. Out on the sidewalk it ain't that mild."

"So what? You have warm clothes, don't you? I'll buy you some coffee. All you want."

"Then I can take a leak on the sidewalk, I guess."

"Come on, Jer. Strength in numbers."

"Look, Zit, I'll tell you what. You go out there by yourself once or twice, and if you don't get arrested, then you call me back."

"Will you come then?"

"I'll consider it. No guarantee."

Eddie figured this was probably the best he would get out of Jerry. "Okay, deal. I'll call you after I try it once or twice."

"Deal. So, Zit, what else is happening? Are you still at your brother's place?"

"Yeah, I'm staying in his spare bedroom. And I'm working as a temp in a bookstore."

"No kidding. You been in touch with Alison yet?"

"No, not yet. But, Jerry, guess what? I met a girl."

"You met a girl? No shit?"

He could tell he'd regained Jerry's attention. "No shit, Jer. I had lunch with her today."

"Zit. Let me remind you that you're still married."

"So? Alison walked out on me, didn't she?"

"I guess you could say that. Technically."

"So, what's the problem? I just had lunch with the girl."

"How'd you meet her?"

"On the internet."

"No shit?"

"No shit. She's the one that had Fagen's address."

"You son-of-a-bitch. Hey, Zit, just remember that you're still married. Okay? To a beautiful woman, I might add."

"I'll try to remember."

"Yeah. You do that. Zit, look, I gotta go. I've gotta get back to work."

"Let me guess: your staff needs more of your guidance."

"Yeah, something like that."

"Okay, Jer, take it easy. I'm gonna call you next week."

"Okay, Zit, you take care."

13

Thursday, March 9, 2000

    Eddie literally bounced along the sidewalk as he worked his way along Third Avenue toward the bus stop. *This is the day. This is the day I meet the Dan Man.*
    Even though it looked like reasonable weather—the forecast was for cloudy skies with a high of forty-five degrees—he was prepared for the worst. He was wearing a black sweater over a red flannel shirt, navy corduroy pants, ski-style wool socks, and black hiking boots. He had his heavy winter coat on, a forest green monstrosity with wooden pegs for buttons. He had a scarlet-red Rutgers scarf around his neck, his CD player, earphones, and a pair of lined gloves in his pockets, and a Steely Dan baseball cap on his head. A handmade sign—with *Steely Dan Rules!* hand-printed on both sides—was tucked under one arm; Eddie had cobbled it together with a broomstick, poster-board, thumb tacks, and duct tape. He was ready for anything.
    It was mid-morning, and the sidewalk was crowded with shoppers, but no one glanced at him as he boarded the uptown bus. Even with the sign, he looked normal compared to some of the characters on the streets of Manhattan. Twenty minutes later, he got off at 88th Street and headed west.
    Fifty-nine East 88th Street sat in a quiet neighborhood that was primarily residential, a mixture of high-rise apartments, condominiums, and elegant brownstones. Some of the brownstones had been converted to the swank offices of lawyers, doctors, and trading companies. But it was still Manhattan, and the streets were dotted with restaurants, coffee shops, and boutiques. Stopping at the corner of 88th and Park Avenue, he took a minute to adjust his earphones—he was listening to *Pretzel Logic*—put on his gloves, and deploy his *Steely Dan Rules!* sign, drawing a few stares from nearby pedestrians. He watched as clouds rolled across the sky. *It won't reach forty-five degrees today.*
    Continuing west on 88th Street—parading, as Marcie had described it—Eddie spotted the canopy that led into the main entrance of the building. It was a modest structure—fourteen or fifteen stories, he thought—of red brick faced with white marble at street level. As he approached, he noticed a loading zone at the curb, and a pair of giant shrubs in ornate ceramic pots straddling the building's entrance. Passing under the canopy, he glanced to his left and saw a doorman standing just inside the glass doors. He continued past, walked all the way to Madison Avenue, turned, and headed back. It was relatively quiet, with few people on the sidewalks.

After passing the building perhaps half a dozen times, he drew the attention of the doorman, who had come outside and was now standing under the canopy, watching him. He hesitated for just a second, but then, remembering his civil rights, he continued on, moving steadily forward. The doorman was tall and thin, and, dressed in a grey uniform with gold trim and a neat blue tie, somehow reminded him of Abraham Lincoln. All that's missing, he thought, was the top hat and beard. As Eddie approached, he wondered how cold this guy must be without an overcoat, gloves, or, for that matter, any kind of hat.

Old Abe folded his arms across his chest and addressed him: "Hey, what gives?" Breath steamed out of his mouth.

Eddie pulled his earplugs out. "What?"

"I said, what gives?"

"What do you mean?"

"I mean, what are you doing out here?"

"I'm walking up and down the sidewalk minding my own business."

"What's with the sign?" the doorman said as he rubbed his hands together.

Eddie could see that the man was uncomfortable. His cheeks were beginning to turn blue. "What about it?" he replied.

"You can't demonstrate out here."

A few passersby glanced at them, but kept moving. An old gentleman walking a wiener-dog stopped to watch and listen. *The man looked Chinese, and the dog was some kind of dachshund mix.* Eddie looked more closely. *The dog . . . the dog had a giant penis!*

The doorman turned to the man and said, "Hello, doctor. Did you enjoy your walk?"

"It's a little too cold for walking today," the doctor replied.

The dog growled and jumped at Eddie, only to be pulled up short by his leash. Eddie's jaw dropped as he watched the dog's penis bounce just millimeters above the sidewalk. *It's enormous! I should be so lucky!*

Eddie gave Old Abe a "did you see that?" look, but the doorman, apparently having seen the dog many times, wasn't impressed. The two men watched as the doctor entered the building dragging the dog behind him. The dog's dick barely cleared the threshold. Eddie sighed. *I guess nuisance is in the eye of the beholder.*

As the glass doors closed, Old Abe turned his attention back to Eddie. "Like I was saying, you can't demonstrate out here."

"I'm not demonstrating."

"You're demonstrating. You're making a public nuisance."

"What public nuisance?" Eddie replied. "I don't see any nuisance. There's hardly anybody around."

"Doesn't matter," said the doorman, now visibly suffering. "You can't demonstrate out here."

"I'm walking up and down the sidewalk with a sign. What's the big deal?"

"Look," said the doorman, quickly realizing that he was going to freeze to death in another minute or two, "I guess I can't stop you from walking on the sidewalk." He backed toward the glass doors. "Just remember, no disturbances. You hear what I'm saying?"

"I hear you."

The glass doors opened. The doorman, still backing up, pointed a finger at him and repeated his admonition: "No disturbances."

"Got it," Eddie replied, counting this as a victory, however small.

*****

The next hour was uneventful. Eddie paraded up and down the sidewalk, and was pretty much ignored by everyone who passed, except for one elderly man who called him "Bozo" and told him to get a job. Few people entered or left the apartment building, and none of them looked remotely like Donald Fagen. The doorman occasionally left his desk to greet residents, and gave Eddie the hairy eyeball every chance he got.

Tired from parading in the near-freezing cold, and hungry from the exertion, Eddie walked over to Lexington Avenue, where he spotted a hot dog stand. The man tending the stand, an elderly guy built like an extra-wide fireplug, was wearing bulbous white sneakers, a red sweatsuit, and a black pullover hat that covered his head, ears, and most of his forehead. Eddie saw that the man's already ample belly looked like it was wrapped with a garden hose. As he got closer, he saw that the man was wearing layers of clothing—thermal underwear for sure, he guessed—and the clothing had bunched up around his waist.

As he approached, the man waved to him and shouted, "Hey, Steely Dan, how about a hot one? All beef!"

Eddie looked up and down Lexington, but didn't see anything better.

The man continued, "I know those Steely Dan guys."

"Yeah? How?"

"They come around here all the time, you know? For hot dogs."

"No kidding?"

"No kidding."

"So," Eddie probed, "what do they look like?"

"Steely Dan? A tall guy and a shorter guy."

That could be Fagen and Becker. "What do they look like?"

The man put a finger to his lips, thought for a few seconds, and replied, "The tall guy is dark, and the shorter guy is not so dark."

That could be them! "What else?"

"They usually wear raincoats." The man's eyebrows bounced, and he pursed his lips to stifle an impending grin. "You know what I mean? So they don't rust when it rains?" The man winked at Eddie, and asked him what he wanted to eat.

Everybody's a comedian. He ordered a hot dog with mustard and sauerkraut, and a root beer. As he stood on the sidewalk eating, his cell phone rang.

"Hello?"

"Eddie, it's me, Dad."

"Hey, Dad," he replied, immediately feeling guilty that he hadn't called his parents since he'd moved in with Mark. But he was always happy to hear his father's voice. "How's it going?"

"Well, I'm doing better than John McCain. How about you? And where are you?'

Eddie knew that his father followed politics closely. McCain had been hammered on Super Tuesday. The newspapers speculated that he was about to drop out of the presidential race. "I'm fine, Dad. I'm just standing on a street corner eating a hot dog."

"So you're not working yet?"

"No, I found a job, Dad. I'm working as a temp at a bookstore. I'm just not working today."

"Well, that's good."

"Yeah. Have you spoken to Mark?"

"No," Harry Zittner lied. In fact, he had called Mark to see what was happening with Eddie, and then sworn Mark to secrecy.

"Well, I'm going to be staying at his place for a while."

"That's good," his father said, having already heard this from his younger son. "At least you won't be spending an arm and a leg on some crummy apartment."

"Yeah. Mark said I could crash in his spare room, for a few weeks, anyway."

"Eddie," his father said, the preliminaries over, "Your mother and I need to talk to you."

Something tightened in Eddie's stomach. He tossed the last bite of hot dog into a nearby trash can. "Are you okay, Dad?"

"Yeah, I'm okay. My health is fine." Eddie took a deep breath of cold air as his father continued, "Look, can you come to the house for dinner tonight? Around seven?"

Eddie checked his watch. Time was not the problem. He thought about how he might get from Manhattan to Saddle River, and concluded that he'd need to take the train over to Jersey, and then a cab to the house. "What do you want to talk about, Dad?" he probed. "And what about Mark? Do you want him to come, too?"

"No, just come by yourself. Your mother and I want to talk to you."

"Okay, Dad." He thought he had a fair idea of what they wanted to talk about. "I'll be there. I'll see you later. You and Ma."

"Okay, Easy, take care. Dress warm."

He flipped the phone closed, drained the root beer, tossed the bottle into the trash, and looked around for a bus stop.

14

As the taxi stopped in front of his parents' house, Eddie glanced at his watch. He was ten minutes early. He paid the driver, got out, hunched his shoulders against the cold, and began climbing up the granite walkway. As he neared the house, he saw his father open the door, step outside, and wave a greeting. He waved back, noting that his father was dressed for the occasion. Well, not exactly dressed up, but he was wearing a powder blue shirt with a button-down collar, a navy sweater vest, charcoal grey slacks, and a well-shined pair of black loafers. *This must be important.*

Arriving at the entryway, Eddie offered his hand, which his father took as he pulled his son closer. "I'm early," he gasped as his father gave him a bear-hug.

"I know." His father released his grip. "I saw the cab pull up. How long did it take you to get here?"

"About an hour. I took the train from Penn Station to Woodcliff Lake and then grabbed a taxi."

"That's not bad from Mark's place." Harry Zittner forced a smile. It was uncomfortable for him to concede, even to himself, that his son was separated from his wife.

They walked through the dining room, and Eddie noticed that his father was limping. *Maybe his gout is acting up . . . again.* He made a mental note to ask his mother about it, if he could get her alone for a minute or two. There was red wine breathing in a large carafe, and he saw that the table was set for three. He relaxed a little bit. At least there wouldn't be any unexpected guests.

Father and son proceeded into the kitchen, where Elaine Zittner was preparing dinner. Hearing the men come in, she had turned, wiped her hands on an apron—*she was wearing an apron!*—and walked over to Eddie and gave him a hug.

"How's my oldest son?" she asked.

"I'm fine, Ma, how are you?"

"I'm good. A few aches and pains, but who's complaining?"

"Ma," he said, glancing at covered pots on the stove, "you didn't have to go to all this trouble."

"What trouble? You think I forgot how to cook?"

Ten minutes later they were seated: his father, as always, at the head of the table, Eddie on his father's right, and his mother on his father's left. His mother had prepared pot roast, one of his favorites, with mashed potatoes and green beans. She served the two men generous portions of each, and took smaller portions for herself. Eddie picked up his plate and ladled spoonfuls of gravy, fragrant and thick with chunks of onion, over the meat and potatoes. His father poured the wine, and began slicing a rye bread that smelled like it was just out of the oven. His parents had gone to quite a bit of trouble preparing all this. And then he realized: *I'm being set up . . .*

Small talk about big disasters: his father complained about the Dow, which had dropped below ten thousand, and his mother *could not believe* that Kathie Lee was leaving *Live with Regis* after all those years! But the conversation soon turned serious.

"Eddie," his mother began, "we want to talk to you about Alison, and your marriage."

No surprise there.

"Easy," his father said, "I talked to Alison this morning."

"Did she call you?" he asked.

Harry Zittner looked uncomfortable, and glanced at his wife, who was staring at her plate. "No, Eddie, I called her."

"Dad . . ."

"I'm sorry, Eddie. You know we hate to interfere in your personal life, or Mark's for that matter, but, well, you know, we felt we needed to get involved. This one time."

He couldn't argue with that. His parents were generally very good about leaving him alone to work out whatever issues he had in his personal life. He glanced quickly at his mother, who was sipping her wine. She met his glance, but gave nothing away with her eyes.

He addressed his father again, "Okay. What did you and Alison talk about?"

His father took a sip of ice water and wiped his mouth with a linen napkin. "We just talked about what's going on between the two of you. You know, with the marriage and your careers, that kind of thing."

His mother interrupted, "Eddie, look, I'm sorry for the way I acted that night you came over. You remember?"

"Yeah, Ma, I remember." *How could I forget?* He was a little surprised; it wasn't like his mother to apologize without a good reason.

"Well," she continued, "I admit I over-reacted that night."

"Okay, Ma, no big deal."

"But Eddie, look, your father and I think you have serious problems with your marriage."

"Were you on the phone call, too?"

"No, I wasn't, but your father filled me in. We talked about it for quite a while this morning."

"So," he addressed his father again, "what did Alison say?"

"Well, she said that the two of you had grown apart in the last few months." He nodded as his father continued, "You know. With her new job, she thinks that, well, you might be feeling threatened." Harry Zittner took another sip of water. "And, she's concerned that you're not writing anymore."

"And," his mother jumped in, "she's concerned that you can't hold a job, and won't get a better job. And that you spend so much time surfing the internet. And the craziness with the music. I'm sorry to bring it all up again."

"Is that Alison talking, Ma," he asked her, "or you?"

His father responded. "It's Alison talking . . . her words."

Eddie saw the concern on his father's face. "I didn't think she was that unhappy."

"But, Eddie," his father continued, "what concerns me is her mood."

"What do you mean?"

"I don't know, Eddie. I just got the feeling that she's losing interest. I got the feeling that she's fed up, at least to a certain extent. You know what I mean?"

No, not really. Deep down, there had always been a strong bond between them . . . for most of their married life, anyway. *Were those days gone forever?*

"Eddie," his father continued, "I think—we think—you should meet with her and, you know, talk things over."

"Eddie," his mother said, "I hate to say it this way, but, well, maybe she'll take you back, if you agree to focus a little more on your career, and stop with the craziness about the music."

"Take me back? Ma, she walked out on me."

"Eddie," his father said, "you know, these situations are complex. Who walked out on who? Does it really matter?"

There's no good answer to that. "Okay, Dad, I guess you're right. It doesn't really matter."

"So will you call her?" his mother asked.

"I'll call her in the next few days. Let me think about it."

Harry Zittner sighed as he reached for the mashed potatoes. "Don't wait too long, Eddie."

15

Saturday, March 11, 2000

After working a three-to-eleven shift at the bookstore, and then another hour re-stacking books, Eddie slept in on Saturday morning. Finally dragging himself out of bed, he showered and dressed and was back on the street at noon, hopeful that this would be the day he met the Dan Man.

Third Avenue was jammed. *That's what I get for going out on Saturday*. But then again, what choice did he have? This was his day off. A few people stared at him as he passed with his new, hand-lettered sign, this one with *Donald Fagen, Meet Your Biggest Fan* on one side, and *Donald Fagen, I Want Your Autograph* on the other. *Not particularly original, but more to the point.* Maybe someone would see the sign and get in touch with Fagen. It wasn't as cold as Thursday, but it threatened to rain, and the wind had picked up. He was again wearing his forest green winter coat over shirt, sweater, corduroy pants, and heavy boots. And his Steely Dan hat, of course. He thought he might need an umbrella in an hour or two.

He stopped at a Bagelry, and the manager, a dour-looking woman—Korean, Eddie guessed— asked him who Donald Fagen was. I'll tell you, he replied, if you give me a discount on a bagel and coffee. No discounts, she replied, making a face that would scare a hardened criminal. He took his bagel and coffee and got the hell out of there before she did something worse.

Eddie arrived at 59 East 88th just after one, and started to parade. *The Nightfly*, Fagen's first solo album, was playing softly on his Walkman. And five minutes later, like clockwork, Old Abe was back on the sidewalk, standing under the canopy, pulling on a pair of leather gloves as he watched him approach. Eddie noted that Old Abe was prepared today, wearing a heavy overcoat and what looked like a captain's hat, which, he realized, was part of the doorman's uniform.

"Hey," Old Abe said, doing his best to position himself directly in Eddie's path.

What now? Eddie stopped and pulled his earphones out. "Hey," he replied.

"I remember you from a couple of days ago."

"No kidding. I remember you from a couple of days ago."

"Well isn't that nice?"

"I don't know about nice, but it proves we both have memories."

We both have memories?

Old Abe ignored the remark, and decided to re-assert his authority, this time in a more diplomatic way. "Remember what I said before? About no disturbances out here on the sidewalk?"

"Yeah, I remember. I'm not disturbing anything."

"Good." Old Abe looked up and down the street. There were people on both sides of 88th, some walking and some just loitering, and a couple of people on bicycles, but there was virtually no street traffic. "Like I said before, I can't stop you from walking up and down the sidewalk. Just don't make any trouble out here."

"I don't plan to."

"Good," the doorman said, apparently satisfied that the requirement of his tenants for peace and quiet was being met. Old Abe looked up and down the street again. "Do you mind if I ask you a question?"

"No problem," Eddie said.

"Who are you? I mean, what's your name? And where are you from?"

"What difference does it make?" he replied. "And anyway, that's two questions."

"Two questions." Old Abe thought for a moment. "Yeah, so what?"

"You said you'd ask one question."

"Oh, yeah, right. Well, what's your name, anyway?"

Figuring that telling Old Abe his name might be a step in the direction of improving relations out here on the sidewalk, he decided to answer. "Eddie Zittner. And I live downtown."

"Downtown. So why come all the way up here to demonstrate?"

"Well, because this is where Donald Fagen lives. I'm trying to meet him, you know, and get his autograph, like the sign says."

Eddie stared at the doorman, who seemed to be concentrating, his mind processing more information than it was probably used to. Old Abe started to speak, then stopped, and then, as if a light bulb had switched on inside his head, said, "What makes you think this Fagen person lives here?"

"I have it on good authority."

"You do?"

"I do," Eddie replied, and then decided to take a shot in the dark. "I think it's pretty well known around town that he lives here with his wife."

He watched closely for a reaction, but Old Abe was looking down the street. Eddie watched as a police cruiser rounded the corner and, a few seconds later, pulled into the loading zone in front of the building. A policeman climbed out of the car, slammed the door and walked toward the canopy. Eddie noted the policeman's pencil-thin mustache and dark complexion. *Italian.*

Eddie looked at the doorman. "You called the police?"

"Don't get your balls in an uproar," Old Abe replied, and then addressed the policeman, "Hey, Vince."

"Hey, *paisan*," the policeman replied, and then it was reunion time as they shadow-boxed each other. The policeman crouched and threw a left jab followed by a right cross, both punches stopping a few inches from the doorman. The doorman reacted with exaggerated flinches, and then staggered backwards as both men laughed.

Eddie watched as they stepped toward the glass doors, which opened with a whoosh, and then into the lobby, the doors closing behind them. The men talked for perhaps a minute, and then came back outside. As they approached, Eddie said, "I'm not breaking any laws, officer."

The officer, Vince, towering over Eddie, took a deep breath and exhaled into his face. He detected garlic under the strong odor of cigars. *Definitely Italian.*

"I didn't say you were," the officer replied, rubbing his hands together to stay warm. He was in full uniform, and wore a heavy leather waistcoat, but no gloves. "Do you have any identification on you?" he asked.

"Sure," Eddie said, reaching toward his back pocket.

"May I see it, please?"

He pulled his wallet out and extracted his driver's license, which he handed to the policeman. The policeman examined it front and back.

"Edward Zittner. So you're from New Jersey?"

The doorman interrupted, "You said you were from downtown."

Eddie turned to him, "I'm living in Manhattan temporarily."

"No shit," the policeman said, handing the driver's license back. "It sucks downtown. Just like Jersey."

Three teenagers had stopped to watch and listen. Two of them appeared to be brothers—Hispanic by the looks of them, Eddie thought— and the third was an attractive Asian girl. They were all wearing heavy boots, jeans, and a variety of sweatshirts, jackets, and pullover caps.

"So," the policeman nodded at the sign, "who's Donald Fagen?"

"Donald Fagen? He's a musician, a very famous one."

"Famous?" the policeman replied, "How famous? I never heard of him."

"Me neither," the doorman added. Eddie wondered if Old Abe was agreeing to help intimidate him, or was just outright lying. Likely the doorman knew Fagen very well, or at least well enough to say hello to him as he came and went.

The policeman continued, "So I hear from Ralph that you're having a little demonstration right here on the sidewalk."

Ralph? "I wouldn't call it a demonstration. I'm walking up and down the sidewalk carrying a sign."

"And you think this Fagen character is gonna come out?" The policeman looked doubtful.

The doorman—Ralph—chimed in. "Maybe he'll dive out the fourteenth floor window."

The fourteenth floor . . . is that where he lives? Eddie stared hard into the doorman's eyes.

The policeman smiled. "Look, Edward, this is a very quiet neighborhood. Residential. Wealthy tenants. They pay a lot of money for these places. Capishe?"

Capishe? "What about that guy over there?" Eddie asked, gesturing across the street toward an elderly man, seated on a wooden chair, with a boom-box at his feet, playing some kind of turn-of-the-century New Orleans jazz. The man was completely covered by a couple of worn blankets. He was, in fact, so well wrapped that he could have been naked under the blankets. He looked like a dirty grey burrito topped with a brown Cossack-style hat. The boom-box was playing loud enough to be heard from across the street, but not loud enough to keep burrito-man awake.

"I'm going to roust him next, right after I'm finished with you," the policeman said.

One of the teenage boys started to mutter something about "police brutality." The girl picked up on the idea and started chanting "Attica! Attica!" as she punched the air with her fist. The policeman turned toward them and said, "Hey! Shut the hell up!" The teenagers stopped, and looked at each other, trying to decide what to do next. The policeman turned back to Eddie and said, "You see what you started?"

"I started?" he said. "I didn't start anything."

By then, the teenagers, not knowing and not caring who Donald Fagen was, decided that discretion was the better part of valor, and walked away, heading east.

"Look, Edward," the policeman continued, "I can't stop you from walking up and down the sidewalk. But, look, those kids are only the beginning. You're gonna attract all kinds of undesirables. Capishe?" Eddie nodded. Satisfied that he was listening, the policeman continued, "So here's the deal. We make a gentleman's agreement: you limit your demonstrating to an hour a day, weekdays only, and Ralphie and I won't hassle you." The doorman nodded his agreement.

Eddie did a quick calculation in his head. One hour a day was not going to accomplish anything, he figured. He needed more time. On the other hand, it was still pretty damned cold, and windy, today in particular, and who knew when it would get much warmer?

"Four hours," he replied.

"No way," the policeman said.

"Then three hours," he countered, "but every day, Saturdays and Sundays included."

Vince looked at Ralph, who just raised his eyebrows. Then he looked back at Eddie, trying to assess how determined he was.

"Okay, three hours max, but weekdays only."

"No deal," Eddie said, "I need Saturdays, too. I don't work on Saturdays."

"Two hours, then," The policeman said. "Two hours max, weekdays and Saturdays included. Deal?"

"Deal," Eddie said, figuring that two hours out in this weather was all he'd be able to handle anyway, at least until it got a little warmer.

"Thank God," the policeman said, satisfied that he had struck a balance between the right of free speech and the right to privacy and a little peace and quiet. He shook hands with Ralph and walked to his car, got in, started it up, and drove away, forgetting to roust the old man with the boombox.

Eddie nodded at Ralph, who nodded back, and started to parade again, heading east toward Madison Avenue. But, like Thursday, he had no success in smoking out Fagen. Hardly anyone entered or left 59 East 88th. Thirty minutes later it was raining, and, chilled to the bone, he decided to retreat back to his brother's apartment.

16

Sunday, March 12, 2000

To: MarKau55@nyc.rr.com

From: EZEddie32@nyc.rr.com

Subject: Hi

    Marcie, I hope all is well with you. I really enjoyed having lunch with you last week. It was you-know-what!
    Remember my plan to parade in front of Fagen's apartment? Well, I've done it, twice now, and it's gone pretty well. The second day, an "agent of the law" hassled me a little, but after we discussed it, he agreed that I have every right to be out on the sidewalk as long as I didn't create a disturbance. So, no problem. But, no success, either. No sign of Fagen or anyone who knows him. Would you care to reconsider and "parade" with me sometime? If not, would you like to go out sometime? How about dinner? . . . Eddie

****

To: EZEddie32@nyc.rr.com

From: MarKau55@nyc.rr.com

Subject: Hi back

    Eddie, I just got your email. I'm on-line, too. Switch to IM . . . Marcie

****

EZEddie32: Eat any good sable lately?
MarKau55: Not since our lunch together.
EZEddie32: So what did you think of my email?
MarKau55: I think you're wasting your time parading up and down the sidewalk, but who knows, maybe you'll get lucky.
EZEddie32: Any better ideas? Can you get me Fagen's phone number? I called River Sound but all I got was a recorded message.
MarKau55: No, I cannot get you his phone number. Remember, privacy laws?
EZEddie32: So how about dinner?
MarKau55: Hold on a minute . . . I just talked to my roommate. Why don't you come to our apartment for dinner tomorrow? Her sometime boyfriend will join us. We can have a little dinner party.

EZEddie32: I'd love to, thanks for the invitation. That's two meals that I owe you.
MarKau55: You paid for lunch, remember?
EZEddie32: Oh yeah. Shall I bring a bottle of wine? White or red?
MarKau55: Shall?
EZEddie32: What's wrong with shall?
MarKau55: Nothing, I guess. I just don't hear it very often in regular speech.
EZEddie32: This isn't regular speech. It isn't even speech.
MarKau55: I shall call it whatever I choose.
EZEddie32: White or red?
MarKau55: White, chardonnay preferred, but don't spend a lot of money. How about seven?
EZEddie32: Seven is good. I hate to be intrusive, but I will need your address.
MarKau55: You promise not to stalk me?
EZEddie32: Promise.
MarKau55: 43 Avenue A. It's a couple of blocks north of Houston Street. Apartment 3C.
EZEddie32: Got it. See you at seven tomorrow.

17

Monday, March 13, 2000

Eddie found 43 Avenue A easily enough, a nondescript apartment building surrounded by other nondescript apartment buildings. He buzzed Marcie's apartment, and was in turn buzzed through the inside glass door. Bypassing a decrepit-looking elevator, he bounded up two flights of twisted stairs, and was winded by the time he reached the door. He took a couple of deep breaths, smoothed his hair, rolled his shoulders under his leather coat, and knocked. A few seconds later, he heard deadbolts slide, and the door swung open.

"You're right on time," Marcie said, smiling.

"With wine," he replied, and felt a flush of embarrassment rise on his cheeks.

She ignored the remark. "Come on in, I'll take the wine and your jacket." She led him into the living room, which was decorated with contemporary furniture that, to him, looked vaguely like Ikea. The artwork, though, was stunning: a large abstract painting, an outrageous study of red, grey and black swirls, dominated one wall, and the smaller paintings, lithographs, and metal sculpture were also "avant garde." A few potted plants and a couple of small trees—*which must be artificial*—softened the effect of the artwork.

Marcie was wearing a black blouse and a denim skirt, and an array of earrings that dangled as she moved. Her dark hair was swept back and jelled, in a style that vaguely reminded him of someone he'd seen in a movie. *Someone in a James Bond flick . . . Grace Jones? . . . yeah, maybe.*

"It's just the two of us," Marcie said. "It won't be much of a dinner party."

"What happened to your roommate?" he asked, wondering if there really was a roommate. The apartment was tiny, with the living room seamlessly leading into a combination kitchen and dining area. He spotted a hallway, which, he assumed, must lead to the bedroom. Or bedrooms.

"She and her boyfriend decided to go out."

"She doesn't like your cooking?"

"I hardly know her. She's only been here three weeks."

He glanced at the dining room table, set for two. He could smell something cooking—something with garlic and lemon and . . . some other stuff.

Marcie moved into the kitchen. "Yeah, my former roommate graduated in December, and just moved to Boston." The cork popped as she opened the bottle of chardonnay and poured two glasses.

"What's for dinner? It smells great."

She grinned at him. "Again with 'great'?"

He struck a serious pose. "How about 'wonderful'?"

"It's lemon chicken." She sipped her wine. "Tell me later how wonderful it was."

After finishing their wine, they sat down and ate—very good, Eddie thought: lightly breaded chicken breasts, sautéed and then baked—with red potatoes and a green salad. They talked about Marcie's art, which she had purchased at a couple of obscure galleries she had 'discovered' in the Village. He was no expert, but he favored more traditional art, like that of Cezanne, and Matisse, and even some of the early Picasso's.

After finishing off one bottle of wine and starting another, Marcie cleared the table and brewed a pot of decaf. Eddie relaxed on the sofa, starting to feel comfortable as he listened to some soft jazz he couldn't recognize. Marcie brought the coffee and sat down at the opposite end of the sofa.

"I noticed you haven't played any Steely Dan," he said.

"It doesn't really set the mood. This is Warren Hill. I've got Grover Washington coming up."

"Good stuff. I listen to jazz every now and then."

"Speaking of good stuff, you want a little weed?"

"Weed? You mean marijuana?"

"Yeah. Want some?"

He thought about it. He'd smoked some in high school and college, but only once or twice since then. It had been a few years. He didn't know how he'd react, but decided to give it a shot anyway.

"Sure, why not?"

"Back in a minute," Marcie said as she got up and disappeared down the hallway. She came back a minute later, switching off lights as she moved. She was carrying what to Eddie looked like a very large joint.

"That thing is huge."

"Big enough for two," she said as she lit up and sucked smoke into her lungs. As she held her breath, she leaned back and closed her eyes. Finally, she coughed, exhaled, and handed the joint to Eddie.

He took a tentative pull, coughed, and then took a large pull, filling his lungs. In a few seconds the harshness overcame him, and he coughed out the smoke. His eyes watered. Trying to sound at least a little bit worldly, he choked out, "That's some good shit. Strong."

"You didn't even hold it," Marcie said, taking the joint back. "When was the last time you smoked?"

"I can't remember. I must've been too stoned."

"Yeah, right."

"Hey, I smoke every now and then."

"With your wife?"

"No, with my friends," he said, stung that Marcie had referred to his marital status. *Where'd that come from?*

Soon the joint was gone. Marcie put the doobie in an ashtray and went into the kitchen. A minute later she returned with two glasses of wine. This time she sat close to him. "I thought you might want to go back to the wine."

He put his arm around her, and she responded by kissing him lightly on the cheek.

"This is nice," he said, lamely. He didn't know how to act, or how to feel, or what to say. He thought of Alison, and wondered what she was doing this evening.

Marcie leaned over and kissed him full on the lips. It was a gentle kiss, not passionate, but not tentative either. For an instant, their lips clung together as she pulled slowly away. Then he leaned over and kissed her, deeply, and she responded by putting her hand on his thigh. Soon they were groping each other, and he had his hand under her blouse. *No bra.* She moved her hand along the inside of his thigh, and he felt himself getting hard. He fought a battle within himself, but the wine and the weed and the perfume made his head spin. And now his penis was starting to throb, and he was getting that feeling, that irresistible urge that, once started, was nearly impossible to turn off.

"Touch me," she whispered.

"What?"

"Touch me. Down there."

Breathing hard, he slid his hand between her legs. Her thighs were cool and smooth, and he tried to remember if she was wearing pantyhose when he came in. She leaned back, slightly, and moved her hips forward, and he felt her. He felt moisture as he moved his fingers over her. Then, suddenly, he pulled away.

"I'm sorry, Marcie, I can't do it."

"What's wrong?" She sat up.

He stood in front of her. "I've got to get out of here before I do something I'll regret." He grabbed his jacket and moved quickly to the door.

"You're wife left you, right? So what's the problem?"

But he was already out the door, and then across the landing, and then running down the stairs. He burst onto the sidewalk, and cursed himself as he walked toward the lights of Houston Street. A few minutes later, he found relief, in the men's room of an all-night diner, hunched over a filthy toilet bowl.

18

Tuesday, March 14, 2000

Lois Lane Smith sat at her desk, shuffling papers and trying to stay awake. Lunch with a girlfriend had been nice, but the strawberry cheesecake had knocked her for a loop. *Or maybe it was the wine . . .*

She was startled when the phone rang. "Lois Lane Smith, may I help you?"

"Lois, Phil. How are you?"

She pushed back from her desk and put her feet up on the lower drawer, which was hanging open and jammed with files. She hadn't heard from Phil in a couple of weeks.

"I'm fine, Phil. I thought you'd forgotten about me."

"Lois, how could I forget you?"

She contemplated the question. Their affair had lasted for more than a year. There had been times when he couldn't get away from his responsibilities as District Sales Manager for Gallo Wine, or from his responsibilities as a husband, but he had always called at least once a week.

"You can't," she said, "I'm unforgettable."

"I'm sorry. I should have called last week. We could have had phone sex." Before she could answer, he continued, "Where are you right now?"

"Why, looking for a quickie? Is that what you have in mind?"

"No," he replied, "though I can't think of anything I'd rather be doing."

Always the smooth talker. . . She looked across the city room, which was filled with desks, chairs, and file cabinets. Most of the desks were unoccupied.

He continued, "Lois, I've got a scoop for you."

"Okay," she replied, surprised that Phil would actually try to help with her career. "Let's hear it."

"You ever hear of a rock group called Steely Dan?"

"Yeah, I've heard of them. Weren't they popular back in the sixties?"

"The seventies. They did some tours a few years ago. Anyway, I'm at Second Avenue and 95th Street and there's a guy walking up and down the sidewalk with a sign that says 'Steely Dan Rules.' Right now."

"Have you talked to him?"

"No, I'm across the street."

"Okay, so what?"

"So, here's the big human interest story you've been looking for."

"I don't get it. Is the guy some kind of weirdo?"

"I don't think so. He looks like a normal person. But there's some other guy walking behind him, and he does look like a weirdo. And now they're arguing with each other."

Phil was right; she had been looking for an offbeat story that would get her a little recognition. *And a raise, maybe?* She wasn't working on anything else that couldn't wait a day or two.

"Okay, Phil, I'll grab a cab and be there in twenty minutes. Where exactly are you?"

"Corner of Second and 95th, but Lois, I won't be here. I've got to get back to the office."

"You can't wait twenty minutes?"

"Sorry, honey, I've got a meeting in half an hour."

Honey . . . heard that before . . . here it comes.

Phil didn't disappoint. "I promise I'll call you next week."

"Make sure you have a couple of hours when you do."

"We'll do lunch and then do each other."

"Don't be crude, Phil."

"Take care, hon."

Lois grabbed her jacket and oversized handbag—or undersized briefcase if you will—and started toward the elevators.

*****

Eddie Zittner got off the Third Avenue bus and headed east, looking for 312 East 95th Street. It was another breezy, overcast day, with rain threatening, and he stomped down the sidewalk, still angry with himself for nearly having sex with Marcie—and also for not having sex with Marcie. *She must think I'm a real jerk . . . and she'd be right.*

He had decided to re-think his strategy. He assumed Fagen and Becker were both in the city, working more promotional angles for *Two Against Nature*. Parading in front of Fagen's apartment hadn't gotten him anywhere. He had decided to try parading in front of their studio, on the chance he might spot one or both band members, or perhaps meet someone who knew them.

Arriving at 312, which was between First and Second Avenue, he looked around, noting that there was no sign announcing "River Sound" or, for that matter, any other business. He stepped into the tiny landing, which led to a stairwell, and checked the names on the mailboxes. Sure enough,

River Sound was listed next to one of the buzzers. He stepped back out onto the sidewalk, deployed his *Steely Dan Rules!* sign, and began to parade.

The building that housed River Sound was painted a gun-metal grey, which, in a crazy way, fit right in on a street that featured small apartment buildings painted royal blue, white-wash white, and a rainbow of other colors. The sidewalks were dirty, winos having left crumpled bags and broken bottles at their favorite "flops," and the smell was typical low rent Manhattan. *Lousy neighborhood.*

He paraded up and down the sidewalk, ignoring the stares of residents lounging on stairways. He tried to decipher the graffiti on the walls as he listened to *Countdown to Ecstasy*. Ten minutes into his parade, he heard what sounded like someone barking "Who let the dogs out?" followed by owl-like hoots of "Who? Who?" He glanced over his shoulder and saw a man marching behind him—but this was no normal march. This guy was high-stepping and swinging his arms. *Goose-stepping . . . and snapping his fingers like a fool.*

The man was a blur of red, white, and blue, like a flag flapping in a breeze. Eddie stopped at the corner, turned, and faced the man, who stopped a few feet away, grinning like Mickey Mouse on acid. They stared at each other. Eddie got his first good look at "Flagman." He was tall and thin—rail-thin—in his early twenties, and dressed in a rag-tag collection of sweat clothes, vests, and sweaters, all hanging on his stick-like body. He reminded Eddie of a wooden soldier, right out of the *Nutcracker*. And although Flagman was wearing thick, horn-rimmed glasses, Eddie could see that his eyes were bulging, practically out of their sockets.

He decided to challenge this wacko. "What do you think you're doing?"

"Marching with you." The man's grin got wider.

"What you're doing," Eddie growled, trying to scare him off, "that's not marching. That's . . . crazy."

"That's the way I march." Flagman proceeded to demonstrate, marching in a small circle. He stopped where he had started, and pushed his hands into his pockets.

"Are you a Steely Dan fan?" Eddie asked.

"No, never heard of them."

"Well, then," Eddie cranked it up a notch, "why don't you go the fuck away?"

Flagman smiled nervously. "I've got the right to walk anywhere I want. Just like you."

A few people stopped to watch as they tried to stare each other down. Perhaps a minute passed. Eddie knew that he couldn't stop this wacko from marching with him. *But maybe, just maybe, I can keep him under control...*

"Okay." Eddie tried to strike a tone that was firm, but hinted of acceptance. "You can march behind me, if you quit your goose-stepping, or whatever it is you're doing."

"It's not goose-stepping."

Remain calm... "Well, it will attract attention." Eddie emphasized each word, hoping his logic would get through the man's blank stare. Flagman finally smiled and nodded.

Eddie resumed parading, and Flagman followed—walking almost like a normal person—before he lost interest, presumably disappointed by the lack of reaction from other street-people. Eddie watched as Flagman crossed the street and disappeared down Second Avenue. *All that hazerai for five minutes of parading?*

Minutes later, a taxi pulled up at the corner and disgorged a woman, who started walking toward him. She was perhaps fifty feet away, and Eddie could see that she was about five foot six, with a decent figure. Nice walk. He slowed down as she approached.

"Excuse me." She smiled at him.

He stopped, taking her in. She was one of those attractive women of indeterminate heritage. Her eyes were brown—no, more like green—and her blonde hair was pinned up in one of those half-ponytail things. She wore a tan leather jacket over what looked like a black business suit.

"I'm from *The Post*. Do you mind answering a few questions?"

"*The Post*? You're a reporter?" *She must be in her mid-twenties...*

"Yes," she said, taking a business card from her handbag and handing it to him. "Lois Lane Smith. I write human interest stories, things like that."

"Lois Lane." He cracked a smile, "like in Superman?"

She returned the smile. "The same. A little joke my parents played on me."

"So what do you want with me?"

"A friend called me and said he saw you marching with that sign."

"So?"

"So, I thought it might make a good human interest story."

A newspaper article... publicity... maybe it would help his cause. How could Fagen and Becker ignore a newspaper article?

"Well?" she asked.

"Okay. What do you want to ask me?"

She gestured toward Ray's Famous Pizza at the corner of 95th and Second. "Why don't we go over there?" Soon they were seated across a table, Eddie with a greasy slice of pepperoni and a coke, and Lois with a cup of coffee. Eddie's *Steely Dan Rules!* sign was leaning against the wall a few feet away.

She took out a pen and notepad. "Let me start by asking you who you are, where you're from, and what it is you're doing?"

"That's a lot of questions."

"Well, I am a reporter."

"Okay. My name is Eddie Zittner. I'm from New Jersey, living temporarily in Manhattan."

"Zittner with one 't' or two 't's?"

"Two."

She started taking notes. "And what is it you're doing out here?"

"I'm trying to get the musicians from Steely Dan to come down from their studio and give me their autographs."

"Their autographs. Who's autograph? And why do you want their autographs?"

"Do you know who Steely Dan is?"

"Yeah, they're a rock and roll group. They have some good tunes."

"Good tunes?"

"Yeah, tunes. Songs."

Eddie stood up. "You don't know anything about them, do you?"

"I'm not an encyclopedia," Lois replied, giving back a little attitude. "I've heard some of their songs. Okay?" She stared hard at him.

"No, not okay." Eddie grabbed his sign, ready to resume his quest.

Lois stood and confronted him. "Hey! I'm a reporter. I can't know everything about everything."

"Obviously." He returned her stare. They stood there, eyeball to eyeball. An elderly couple at the counter turned and watched them.

"Hey!" She said, almost shouting. "Take it easy. I'm just trying to do my job."

The elderly couple flinched and hurried out of the store. The man behind the counter hollered at them: "You two! You're costing me business!"

Eddie ignored the man and continued to glare at Lois. "Tell your boss to send someone who knows music next time."

Lois glared back. "Well, fuck this. I didn't come all the way up here just to have you jerk me around." She shoved her pen and notebook into her handbag, and headed for the door.

Eddie, shaken, did some quick thinking. *Remember, idiot, that a little publicity might help your cause?* And he hadn't meant to come across like a jerk. "Wait a minute," he said.

She turned back to face him. "What?" She spat the word at him.

"Hey . . . I'm sorry," he said, calming down. "I've had a bad week. I'm sorry I lost it there."

She took a deep breath. "You gonna cooperate?"

"Yeah," he said, contrite. He sat back down and composed himself. Then she sat back down and took out her pen and notebook .

"Okay. Where were we? Tell me about Steely Dan."

"Steely Dan . . ." He gathered his thoughts. "Steely Dan is probably the best rock group of all time."

"Of all time. That's your opinion, right?"

"Yeah, and the opinion of lots of other people."

"Are you part of a fan club or something?"

A fan club? He'd never join a fan club. "No."

"So you're doing this on your own."

"Well, sometimes other people join me while I'm walking."

Lois looked out the window, down 95th Street, as if searching for his followers. "It's pretty quiet around here. Not many people."

"There are, sometimes."

"Let's go back to Steely Dan. What makes them so good?"

This was the question he had contemplated on-and-off for months—years, really. "It's a lot of things. The music is excellent. Exceptional. And the lyrics are, well, unique. Sometimes funny, other times sarcastic."

"So it's really good music, with clever lyrics?"

"It's hard to explain."

"Okay, let me ask a different question. Why are you on this particular street?"

"River Sound, their studio, is just down the block."

"River Sound." She wrote the name in her notebook.

"Yeah."

"And how do you know River Sound is their studio?"

"Research."

Five minutes later the interview was over, and they were back on Second Avenue. Lois pulled a camera out of her handbag. "Do you mind if I take a picture of you holding that sign?"

He thought for a moment. A newspaper article was one thing, but his picture in the paper? After some discussion, she took a picture of the sign as it leaned against a tree. They said their good-byes, Lois thanking him and telling him to look for the article in tomorrow's paper. She turned and walked down the street, looking for a taxi.

Uninformed, but she had a really nice walk.

19

Wednesday, March 15, 2000

Searching for Steely Dan

Exclusive
By Lois Lane Smith

Eddie Zittner is on a quest. He is marching up and down the sidewalks of Manhattan, trying to get the autographs of two of rock's most reclusive stars.

"My goal is to meet them, shake their hands, and get their autographs," Zittner said, referring to Donald Fagen and Walter Becker, founding members of the rock group Steely Dan.

Zittner, 29, marches in front of River Sound on East 95th Street. He believes that he will spot Fagen or Becker coming out of the studio. He has marched three times in the last week, dressed warmly and clutching a sign that states "Steely Dan Rules." So far, no luck.

"I'm doing this on my own," he said, noting that occasionally people march with him.

Zittner has been a fan of "The Dan" since he was a teenager. He is not associated with a fan club, or any other group. He is a New Jersey native, living temporarily in Manhattan, and manages the Borders bookstore in Murray Hill. He said he is married, but would not comment further on his personal life.

When asked if anyone objected to his marching, he said "I know my rights. I have the right to walk on the sidewalk, like anyone else."

Steely Dan was well known in the 70s, when they had a number of hit records. They fell into obscurity in the 80s, but made a comeback in the 90s, playing oldies as they toured the United States. Zittner noted that the rock group has just released a CD—Two Against Nature—their first release in almost 20 years.

Zittner said, "Steely Dan is probably the best rock group of all time." He plans to continue his lonely quest until he gets those autographs.

****

Eddie woke up early—it was eight-thirty, and his brother was already gone—dressed, and went downstairs to get a copy of *The Post*. He buzzed with anticipation as he walked a block to the nearest newsstand. It was warm and breezy, so humid there were wisps of fog in the air. He bought a paper and stood on the sidewalk flipping pages. He found the article at the bottom of page seven, beneath a picture of his *Steely Dan Rules!* sign. He tingled with excitement as he read the article. *His name in the paper! Publicity for his cause! How could Fagen and Becker ignore this?*

He read the article a second time, and a feeling of concern began to creep over him. He wasn't the manager at Borders, and he wondered how his boss would react to that. On the other hand, a little free publicity for the store wouldn't hurt, would it? And Lois wrote that The Dan had fallen into obscurity in the 80s. Where did she get that idea? And oldies? He'd never thought of The Dan's music as old. He folded the paper and tucked it under his arm as he hurried back to the apartment. Maybe he should call *The Post* and set Lois Lane Smith straight. Maybe they would print a clarification tomorrow.

Two hours later, he was sitting on the sofa, reading Harlan Coben's *Drop Shot* and listening to *Katy Lied* on the stereo, when his cell phone rang. He used the remote to switch the stereo off, and noted the time: just before eleven. He needed to be at work by one. It was his father. After quick hellos, Harry Zittner came right to the point.

"I saw that article in *The Post*."

Eddie could only respond with a tentative "Uh-huh."

"What the hell were you thinking?" He kept quiet as his father began the ass-chewing. "How do you think Alison will react when she sees this? Have you totally given up on your marriage?"

He swallowed, trying to get the saliva flowing again. "No, Dad, I haven't."

"Then how do you think she'll react? Did you ever call her?"

"No, not yet."

"I don't know what to say to you anymore."

Eddie took a couple of breaths, thinking how he might respond. "Dad, listen, the reporter came to me, and asked to interview me. That's how it happened."

"Three times you've been out on the sidewalk, carrying a sign?" Eddie couldn't think of an answer to that. His father continued, "I don't remember you telling me or your mother about your plan to do this."

"Well, I was trying to keep it quiet."

He heard his father cough, or laugh, or maybe choke. "And this article, that's part of keeping it quiet?"

In his mind, Eddie conceded that he'd lost this argument. He was never really in it. But he did want to try to have an adult-to-adult conversation with his father. "I see your point, Dad."

"Well, it's about time."

"Has Mom seen it yet?"

"I don't know. She hasn't called me about it. But I'm sure someone will show it to her." Eddie could tell that his father was calming down.

"Do you think I should call her?"

"I don't know. Look, Eddie, I've gotta go. Tax time, remember?"

"Yeah," Eddie remembered that he needed to get his and Alison's tax records together. He'd have to get in touch with her about that. All the tax stuff was at the apartment in Somerset.

"I just don't know anymore, Eddie," his father said, hanging up.

*****

At three, his cell phone rang again. He had just finished unpacking the day's shipment of hard covers and paperbacks. He glanced at the display: it was his brother. He picked up and said hello.

"Eddie," Mark chuckled, "you sneaky son-of-a-bitch."

Nothing like being subtle. "You saw the article?" *Not really a question, was it?*

"Yeah, I saw the article. I was wondering what you were doing in your spare time."

Well, now you know.

Mark continued, "So where were you hiding the signs?"

"Under the bed."

"And you usually come and go while I'm at work."

"Yeah."

"Like I said, you're a sneaky son-of-a-bitch."

Eddie detected a lightness in his brother's voice. He wasn't angry, he thought, he was just giving him the business. "I wasn't trying to hide anything. I just didn't think you'd be interested."

"Hey, it's okay with me. You can do whatever you want. Have Mom or Dad called?"

"Dad called. He wasn't very happy."

"I bet he reamed you out pretty good."

"Yeah, he did."

"*The Post.* You're dragging the good name of Zittner through the mud." Eddie could tell that Mark was having fun now. "Why didn't you go to the *Times*?"

"She found me, Mark. The reporter came to me."

"I believe you, Eddie. Look, I've got to get back to work."

"Mark, will I see you tonight?"

"Yeah, I'll be home. You take care of dinner, okay?"

"Will do."
"Eddie?"
"Yeah?"
"One more question. What did she look like?"
"Who?"
"The reporter."
"Not too bad."
"Sweet. I've gotta go."

****

From: MarKau55@nyc.rr.com

To: EZEddie32@nyc.rr.com

Subject:!!!!

Eddie, I saw the article in the newspaper. I must say I'm impressed. And you haven't been arrested. With this publicity, maybe you will have some success meeting Fagen and Becker.
I wanted to talk to you (face-to-face) about what happened on Monday night, but maybe it would be easier in an email. I am sorry that I came on so strongly. All I can think to say is that I am attracted to you, and I didn't realize you weren't ready for "that kind" of relationship. You never told me how long you had been separated from your wife. I now know (I'm guessing) that it must not have been too long. Am I right?
I would like to start again, if you are willing, and to take it slower (a lot slower if that is what you want.) How do you feel about meeting somewhere, a public place, this time?
Please let me know....Marcie

****

Just before midnight, a buzzing sound woke Eddie from a fitful sleep. *Where the hell am I?* He fumbled with the light and then managed to locate his cell phone.

"Hello," he mumbled, glancing at his watch.

"Eddie? It's your mother." Words that were the rough equivalent of ice water running down his back.

He gathered himself. "Oh, hi, Ma." *And to what do I owe the pleasure of this call?*

"I'm sorry to call this late. Did I wake you?"

"No, Ma, it's all right. I was just, uh, reading."

"Eddie, I've been lying here in bed, but I can't sleep thinking about that newspaper article."

"Oh, you saw it?" He cringed. *Could I have asked a dumber question?*

"Yes, I saw it. I believe everyone in the office tried to show it to me at least once. Some people more than once."

That can't be good.

His mother continued, "I don't think I'll be able to sleep unless I get this off my chest."

Resigned to whatever fate awaited him, he replied, "What is it, Ma?"

"You're an idiot, Eddie."

He couldn't think of a good response to that.

"You're an idiot. You call me when you come to your senses."

"Okay, Ma."

He heard her breathe a sigh of relief. "There. Now maybe I can get some sleep."

"Okay, Ma," he said, as he heard his mother hang up the phone.

20

Thursday, March 16, 2000

Eddie sat on the sofa, sipping coffee and staring out the window. Across the river, Brooklyn and Queens spread out like a vast urban desert. The apartment was as quiet as a tomb. He thought about yesterday's events: the newspaper article, the call from his father, the call and then dinner with his brother, and the email from Marcie. *Not to forget the late-night call from his mother.* He knew that what he really needed to do was call Alison. It had been more than two weeks since she had thrown him out, or had walked out on him—however he wanted to think of it—and if he was going to try to save his marriage, now would be a good time to start. He picked up his cell phone and speed-dialed her number.

She picked up. "Alison Zittner."

"Alison, it's me, Eddie." Silence on the line. "How are you?"

"I'm fine, Eddie. I see you've been busy."

He had assumed she'd seen the article—God knows, everyone else had—and that she would give him some shit about it. "You saw the article?"

"Me and a few hundred thousand other people."

He thought for a few seconds, but couldn't come up with a meaningful response. Finally, he said, "What can I say?"

"There's not much you can say, is there?"

"Look, Alison, I think we should sit down and talk."

"Talk about what?"

"Us. Our marriage."

After a pause, she replied, "I've been thinking about that."

"I have, too. I've been thinking about it a lot."

"You must have plenty of time as you're marching up and down the sidewalk."

"As a matter of fact, yes, I was thinking about you as I marched."

"Whatever."

"Is this how you're going to be? Nasty?"

"As opposed to stupid?"

"Look. Do you want to talk, or not?"

She paused for a few seconds, then replied, "Yes, Eddie, I think we should talk."

"Okay," he said, relieved. He didn't think he could meet her today; he was scheduled to work a full shift. *And Alison's schedule . . . she might be anywhere.* "Where are you tomorrow?" he asked.

"Where are you right now?"

Right now? "I'm at my brother's apartment. East 32nd Street. Where are you?"

"I'm in Midtown. I've got a meeting with a client in half an hour. I could meet you after that."

He glanced at his watch. *Just after nine-thirty.* "What time?"

"Say, eleven?"

"I can do that. I don't have to be at work until one."

"You have a job?"

"Yeah. I'm working at a bookstore. As a temp."

"Another bookstore?"

Is that sarcasm? "Yes, another bookstore."

"Well, at least you're working. How about eleven o'clock at the corner of 50th and Broadway? In front of the Denny's?"

"I'll be there."

"Okay. See you then." She hung up.

*****

He arrived at Denny's just before eleven, and stood near the entry, scanning the sidewalks as he tried to keep warm. The sun had disappeared behind ugly grey clouds, and a cold front was on the way. He soon retreated into the warmth of the restaurant. Alison showed up at eleven-fifteen, spotted him through the window, and pushed through the revolving door.

"Sorry I'm late," she said, "the meeting took longer than I expected."

Right. She took off her scarf, gloves and overcoat, revealing a well-cut business suit. *No skimping when it comes to dressing for work.* Five minutes later, they were seated in a booth, opposite each other, waiting for coffee. Since sitting, Alison had busied herself making notes in her personal organizer. He tried to read her mood, but she was giving nothing away.

Finally, she put down her pen. "Eddie, I've been thinking about our marriage, too. I think I still love you, but . . ."

But what?

She looked around the restaurant before finally locking her eyes onto his. "But, we've just grown apart."

That sounds rehearsed. The waitress arrived with coffee, and Eddie watched as she filled two cups and moved to the next table.

Alison continued, "I think we're going in different directions."

He felt a twinge of fear. "What do you mean?"

"Can't you see it? Haven't you felt us growing apart, these last few months?"

Since that night at their apartment, he'd done a lot of thinking. He believed that he was still in love with her. She was the only girl—the only woman—he had ever loved. Sure, he'd gone out with lots of girls in high school and college, but Alison was the only one he'd ever fallen for. And he'd fallen hard. But he had to be honest with himself, as much as it hurt: they didn't seem to be on the same page anymore.

"I guess I agree with you, to some extent."

"To some extent? Eddie, I'm trying to build a career. I work all the time trying to get ahead. I was trying to get us to the point where we might have been able to move to a nicer place. And what are you doing to help? You can't hold a job, and you don't even try to write anymore."

"Alison—"

"And need I mention your fixation on Steely Dan? Parading up and down the sidewalk carrying a sign?"

"I just do it in my spare time. It doesn't interfere with my job or anything."

"Eddie, listen. You're twenty-nine years old and you still act like a teenager." He could see her anger building. "I'm not sure I want to be married to a person like that. I don't understand you anymore."

Don't bother to understand . . . "Alison, it's just a hobby. I don't see why you object to me having a hobby."

"A hobby? That's no hobby, Eddie, that's an obsession."

He felt a narrow blade slide slowly and painfully into his belly. He took a deep breath. "Alison. I know I still love you. And you said you think you still love me. Doesn't that count for something?"

"Yes, Eddie, it counts for something, but it's not enough anymore. Not for me, anyway." She drained her coffee. "And I'm not really sure I'm still in love with you."

Eddie felt the blade twist. "Alison, is there someone else?"

His wife looked uncomfortable. Maybe she blushed a little; it was hard for him to tell with all the make-up she wore. "No, Eddie." She tapped her fingers on the empty cup.

There wasn't much to say after that, and it quickly became uncomfortable to sit across from one another. Alison glanced at her watch and stood up. She had to get to her next meeting, she said. Eddie watched as she picked up her handbag, scarf and overcoat and headed for the door.

The rest of the day was a blur. Having lost his appetite, Eddie decided to skip lunch and go directly to work. Arriving just before noon, he worked straight through to six—no breaks, no nothing—and then hit the wall. Starving and exhausted, he told his boss he had to leave, and was surprised to find out that he'd been scheduled to work from one-to-five, not one-to-nine. Not a problem, his boss said; he appreciated the initiative.

Eddie walked west toward his brother's apartment. Stopping at a hole-in-the-wall Chinese restaurant, he gorged on half a dozen egg rolls dipped in sweet and sour sauce laced with hot mustard. He washed the egg rolls down with a Coke, and belched the rest of the way home. Mark was out—another dinner date, he had said—so he could suffer alone. He decided to put on some Santana. By seven, he was stretched out on the sofa, popping Rolaids and listening to "Fried Neckbones and Home Fries" until he couldn't stand it anymore.

21

Friday, March 17, 2000

It was a strange noise. Eddie opened his eyes. *A fly in the room?* He glanced out the window. The office building across the street was shrouded in mist. *A buzzing sound . . . a bumblebee under the bed?* His brain, foggy from sleep, finally kicked into gear. Still lying under the covers, he reached down and walked his fingers along the carpet until he found his cell phone. He picked it up and brought it to his face.

"Hello?" he mumbled.

"Eddie? Did I wake you?"

"Who is this?" *Alison?*

"It's Marcie. Did I wake you?"

Marcie . . . "Oh, hi." He sat up. "No, I was just getting up. What time is it, anyway?"

"It's almost ten."

"Almost ten. Man, I must have been zonked."

"Out drinking?"

"Uh, no." *Think fast.* "Just working too hard."

"Oh. I thought you might have been out celebrating that newspaper article."

"That article . . . . No, no celebration."

"Did you get my email?"

"Yeah." His mind was clear now. "Yeah. I'm sorry I didn't get back to you."

"Busy, huh?"

"Yeah. Like I said, working some long hours."

"Eddie?" He heard hesitation in her voice. "I just wanted to apologize, again, for coming on so strong last week."

"Uh, it's okay, Marcie. I guess I'm just not ready yet. You caught me off guard."

"Well, like I said, I'm sorry."

"It's okay."

"So, what do you think? Can we start again? A little slower this time?"

Slower . . . Eddie had been thinking about Marcie for days. Yeah, there was too much going on in his life right now. He did need to take it slower. But he felt his penis getting hard.

"Yeah, Marcie, I'd like that."

"Me, too."

"Well, you cooked last time. How about letting me take you out to dinner one night?"

"How nice. Thank you for asking."

"There's a good Chinese place I know, Ming's, on Third Avenue at 34th. How about next week?"

"How about tonight?"

Tonight . . . He thought for a few seconds. He was working another one-to-five shift today. It felt a little sudden, but, what the hell.

"Yeah. I guess I could do tonight."

"Chinese sounds great. What time?"

"Uh, why don't we meet there at seven?"

"Ming's on Third Avenue at 34th."

"Yeah. You know the place?"

"No, but I'll find it. Casual dress, I assume?"

"Yeah." *Yeah, why don't you wear that denim skirt again . . . with no pantyhose.* He remembered how smooth her skin felt that night. He was getting harder.

"Okay, I'll see you tonight, Easy Eddie."

"Oh, yeah. No one's called me that in a while."

"Easy Eddie. Take it easy, Eddie." She hung up.

Two minutes later, he was in the shower, all soaped up and masturbating.

*****

Eddie arrived at Ming's just before seven. Before he could get his name on the waiting list, he heard his name being called. He looked toward the windows and spotted Mark, sitting with a woman, waving him over. He waved back and started toward them. As he walked between the tables, he took a good look at his brother's date. She was pretty enough—nice figure, as far as he could tell from far away—with a light complexion that contrasted sharply with jet black hair, deep red lipstick, and heavy, dark make-up. She was wearing black slacks, a red blouse, and a short black leather jacket. An average face, he thought, but the overall effect was striking. *Almost Gothic.*

The scene was, Eddie thought, a virtual riot of colors. The restaurant was decorated in traditional Chinese red, with gold trim and lots of wood paneling. Mark's date was drinking something purple. *Cranberry juice?* And his brother was looking sharp in a navy blue suit—Mark must have owned dozens of suits—with a white shirt and a green tie. And drinking a large mug of green beer. Eddie realized that he had never seen his brother "out on a date." He looked a little closer—did Mark's hair appear to be a little thicker? Was he wearing a weave? Using Rogaine? And his skin . . . *was Mark going to a tanning salon?*

Mark raised his mug and said "Cheers."

"Hey, Mark." Eddie stopped beside the booth. "I almost forgot it was St. Patrick's Day."

"How could you forget that?" Eddie glanced at Mark's date, who was eyeing him as she sipped her drink. His brother continued, "Eddie, this is Connie Lee Wilson. Connie, this is my brother, Eddie. Easy Eddie."

Eddie offered his hand. "Nice to meet you, Connie."

"Connie Lee," she corrected.

"Connie Lee," he repeated, nodding. She nodded back.

"So what brings you here?" Mark continued. "Take-out?"

"No, as a matter of fact, I'm meeting someone."

Mark grinned. "You have a date?"

Shit! Eddie coughed, glanced at his watch, and tried to think of some way to avoid answering that question. But he was trapped. And he knew it. After another cough, he replied, "Uh, yeah, I guess you could call it a date."

Mark raised his eyebrows, wondering, Eddie was sure, why his married brother was "out on a date." Mark glanced at Connie Lee—who had a blank look on her face—and turned back to Eddie. "Well, why don't you join us?"

Join us? "Uh," Eddie stammered, glancing toward the restaurant's entrance. Marcie was just coming through the door, wearing tightly woven fishnet stockings under a leather skirt. He felt a tingle in his groin. "Uh . . . sure, why not? Hold on," he said, moving away from the booth. "My date just arrived."

Minutes later, after a round of introductions, smiles, polite handshakes, and the ordering of food and drink, the couples were settled in the booth, Mark and his date on the window side, Eddie next to his brother, and Marcie, looking a little uncomfortable, sitting next to Connie Lee. The drinks arrived; Marcie going with a glass of chardonnay, and the brothers splitting a pitcher of green beer. Connie Lee had ordered another Portuguese Breeze; which, she said, was a mixture of madiera, vodka, and cranberry juice that she herself had "invented."

Eddie tried to jump-start the conversation by asking how long Mark and Connie Lee had been seeing each other. A look passed between them, and Mark finally responded, "Oh, a few months," with Connie Lee adding, "We work at the same place." More details followed: Connie Lee had been hired a year ago by Mark's boss, as secretary of the department. They had dated on-and-off, trying to keep it quiet, but their "thing" had soon become the worst-kept secret in the office. So now they were open about the fact that they were dating, but played it cool at work. It wouldn't be long, Connie Lee figured, until she was transferred to another department.

When Mark had mentioned that he was in investment banking, Marcie's eyes lit up like Chanukah candles. "That sounds so interesting," she said. "What kind of deals are you working on?" This was an open invitation for Mark, who presented Marcie with one of his business cards and proceeded to describe his latest project, a merger between restaurant chains, and his recent trip to Miami as part of the negotiating team. That led to "Where did you stay?" and "What did you see?" and "Where did you eat?" kind of questions. It turned out that, as a teenager, Marcie's family had vacationed in Miami Beach just about every year. She loved Cuban food—paella, fried plantains, the works.

And Mark was fascinated to hear that Marcie was in law school. "How long until you graduate?" he asked, and then, "What branch of law are you specializing in?" The word "branch" had gotten a chuckle out of Eddie, who remarked that he thought branches only grew on trees. Marcie politely ignored him, and responded to Mark with, "Well, I've always been interested in mergers and acquisitions."

Eddie tried to engage Connie Lee in conversation, but now working on her third, or maybe fourth, Portuguese Breeze, she seemed oblivious to her surroundings. Finally, he shut up, occupying himself by pushing chunks of orange beef around his plate. He was miffed and embarrassed, but still smiled, nodded at the appropriate moments, and jumped into Marcie's conversation with Mark whenever he could, which wasn't very often.

On the sidewalk, they hailed a couple of taxis. Connie Lee was hanging all over Mark—eyes shining, cheeks glowing—perhaps, Eddie thought, anticipating another drink or two and some deviant sex before passing out. Mark guided her into the back seat, and then winked at Eddie and told him not to wait up.

As the first cab sped away, Eddie turned back to Marcie, who mumbled something about needing to get some sleep. Her shift at Zabar's began at eight the next morning, she explained. After a polite good-bye kiss, Eddie helped her into the second cab, and watched as it pulled slowly away. Then he turned and began walking back to his brother's apartment. *At least the sizzling black pepper shrimp had been good.*

22

Saturday, March 18, 2000

After another night of tossing, turning, and wrestling with sheets and blankets, Eddie dragged himself out of bed just after nine. He walked into the kitchen and spotted a post-it on the counter with *I'm at work—Mark* printed on it. He poured a cup of coffee—at least his brother had left him some—and scanned the headlines of *The Times*, noting that now it was The Reverend Al Sharpton who was blasting Mayor Guiliani and the New York Police Department. By the time he looked up, it was almost ten. He was working an eleven-to-five shift today. *Time to get moving.*

*****

Just after five, Eddie let himself back into the apartment, and was surprised to see his brother sitting on the sofa, sucking on a Heineken, and watching what sounded like CNN.

"Hey, Eddie, why don't you grab a beer and join me?"

"Will do." He perked up a little. He'd been depressed all day thinking about Marcie and last night's dinner. He got a beer out of the refrigerator, walked back to the living room, and plopped down on the loveseat.

Wolf Blitzer was rambling on about the Middle East. "So, Mark, you worked today?" Then remembering that his brother had left him a note to that effect, he added, "I mean, how many hours did you work today?"

Mark used the remote to mute the television. "Nine to three."

"Mmm." Eddie tried to lip-read what Blitzer was saying.

A few seconds later, Mark switched the television off. "Eddie . . . we need to talk."

Eddie looked at his brother. Mark looked a little tense, and cleared his throat before speaking: "Eddie, look, I don't know any good way to tell you this. Marcie and I have been in touch with each other."

Eddie stared at his brother. *Shit.* He had entertained hopes that Mark might apologize for coming on to Marcie over dinner. "And?"

Mark drained his beer. "I want to be straight with you, Eddie. We want to begin seeing each other."

"Uh . . . how did she contact you?" Eddie remembered that Mark had given her his business card, but he thought he'd ask anyway.

"Email. She sent me an email at work."

"I thought she was working today."

"I guess she sent it before she went to work."

"So you exchanged emails?"

"Well, she sent me an email, and then I called her on her cell. Hey," he grinned nervously, "it's hard to communicate with emails."

Yeah.

Mark continued, "So, anyway, I hope you understand."

Eddie thought back to last night's dinner. At the time, he couldn't tell whether Marcie had been flirting with Mark, or Mark with Marcie, or whether they had just "hit it off." *But what did it matter?* He took a long pull on his beer. *Act natural, like you don't care.* "Yeah, I understand. I saw that you guys were interested in each other." It hurt to say it out loud.

"I know things have been rough on you, Eddie."

"It's okay, Mark. Hell, Marcie and I weren't going together or anything." *Past tense.*

"She said she was going to call you."

"Mmm," was all he could manage. He drank some more beer and stared out the window.

Mark got up. "Well, look, I've got to get dressed." He turned and moved toward the master bedroom.

****

From: MarKau55@rr.nyc.com

To: EZEddie32@rr.nyc.com

Subject: (no subject)

Eddie, I told your brother that I would call you, and I intended to call you, but maybe it will be easier in an email.

I assume by now (I'm writing this Saturday at 6 PM. I just got home from work) Mark has spoken to you. I am sorry things worked out this way. Maybe you saw it over dinner, that Mark and I were interested in each other. You know, chemistry between people is what it is. I can't explain it. It just happened.

I know you are going through some tough times, what with the separation from your wife, etc. I feel guilty that I have contributed to your unhappiness. Eddie, I wish the best for you, however things turn out with your marriage. And I hope we can remain friends.

…Marcie

****

<u>From</u>: EZEddie32@rr.nyc.com

<u>To</u>: MarKau55@rr.nyc.com

<u>Subject</u>: Thanks for the email

    It's okay, Marcie. Mark did talk to me, and I do understand. Hey, I learned something: not to take your date to your brother's favorite restaurant.
    Seriously, I want you to be happy, and I want my brother to be happy. If you guys hit it off, well, then, I'll be happy, too.
    …Eddie

23

Working title: <u>The Story In Your Eyes</u>

An unpublished short story
by Eddie Zittner

    I met her in an internet chat room. We were debating the merits of Steely Dan's new CD, *Two Against Nature*. She thought it was too jazzy; she liked the old stuff better. I agreed with her—it is too jazzy—but I thought I'd argue the point, just for the sake of arguing. So we argued, and when we got tired of arguing, we chatted, which is what I assume you call it when you're in a chat room.

    She said her name was Marcy, that she was 25 years old, and that she was in law school. Right! Did she take me for a fool? For all I knew, she was a bleached-out housewife, swilling bourbon and looking for some extra-curricular action. Or some teenager jerking my chain. Or some gay caballero really looking to jerk my chain. And what a coincidence: we both lived in Manhattan. So, after some more "chatting," we agreed to meet Saturday morning for a "get acquainted" breakfast at The Stage Delicatessen, a tourist spot in Midtown. I don't know why she insisted on The Stage, but she did. Maybe she knows someone there. Or maybe she gets a discount there. We agreed to wear our Steely Dan hats so we would recognize each other. She bought hers during the 1993 tour; mine's from the 1994 tour.

    Who knew if she really was twenty-five? Who knew if she would show up? Who knew if she was even a "she"? Nonetheless, I decided to go. Maybe I'd get lucky.

    I arrived shortly before nine and stood waiting in the entryway. A few minutes later, here she comes, wearing the SD hat. And she hadn't lied: she was definitely a woman, in her mid-twenties, I guessed, and pretty good-looking. I mean, I couldn't be sure she was 100% female—if you know what I mean—but maybe I would get the chance to find out.

    We introduced ourselves. She said her name was Marcy Koffman—probably Jewish, I guessed. We went inside, hung up our coats, and the hostess seated us.

    I took a good look at her. Her most striking feature was her eyes—beautiful blue eyes, with soaring, dramatic eyebrows, just like Liv Tyler, whom I have worshipped, from afar, ever since I saw *Armageddon*. She had a pretty face, with a dimple on her left cheek, and she wore an array of earrings—half a dozen, at least. Her auburn hair fell around her shoulders. And, from what I could see, she had a nice figure.

    The waitress brought coffee. I ordered my usual deli breakfast, nova with cream cheese on a sesame bagel. She ordered a plate of sable with an onion bagel, sliced but not toasted, on the side. This got my attention.

I didn't want to appear completely ignorant, but I had to ask. "What is sable?"

"You don't know what sable is? Sable Carp? It's a kind of smoked fish."

"No, I've never heard of it."

"I'll let you have a taste." Her marvelous eyes narrowed. "Didn't you say you were from the city?"

"Jersey. I grew up in Jersey. But I'm living here now."

"Jewish?"

"Yeah. You?"

"Yeah. You grew up in Jersey and never had sable?"

"I was deprived as a child."

"You must have been."

She sipped her coffee, and her eyes twinkled, and I started to fall in love.

(to be continued)

24

Monday, March 20, 2000

The ride uptown was slow and painful. As the bus snaked through horrendous mid-morning traffic, Eddie ate his jelly donuts, drank his coffee, stared out the window, and wondered how fate could have brought the unlikely trio of Alison, Mark, and Marcie together to make his life a living hell. Well, correct that; as far as he knew, Alison and Marcie had never met.

He got off the bus at 95th Street, and, carrying his *Steely Dan Rules!* sign, headed east. It was a mild, breezy day, and he kicked his way through dead leaves and blowing newspapers. The streets were crowded—cars double-parked, trucks jockeying for space, and delivery men pushing dollies overflowing with fresh produce. He walked past a teenager who was either trying to fix a car or steal it.

As he approached River Sound, he heard a window slide open across the street.

"Hey, Steely Dan person!" An old guy stuck his head out a third floor window. He was wearing a New York Rangers cap.

Eddie looked up and spotted the man. "Hey."

"I saw that thing in the newspaper about you."

"No kidding." *Maybe this guy knows something.* "You ever see Fagen or Becker around here?"

"Who?"

"Steely Dan? You know, the musicians?"

The old man took off his cap and looked inside it, seemingly lost in thought. *Maybe the answer to the question is in the hat?* Finally he looked back toward Eddie.

"No, can't say that I have."

"You sure?"

"Wouldn't know what they looked like."

Then why bother me? Eddie started moving down the sidewalk.

Ranger fan continued, "Can't say as I ever heard of Steely Dan."

Then why the fuck bother me? He walked a little faster.

"That is, before I saw that thing in the newspaper."

Then why not shut the fuck up? He stopped and turned. "Well, thanks anyway . . . for your *help*." Sarcasm dripped from his voice.

"Glad to oblige," the old man said, a satisfied look on his face. He pulled his head back inside and slammed the window shut.

Eddie began to parade.

Minutes later, Flagman was back, this time with two of his cohorts. Flag was wearing what must have been his traditional array of red, white, and blue clothing. His friends were less colorful, wearing jeans, grey hooded sweatshirts, and fake leather jackets, but all three sported the same "wild hair and thick glasses" look. *An invasion of the nerds.*

Flag led the group, shouting "my main man" as he raised his hand, expecting Eddie to high-five him.

Eddie was in no mood to high-five anybody. "What the fuck are you doing here?"

"Hey, man," Flag replied, "I saw that article about you in *The Post.*"

"No shit." Regret crept into Eddie's gut.

"No shit, man! You're famous! Eddie something, right?"

Regret gave way to resignation. "Yeah. My name is Eddie."

"I knew it!" Flag smiled like he had made a new friend.

Eddie, not accepting defeat, decided to change tactics. "You guys must live around here, right?"

"Right. Right up there." Flag gestured across the street at the building where Ranger fan lived.

"All three of you?"

"Yeah. All in the same building."

The heartbreak of inbreeding. "You guys know the old man wearing the Ranger cap?"

Hooded Sweatshirt, looking proud, replied, "My old man."

The four of them stood in a small circle, eyeing each other. Eddie did some quick thinking: He probably couldn't get rid of them—hell, he figured, they were part of the neighborhood, just like stray cats and overflowing bags of garbage.

"Look, you want to parade with me?"

Flag, Hood, and Wild Hair looked at each other, shrugged, grunted, and nodded—lots of non-verbal communication between these guys—until Flag, obviously the leader, said yeah, why not.

"Okay," Eddie continued, "but listen, you've got to be cool. No craziness."

More shrugs, grunts, and shuffling of feet. "Oh yeah," Flag said, "No problem. Just like last week."

"No, not like last week." *Try to be diplomatic, Eddie . . .* "We've got to be cool. Okay?"

"Okay . . . cool," Flag replied. "Yeah, we can be cool." More nodding, grunting, shuffling, and a belch from Wild Hair.

"Then let's go. Follow me." Eddie started down the sidewalk.

"Cool," Flag said, leading his cohorts forward.

Eddie glanced at his rag-tag collection of followers. *What the fuck am I doing?*

Soon the procession was marching in a rectangle: East along the south side of 95th Street to River Sound, then across the street, then west back to Second Avenue, then across 95th again, and so on and so forth. To break the monotony, Eddie told them a little bit about The Dan, and seconds later heard soft chanting behind him, first "Steely Dan" and then just "Dan, Dan, Dan" over and over. Between chants, Eddie found out that his three "helpers" were just friends—not first cousins as he had suspected—and all lived with their parents. Flag and Wild Hair were part-time students with part-time jobs. Hood seemed to be more into web surfing and game playing. Eddie suspected that smoking weed occupied a good deal of their time—and he felt a twinge of sadness as he remembered his dinner date with Marcie.

But the parade was unproductive. There was no sign of Fagen, Becker, or anyone who remotely resembled them. No one approached them with news of The Dan. Other than a few curious stares, and an occasional "get out of the way," they were pretty much ignored.

Just before noon, the four men stood in front of Ray's Famous Pizza, discussing the improbable concept of having lunch together, when a police cruiser pulled up. The policeman rolled down his window and turned toward them. Eddie saw his reflection on a pair of aviator sunglasses.

The policeman addressed him. "Are you the ringleader of this motley crew?"

Eddie grinned nervously as Hood stepped forward and mumbled something about that being a good band, too.

The policeman got out of his cruiser, whipped off his sunglasses, and eyed Hood. "You better step back, son."

Eddie stepped in front of Hood. "I'm the leader, officer." *Hood was going to fuck this up.*

The policeman asked Eddie for some identification, which he handed over. After glancing at the driver's license, the policeman handed it back and said, "You can't demonstrate out here."

Eddie studied the policeman—Officer Gregory, by his name tag—young, blond, and intense. *This guy could have been a storm trooper in another life.* "Officer, I was told that there was no problem with a peaceful demonstration."

"Who told you that?"

"A policeman."

"What policeman?"

"His name is Vince. That's all I know."

"Well," Officer Gregory stood with hands on hips, "this is my beat, and I don't allow any demonstrations."

This is my beat?

Hood mumbled something about police brutality. Office Gregory gave him a quick glance and then turned back to Eddie. "Shut your friend up."

Eddie turned toward Hood and told him to shut up. Unfortunately, he was still holding his *Steely Dan Rules!* sign, which caught Officer Gregory flush across the face. The policeman grabbed his nose, and things quickly spun out of control. A minute later Eddie was leaning up against the police cruiser, hands cuffed behind him. Flag, Hood, and Wild Hair—neighborhood guys who were just passing by, they had pleaded—beat a hasty retreat into Ray's.

25

The back seat of the police cruiser smelled like a sewer. *The key word is survival...*

Eddie cursed softly to himself as Officer Gregory drove to the 19th Precinct on East 67th Street. The policeman seemed to be calming down. He couldn't remember the last time he'd seen anyone that angry. He'd been lucky; Officer Gregory hadn't suffered anything more serious than a bruise. *Maybe that would work in his favor, come trial time.*

Arriving at the station, Officer Gregory un-cuffed him, shepherded him through the booking process, and put him in a one-man holding cell. Before his cell phone was confiscated, he was allowed one call, which he placed to his brother. Mark, in a meeting in Connecticut, said he would leave immediately. *Not much I can do except wait...*

Just after two, another policeman escorted him to an interview room, a windowless, puke-green cube perhaps eight feet on a side, with a metal table and four metal chairs all bolted solidly to the floor. He watched as the officer stepped into the hallway, closed the door, and locked it from the outside. *The perfect place to work me over while no one is looking.*

Minutes later, he heard the door being unlocked. He looked up, expecting to see his brother. Instead, Lois Lane Smith walked briskly into the room.

"Well, Mr. Zittner." She offered her hand. "We meet again."

Eddie, surprised to see her, and disappointed that she wasn't Mark, nevertheless gathered his wits, stood, and took her hand. "I wasn't expecting you."

She took off her coat, dropped her handbag at her feet, and sat. "Who were you expecting? Your lawyer?"

"My brother. I don't have a lawyer. Never needed one."

"Until now?"

Eddie eyed her. She was wearing a red sweater over a striped blouse, and navy blue slacks. Her hair was styled differently than the last time he'd seen her. She looked different—better. "How did you know I was in jail?"

"The desk sergeant gave me a call."

"No kidding."

"Yeah. He saw your Steely Dan sign and figured you were the guy in the newspaper article."

"Do you know many policemen?"

"A few. I am a reporter."

He thought for a minute. "Yeah, that makes sense."

She reached down and took a pen and notepad out of her handbag. "Will you sit down and answer a few questions for me?"

"What, you're going to write about me being arrested?"

"Yeah, that was the idea."

"Well, I don't want this . . ." Eddie, still standing, gestured at the walls, searching for a way to describe the "experience" he was having. "*This, this, this*, in the newspapers."

"*This*? You mean your arrest?"

"Yeah, my arrest."

"It's news, Eddie."

He circled the table, mumbling "oh, shit" under his breath, much to Lois's amusement. She continued, "Look, I'm going to write this story with or without your help."

He did another circuit around the table. Finally, in a flash of clarity, he realized that if the story was going to be written, at least he could tell his side of it. He sat down opposite her. "Okay. I'll tell you what happened. But, look, you're going to tell the truth about it, right?"

"Right, assuming you tell me the truth. I've already seen the police report."

"What did it say?"

"Why don't you tell me your story first."

Eddie proceeded to tell his version, explaining that it was a mistake, a misunderstanding—an accident, truth be told, that the officer had been hit with the sign. Lois raised her eyebrows; the fact that the policeman had been hit with the sign was not in the police report. She wondered if Officer Gregory—whom she'd never met—was trying to save face. Eddie concluded his story by describing the indignity of being cuffed, finger-printed, photographed, and placed in a holding cell that smelled like, well, the bowels of northern New Jersey.

Lois couldn't resist a smile. "So this hasn't been one of the high points of your life."

"Closer to the low point." He couldn't resist smiling back.

"I guess this means no more parading?"

"I guess not."

"Eddie, look, I'll write the story as truthfully as I can, okay? It does sound like a misunderstanding."

"An accident. I accidentally hit the policeman with my sign."

"I'll probably let that slide. I don't think Officer Gregory wants to see that in the newspaper. Trust me, okay?" Lois flashed her best winning smile.

Eddie grinned his acceptance.

Seizing the opportunity, she continued, "Eddie, listen, since I heard that you were arrested, I've been thinking about you and your search for these rock stars."

"And?"

"And, I'd like to write a feature article about it; more depth, about your search, and you as a person. More detail about Steely Dan, and why you feel the way you do about them. I'll even do some research about them."

"You mean you're gonna write about me being arrested, and then another story after that?"

"Exactly! The story of your arrest will be a great lead-in. You know, drama, sympathy, human interest."

He stretched his legs, crossed them at the ankles, jammed his hands into his pockets, and gazed at the ceiling. *Is this a good idea, or just a bigger pile of shit?* He looked back at Lois, who was scribbling furiously in her notebook.

"Why can't you just skip the story about my arrest?"

"It's the lead-in to the big in-depth interview. Drama? Sympathy? Remember?"

"Embarrassment? Humiliation? Ridicule?"

"I promise it won't be like that. I'll put a positive spin on it." More scribbling in her notepad.

He looked back at the ceiling, as if some clue to his fate was encoded in the myriad of holes that penetrated the acoustic tiles. Finally, with a skeptical look on his face, he said, "I'll think about it."

Then he heard the lock click, and the door swung open, and a policeman stuck his head inside. "Hey, you can go," the officer announced. "We're dropping the charges."

But will my mug shots disappear? He smiled and caught her eye. She smiled back at him, and said she had to run.

*****

Minutes later, having picked up his wallet, keys, cell phone, overcoat, CD player, and *Steely Dan Rules!* sign, Eddie pushed through the doors of the 19th Precinct. He paused on the sidewalk and savored his return to the free world. Then, spotting a bench, he sat and called his brother, giving him the news that the charges had been dropped. Relieved, Mark told him that he was going directly to his office, and might not be home for dinner.

Eddie closed his eyes, put his head back, basked in the sunshine, and thought about his next move. He had fucked up last time. This time, he would do the right thing. He dialed his father's cell phone.

"Harry Zittner speaking."

"Dad, it's me, Eddie. How's it going?"

"The Dow is up, and my office is full of clients. I'm a happy man."

Tax time, Eddie remembered, picturing his father's smiling face. "Dad, I won't keep you long."

"What's up?"

"Remember last week, the newspaper article about me?"

"How could I forget?"

"Well, how can I put this . . . let me just tell you straight out: I was parading again, and got arrested."

"Eddie—"

"Dad, before you say anything, it was all a mistake, a misunderstanding. They dropped the charges."

"The police dropped the charges?"

"Yeah. They drove me to the police station and then released me." *No point going into any more detail.*

"You're all right?"

"I'm all right. And my parading days are over."

"No more of that nonsense?"

"No more. I promise."

"Thank God for that. Look, Eddie, I'm glad you're alright. I've got an office full of people. Can you call me tonight? Or how about tomorrow? That would be better."

"Okay, Dad, but one more thing."

"Go ahead."

"That reporter from *The Post*? She got wind of the story, and may write a follow-up."

"Oy vey. I've got to go."

"I'll call you tomorrow. Tell Mom for me?"

Eddie heard his father groan. "I'll try," his father said as he disconnected.

<u>26</u>

Tuesday, March 21, 2000

Behind Steely Bars

Exclusive
By Lois Lane Smith

Last week, The Post reported Eddie Zittner's quest to meet Donald Fagen and Walter Becker, the reclusive founding members of the rock group Steely Dan. Yesterday, this story took another turn when Zittner was arrested while demonstrating on the Upper East Side.
"I was charged with disturbing the peace," Zittner told The Post, "but I didn't disturb anyone."
The incident occurred at noon at the corner of Second Avenue and 95th Street. According to a source within the NYPD, Zittner was leading a parade of demonstrators when an altercation broke out. After some pushing and shoving, Zittner, 29, was arrested. Other demonstrators were not charged.
Then, just hours later, Zittner's luck changed again when the NYPD dropped the charge and released him. In an interview on the steps of the 19th Precinct, Zittner, still holding his Steely Dan Rules sign, said, "It was just a misunderstanding. I hold no grudge against the police department."
Zittner told The Post that his parading days were over. He plans to continue his search for "The Dan," but has no specific ideas as to how he might find them.
Good luck on your quest, Eddie—and try to stay out of trouble.

****

After a restless night's sleep, Eddie woke just before eight. Lying in bed, he turned over and glanced out the window: grey and overcast, and not a hint of sunshine. He got up, dressed quickly, and walked into the kitchen. There was no sign of his brother—off to work, he assumed—but there was hot coffee left in the pot. *Forget coffee.* Grabbing his jacket and keys, he locked the apartment, took the elevator downstairs, and headed for the newsstand. *Fucking windy . . .* Two minutes later, he stood in a doorway, hunkered down and thumbing through *The Post*.
The article, thankfully, was near the back of the paper. *Maybe fewer people will notice it.* He read the article twice, and then headed for the

Bagelry, where he read it twice more while waiting for his breakfast. *Not bad . . . Lois had done a good job with it.*

Half an hour later, he sat on the sofa in his brother's apartment, contemplating what remained of an egg, cheese, and bagel sandwich. He thought about getting up and making some fresh coffee. *The Best of the Moody Blues* played softly on the stereo. *Magnificent guitar work . . . if they would just ease up on the violins . . .*

Hearing the apartment door open and close, he used the remote to turn the stereo off.

"Mark?"

"Yeah." His brother, dressed in suit and tie, walked into the living room carrying his work-out kit in one hand and his briefcase in the other. "Who else would it be?"

"I figured you'd be at work."

"That was my original plan, but I saw a copy of *The Post* at the fitness center, and figured you'd need some moral support."

Eddie grinned at his brother. "Thanks."

Mark had been out late again last night. Eddie assumed he was seeing Marcie, but was reluctant to ask. He watched as his brother walked into the kitchen, put down his bag, briefcase, and overcoat, hung his suit jacket over a chair, and poured a cup of coffee. A minute later, Mark was sitting on the love seat opposite him, loosening his tie.

"So, did you talk to the folks last night?"

"I called Dad after I spoke to you. He didn't have time to talk."

"Lucky break."

"Yeah."

"And they haven't called today?"

"No, not yet."

Mark sipped his coffee "The article wasn't too bad."

"No, it wasn't that bad." Eddie knew his brother was taking it easy on him; he was even trying to cheer him up, he realized. But who knew how his parents would react? Who knew how Alison would react? And getting arrested was one more thing Alison could use, and would use, to beat him over the head.

Mark continued, "I saw it was the same reporter."

"Yeah."

"How'd she know you'd been arrested?"

"The desk sergeant called her. He saw the sign I was carrying and made the connection."

"Son-of-a-bitch!" Mark shook his head and smiled. "That's probably the first time the police have put two and two together this year."

"Yeah," Eddie couldn't help smiling himself.

Mark turned serious. "Hey, bro, forget about the parents for a minute. How do you feel?"

How do I feel? I'm alive and feeling fine . . . no, let's be honest. "Stupid, I guess. And angry."

"Angry at who?"

"Angry at myself."

"For demonstrating out on the street?"

"For getting arrested. For putting myself in a position where I could get arrested."

"What actually happened?"

"I was telling a guy to shut up. I turned around and hit a cop across the face with my sign."

Mark winced. "Any blood?"

"No."

"So they dropped the charges?"

"Yeah."

Mark drained his coffee cup. "Well, that makes sense. After the Diallo case, the police probably want as little publicity as possible." Eddie remembered the case, which had been all over the newspapers: Diallo, a poor black immigrant from Jamaica, or Africa, or somewhere like that, had been shot forty-one times—*forty-one times!* Or had it been nineteen times? It didn't matter, he figured, since the policeman involved had been acquitted anyway, just last month.

Mark continued, "So why don't you call Mom and get it over with?"

"Believe me, I've thought about it." As if on queue, Eddie's cell phone started to vibrate. Expecting the worst, he picked it up, but didn't recognize the number on the display.

"Hello?"

"Eddie, it's me, Lois."

"Oh, hi." Eddie glanced at his brother, who raised his eyebrows.

"Have you got a minute to talk?"

"Hold for a second." Eddie turned to his brother. "It's the reporter from *The Post*. Lois."

Mark stood up. "I've got to get to work."

"Will I see you tonight?"

"Don't know yet. I'll call you later." Eddie watched as his brother put on his jacket, grabbed his coat and briefcase, and headed for the door.

"I'm back," he said into the phone.

"Eddie. Remember what I said yesterday about doing an in-depth interview?"

"Yeah, but I never agreed to it."

"What if I told you I could get someone from *Rolling Stone* to join us? Someone who knows about Steely Dan?"

"*Rolling Stone*, the magazine?"

"Yeah. What other *Rolling Stone* is there?"

He ignored the sarcasm. "Who is it?"

"I don't know his name."

"So, how do you know him?"

"I don't. My friend, Sheila, works at *Rolling Stone*. She knows the guy."

He turned the idea over in his head. Shit, his name and the story of his quest had already hit the papers twice. How much more damage could a third article do? On the other hand, he might be able to *repair* some of the damage. It might give him a chance to come across as halfway intelligent. And, it might give him a chance to make a public plea for Fagen and Becker's autograph. Meeting someone from *Rolling Stone* who knew The Dan—that sounded interesting.

"When could we meet?" he said.

"Does that mean you'll do it?"

"Yeah, I guess so. You'll put a positive spin on it?"

"Absolutely."

"And I'll be able to make a plea for Fagen and Becker's autographs? In the article?"

"Sure, within reason. You don't want to come across as a psycho, do you?"

"No."

"Okay, then, trust me. You say the words and I'll twirl them like a lasso."

Twirl them like a lasso? "Okay."

"How about tomorrow?"

"Tomorrow?" He did some quick thinking. "Tomorrow I work from nine to three."

"I'll see if I can set something up after three. I'll call you."

"Okay," he said as she disconnected.

27

Wednesday, March 22, 2000

Arriving back at the apartment just after three, Eddie changed his clothes and decided to walk the mile or so to Pete's Tavern, which was located just south of Gramercy Park. Lois had described Pete's as "an ancient and venerable watering hole, replete with dark wood and old whiskey bottles." He figured she was reading that verbatim from a restaurant guide. *It sounded awful, but he could tolerate anything for an hour.*

It was cold and overcast as he worked his way through Little India, catching an occasional whiff of curry as he passed restaurants and take-away shops. Just after four, he arrived at Pete's, pushed through the doors, and looked around. The place was nearly empty—too early for the "drinks before dinner" crowd—and he spotted Lois sitting with the man and woman he assumed were from *Rolling Stone*. Walking toward the booth, he noted the preponderance of dark wood, lots of old whiskey bottles, and a hand-painted sign extolling the virtues of Tendy's Ale. *Tourists must flock to this place.*

Lois stood, quickly said hello, and led the introductions.

"Eddie Zittner, this is Sheila Cheung, my friend at *The Stone*." Sheila, still sitting, offered her hand, which he shook and released. "And this is Bernard Sterling."

Sterling rose and extended his hand. "I hear you're mad about Steely Dan."

Mad? "Uh, yes, I am." *John Denver with a British accent . . . in a Tom Wolfe suit.* He shook Sterling's hand. "Nice to meet you, Mr. Sterling."

"Call me Nardo." Sterling handed Eddie a business card, which identified him as an Editor-at-Large. Soon they were all seated, with the men facing each other by the window, Lois sitting beside Eddie, and Sheila sitting beside Sterling.

Eddie took a good look at Sterling's wrinkled face. *John Denver for sure, if he'd lived to be seventy.*

Lois signaled the waiter, who glided up to the table and asked Eddie what he wanted. Sterling had a glass of whiskey, neat, sitting in front of him. The ladies were sharing a bottle of wine which Lois described as "an acceptable chardonnay," considering the limitations of her entertainment budget. Eddie asked the waiter to bring another wine glass, and then turned back to Sterling. "Are you drinking Scotch, Nardo?"

"Oh, no, dear fellow, Jack Daniels." He lifted his glass and took a sip. "Your most wonderful export, I always say."

Dear fellow? "You're obviously English."

"Astute observation!"

Eddie smiled. "Speaking of observations, do you know you look just like—"

"John Denver, yes." Sterling smiled knowingly. "Quite a coincidence, eh?"

"The resemblance is striking." Eddie grinned.

"So I've been told, so I've been told."

"Did you ever meet—"

"Denver? Never had the pleasure." Sterling's eyes twinkled. "Never even been to Colorado." This set him off, and he cackled like a rooster on speed. Then he raised his glass and toasted his new-found companions. "Rocky Mountain high, chaps!" he proclaimed, setting off yet another round of cackling. Finally calming down, he wiped tears from his eyes and said, "Jolly good."

"Yeah, jolly good." *What a character.* Eddie glanced at Lois, who was grinning to herself as she wrote on her notepad.

Sheila tapped her watch. "Why don't we get down to business."

"Oh, Sheila," Sterling beamed at her, "looking after me, as always."

"It's a job," Sheila replied, which set Sterling off again.

She looked confused. "What'd I say?"

More cackling, and gasps of "please, no more." Sterling once again regained his composure.

Eddie smiled. *The man was a character . . . but likeable.*

Sterling cleared his throat. "Eddie, I'd like to ask you a few questions about Steely Dan, to test your depth of knowledge, so to speak."

"Fire away."

"Well, Lois, who is charming, by the way,"—Sterling blew her a kiss—"has filled me in on some of your background. I guess the most critical question is: Why are you so intent on meeting Mr. Fagen and Mr. Becker? I mean, lots of fans want to meet their favorite rock stars, but most don't pursue it as an avocation."

"Why do I want to meet them? Well," Eddie looked to Lois for encouragement, "the idea came to me a few months ago. I guess I got a little bit angry because it was so hard to find any Steely Dan memorabilia."

"Angry?"

Eddie sensed that Sterling was sizing him up; trying to place him somewhere on a scale between normal and lunatic. "Perhaps frustrated would be a better word."

"Frustrated. Yes, I can see how you might get frustrated."

"And," Eddie played with his wine glass, "I thought meeting them would be a good way to get their autographs."

"And what else would you do, if, indeed, you met them?"

"Well, my idea was to shake their hands, get their autographs, and buy them a cup of coffee. Or a beer. Whatever."

"Coffee. How quaint." Sterling smiled and took a generous gulp of whiskey.

"Forget the coffee. Just meeting them and getting their autographs would be great."

"What is it that makes you like Steely Dan so much?"

"Have you listened to their music?"

Sterling wrinkled his brow. "I listen to gobs and gobs of music. I'm sure I've heard most of it, if not all of it."

Eddie thought for a few seconds. "How about 'Do It Again?'"

"Do it again?"

"Yeah, 'Do It Again,' their first hit single."

Sterling looked uncertain. "Oh, I'm sure I've heard it."

"It's from their first album," Eddie continued. "Do you appreciate the quality of that single? The music almost 'shimmers.'"

"Shimmers?" Now Sterling looked confused.

"Shimmers," Eddie replied. "Like heat waves rising in the desert."

"Music that shimmers . . ." Sterling shook his head and turned to Sheila. "Make a note of that, will you?" Sheila nodded as she reached for her handbag. Eddie glanced at Lois, who was smiling as she wrote furiously in her notepad. Sterling turned back to Eddie, "I guess I need to listen to that one again."

Eddie nodded, satisfied he'd made his point.

"All right, then." Sterling sat up a little straighter. "Other than that one song, why do you like them so much?"

Time to make my case. "Well, if you consider their entire body of work, then, in my opinion, they're one of the best rock groups of all time."

Sterling raised his eyebrows. "One of the best?"

"If not *the* best."

"Oh, come now. What about the Beatles and the Rolling Stones?"

"British bands." Eddie caught himself. "No offense meant."

"None taken, but why differentiate, dear fellow?" Sterling frowned.

Think fast, Eddie. "No reason, really. I like lots of British bands. I was just thinking of American bands."

"Let's see . . . American bands . . . what about the Four Seasons?"

Eddie cringed. "Bubble gum music."

"Ah, right, perhaps that was a poor choice." Sterling thought for a few seconds. "What about the Beach Boys?"

"Bubble gum west."

"Oh, come now, isn't that a bit harsh?"

"I'm talking about serious bands." Eddie decided he would stand his ground.

"Define serious," Sterling snorted. "I'd venture Brian Wilson would take exception to his band being called 'bubble gum west.'" Sterling took another gulp of whiskey.

"Okay. Hold on. You want me to define 'serious music.'" Eddie looked over at Lois, who was rolling her eyes. Sheila poured the last of the wine and looked around for the waiter. Sterling signaled that he was ready for another Jack Daniels. Eddie thought for a minute, grappling with the idea of serious and not-so-serious music. *How did I get myself into this?*

Sterling looked on with amusement. "Try defining commercial, old chap."

"Commercial?"

"Precisely! Let me take it a step further. There's music I would define as commercial, or popular, or mainstream—however you want to say it—and then other music that appeals to a narrower fan base. Then there's the quality factor: there's great music, and awful music, all up and down the scale—no pun intended." Sterling beamed triumphantly around the table. "All up and down the scale . . . oh, that's good! Make a note of that, will you, Sheila?" She nodded.

"Okay, I hear what you're saying," Eddie replied.

Sterling continued, "Steely Dan is one of those groups that never tried to be 'mainstream.'"

"I agree. But wouldn't you say they are among the best of the rock groups?"

"Among the best? Yes, I would say they are among the best. Under-appreciated by most people."

"That's a good way to put it."

"Under-appreciated?"

Eddie smiled. "Precisely!"

Sterling drained the last drops of whiskey from his glass. "You know, they never did much to appeal to a broad fan base. They never toured when they were popular."

"I know."

The waiter arrived with another whiskey and a fresh bottle of Chardonnay. Sheila poured the wine. Sterling sipped his whiskey, smiled, and then took a generous swallow. Eddie wondered how many drinks Sterling had consumed today.

Another thought popped into Sterling's head. "There was a book written about Steely Dan a few years back. Have you seen it?"

"The one by Brian Sweet? Yes, I've read it cover to cover."

"Nice fellow, Sweet. An Englishman, you know."

Eddie glanced at Lois, who seemed to be enjoying herself immensely.

Sterling continued, "Mr. Fagen and Mr. Becker value their privacy, you know. That's why it's so hard to get their autographs."

"Have you ever met them?"

"Once or twice. Yes, twice, I think. Nice fellows. Dry sense of humor. Not your typical rock stars." Sterling took another gulp of whiskey. "Lois mentioned that you were parading in front of Mr. Fagen's apartment building."

"Yes, and near their studio, River Sound."

"If you don't mind me asking, how did you get Mr. Fagen's address?"

"A friend of a friend lives in the same building."

"Really? How do you know?"

"Well, I don't know for sure. I never got a chance to verify it."

"Well, old chap, I guess I should tell you that these kinds of people—celebrities, as we say in the trade—are very good at covering their tracks."

"What do you mean?"

"Diversions. Decoy addresses. Things like that. The address you identified may or may not be a place Mr. Fagen actually lives." Sterling's eyes shone.

Eddie thought for a minute. "I hear what you're saying."

"You were better off parading in front of their studio."

"Uh, huh . . ."

"But that wouldn't get you anywhere. Not now."

"Why not?"

"Because they're not recording right now. They just released an album, remember?"

"So where would they be?"

"Think about it, young man. You're a journalist; at least that's what Ms. Smith told me." He winked at Lois and downed the last of his whiskey.

"I guess they'd be out promoting their new album?" Eddie saw that Sterling was getting a little bleary-eyed.

"Precisely, dear boy! Although Mr. Fagen and Mr. Becker don't do what you would call 'public appearances.' I believe they'd have a good laugh if people began to queue for their autographs."

Queue? "I guess you're right."

"And they'd be preparing for their tour right now, don't you think?"

"There's been no announcement of a tour—"

"There will be, shortly. And check out next week's magazine. We're running a modest article about The Dark Brothers." Sterling began to lean uncertainly toward the window.

"Fagen and Becker?"

"Precisely!" Sterling straightened himself up and raised his empty glass, hoping that Sheila might order one more round.

But Sheila was having none of it. She tapped her watch. "Mr. Sterling, you've got another meeting. We've got to go."

"Ah, Sheila," Sterling beamed at her, "the mother I never had."

Sheila stood and handed him his overcoat. "Mr. Sterling, I'm sure you had a mother." She winked at Eddie. They quickly said their good-byes, and Sheila guided the unsteady Mr. Sterling toward the door.

28

"Well, that was an experience," Lois said as she closed her notepad, dropped it in her handbag, and signaled for the check. "What do you think of Bernard Sterling?"

"A character," Eddie replied. "He seems to know his stuff, though. I like him."

"Loves his Jack Daniels, doesn't he?"

"That he does."

The waiter presented the check, which Lois perused and covered with a credit card. They sipped the last of the wine as they waited. Eddie checked his watch—almost five-thirty—and scanned the room. *The place was starting to fill up* . . . Seconds later, the waiter returned, and Lois signed the check and prepared to leave.

"Going back to work?" he asked.

"No, I've got plenty of time. I thought I'd get a bite to eat and start working on the article."

He started to speak, then stopped, and then blurted out: "Do you mind if I join you?" surprising himself as much as it did Lois. He quickly qualified his statement, adding, "I mean, I skipped lunch. I wanted to get an early dinner, too."

Lois, looking uncertain, sized him up, and finally said, "Well, why not? A business dinner, right?"

"Right," he replied, relieved.

They put on their overcoats and stepped out onto the sidewalk, which was slick from the drizzling rain that had started to fall.

"Did you have any particular place in mind?" He scanned the streets for a taxi.

"Yeah," she replied, "that place right over there." She nodded toward a small restaurant just across the street.

A minute later they walked into Friend of a Farmer, a restaurant that was dedicated, according to the sign, to serving "good, fresh things every day of the week." Predictably, the interior was decorated just like a farmhouse. It was still too early for the dinner crowd, and they were seated immediately, in the front room, their rough-finished wooden table overlooking a street scene framed by bare branches. Nat King Cole crooned softly in the background.

Eddie settled into the wooden chair. "Feels like a 'ladies lunch' kind of place."

"It is," Lois replied, arranging her pen and notepad on the table. "You should see the lines here on the weekends."

"Hmm." He glanced out the window. "Nice view."

"Yeah. If that parking meter were a hitching post, it would be perfect."

"Well, we can't have everything." He scanned the menu. "What's good?"

"Try the chicken pot pie. It's huge, and it's excellent. You look like a chicken pot pie kind of person."

"Which means?" He smiled at her.

"I'll bet you like your basic meat and potatoes, spaghetti and meatballs—"

"Chinese . . . Indian . . ."

"You ever eat a lobster?"

"No, but I've eaten lots of shrimp."

"Eddie Zittner—full of surprises." She scribbled something in her notepad.

The waiter, a Latino who looked uncomfortable wearing a checkered apron, took their order. Eddie went with the chicken pot pie. Lois ordered something called 'country pie' with a side salad.

"So, Eddie, other than shrimp and Steely Dan, what kind of things interest you?"

"Writing. I majored in journalism at Rutgers."

"You already told me that. Yet, you're not a working journalist."

"No." *Even though my wife has encouraged me to try it, at least a thousand times.* "No, I've focused more on writing fiction."

"What kind of fiction?"

"Short stories. Even tried to write a novel, once."

"No kidding. Ever sell anything?"

"No, but I do have a file full of rejection slips."

"I have a few of those, too."

"What did you major in?"

"Journalism, just like you. I went to City College."

"And you're a working journalist. Congratulations." He lifted his glass of ice water.

"Thank you." She clicked his glass with hers.

The food arrived. The chicken pot pie was enormous, served in a dish that was, Eddie guessed, three inches deep, maybe more. The top was crisscrossed with golden-brown strips of pastry. The country pie Lois had ordered was a generous wedge of what looked like the same pastry, oozing with cheese and vegetables. He gave her a 'how am I going to eat this thing?' look, and she replied with a smiling "Try it." He dug into the pot pie, which was filled with chunks of chicken and vegetables swimming in a thick, creamy sauce.

"Mmm . . . delicious," he said, burning his lips on the first bite.

"I told you so." She raised her fork and blew lightly onto a piece of the country pie, trying to cool it off. "Sometimes I wish I were a food critic," she said, popping it into her mouth.

Eddie occupied himself with his dinner, alternating mouthfuls of pot pie with sips of water. He used a spoon to break off pieces of pastry and mix them into the sauce. Halfway through, he took a break and looked up. "How's yours?" he asked.

"Just the way my mother made it. Wonderful crust."

"You don't look like you grew up on a farm."

She frowned. "What do you mean by that?"

"Nothing," he said, raising his arms in surrender. "You just give me the impression that you're one-hundred-percent New Yorker."

"Well, I am. But my mother could cook a mean country pie, although she didn't call it that."

"Tell me about your parents."

"My parents?" She leaned back. "The odd couple. My mother is a Hungarian Jew—I know, I don't look Jewish—with some Italian mixed in. My father is plain ordinary WASP; Swedish if you go back far enough. They're both ultra-liberal, from the 'flower children' days. It was love at first sight. I love them, but they drive me crazy. How about yours?"

"Mine? I guess I'd say the same thing: I love them both, but they drive me crazy—my mother, anyway. They're typical New Jersey suburban Jewish parents. My great, great grandparents are from the old country." Giving up on the pot pie, he pushed his plate away.

"Which old country?"

"Russia, Yugoslavia, Bulgaria; somewhere in there. Borders weren't too clear back then."

A busboy cleared the table. A minute later the waiter came by and poured cups of coffee. Lois thumbed through her notepad. "Let's see if I have this straight now: you like rock and roll—Steely Dan, specifically—marching on the sidewalk, writing fiction, chicken pot pie . . . and shrimp. Did I miss anything?"

"Well, I read a lot."

"Most writers do. What kind of books?"

"Mysteries. Science Fiction. Contemporary novels. And movies—I love old movies."

"Let's see . . ." She tapped her cheek. "I figure you for something like *Caddyshack*."

"Unbelieveable."
"The Godfather."
"Terrific."
"Alien."
"Loved it."
"Animal House."
"A classic!"

She grinned broadly. "I confess, I'm a movie nut, too."

"Let me guess." He thought for a few seconds. "You're probably some kind of romantic . . . am I right?"

"Sometimes."

"I'll bet your favorite movie is . . . *Sleepless in Seattle*?"

She shook her head. "Too sappy, even for me."

"How about . . . *Tootsie*?"

"No, but I love Dustin Hoffman. Actually my favorite movie is *Kramer vs Kramer*. It's got a hard edge to it."

The waiter refilled their coffee cups and dropped the check on the table. Eddie decided to take another leap into space. "The Academy Awards are this weekend. Would you, you know, like to watch it together?"

"You mean, like a date?" Her eyes narrowed, and an unspoken 'what would your wife say' came through loud and clear.

He backtracked. "No, not like a real date. My brother's out of town this weekend. We can watch at his place. That's where I've been staying."

"How do I know I can trust you?"

"Me? I'm harmless." He flashed the most innocent smile he could manage.

"I think you told me that before."

"No, seriously, I'll be a perfect gentleman. I'll even buy dinner—I know a good Chinese place. You know, noodles, egg rolls, the works."

"Shrimp?"

"Shrimp, of course."

"I don't know. What with you getting arrested—"

Now she was pulling his chain . . . "But we're having dinner together *now*." He grinned.

"Yes, but in a public place."

"Come on . . ." *Turn on the charm, Eddie* . . . "I can give you references . . ."

She laughed. "I don't think that will be necessary."

"Then you'll come? My brother's got a fantastic apartment. 'East River View,' as they say."

"No kidding. Where is it?"

"Third Avenue and 32nd Street. His apartment is on the 28th floor."

"Mmm, that sounds elegant. Is he rich?"

"He makes a good living."

She sipped the last of her coffee. "Okay, I'll come. But any funny business?" She waved her fist at him.

He grinned. "As a show of good faith, I'll pay for dinner."

"No thanks—journalistic integrity, remember?" She dropped a twenty dollar bill on the table. "I'll split it with you." She stood and picked up her handbag and overcoat.

"What's your hurry?"

"I've got to get back to the office and get this article filed."

"What about Sunday?"

"The article will be in tomorrow's paper. Call me after that. You can give me directions."

29

Thursday, March 23, 2000

Steely Dan, Where Are You?

Exclusive
By Lois Lane Smith

Why is Eddie Zittner, a self-described "ordinary guy" from New Jersey, trying to meet and obtain the autographs of two of rock's most reclusive stars?

Last week, The Post first reported on Zittner's Quixote-like quest to meet Donald Fagen and Walter Becker, founding members of the rock group Steely Dan. Then, earlier this week, The Post reported Zittner's arrest on the sidewalks of the Upper East Side, the victim of a misunderstanding with the NYPD. A charge of disturbing the peace was quickly dropped, and Zittner was released the same day.

In an effort to understand his motivation, The Post arranged an exclusive interview with Zittner yesterday afternoon. Joining us was Bernard "Nardo" Sterling, Editor-at-Large with Rolling Stone magazine, and an expert on Steely Dan.

"It's been frustrating," Zittner said as we spoke at Pete's Tavern in Gramercy Park. "Not being able to obtain their autographs, or find any memorabilia . . . I guess that's what drove me to demonstrate on the sidewalk."

But what is it about Steely Dan and their music that creates such passion and loyalty in Zittner and the rest of their fan base?

"Their songs are unique," Sterling told The Post. "It's a combination of extraordinary music, and lyrics laced with dark humor and sometimes 'vague' symbolism."

Steely Dan was formed in 1971 by Fagen, Becker, and a handful of other musicians. They had immediate success with their 1972 album *Can't Buy A Thrill*, which included their first hit single, "Do It Again." Zittner describes the song as having a "shimmering" quality unlike anything else he has heard. Steely Dan did some touring in the early 1970s, but life on the road wasn't for them. By mid-1974 they had stopped touring—becoming a so-called "studio band"—and over time, other members left, leaving Fagen and Becker as the remaining core of "The Dan." They continued producing hit albums, using the best session players they could hire, but always keeping control of the final product.

"Fagen and Becker have always been the intellect and driving force behind the band," Sterling said.

In 1980, they released their seventh album, *Gaucho*, and then disbanded, although Fagen and Becker collaborated on each other's solo efforts in later years. In the early 1990s, Fagen and Becker reformed the group using new musicians, and toured the United States, Europe, and Asia, performing mostly old material. Fans would have to wait a long time—almost twenty years—for their new album, *Two Against Nature*, which was released earlier this year.

"Steely Dan is among the best rock groups of all time," Sterling said. "They have an extremely loyal fan base, but, by and large, they are under-appreciated." Sterling, who over the years has become acquainted with Fagen and Becker, described them as nice fellows with a dry sense of humor. "Not your typical rock stars," he added.

Zittner, 29, is the oldest son of—as he describes them—typical New Jersey suburban Jewish parents. A journalism major at Rutgers, so far he has focused on writing fiction. In addition to rock and roll, Zittner is a fan of mystery novels, movies, and Chinese food. He is separated from his wife and living temporarily in Manhattan.

"I'm a law-abiding citizen," Zittner said, noting that he had never been arrested before this week's incident. "I don't plan to do any more demonstrating. But I would love to meet Fagen and Becker, just to shake their hands, get their autographs, and thank them for their excellent music."

A modest request? Steely Dan, if you're out there, you can get in touch with Mr. Zittner by contacting this reporter.

****

Eddie heard the steady beep of the alarm clock, looked up, saw the thing flashing "8:30 AM" at him, and hit the snooze button, buying himself ten minutes of sleep time. A minute later, his mind clearing, he jumped out of bed, eager to get downstairs to buy a newspaper.

By nine-thirty, he had shaved, showered, dressed, locked the apartment, gone downstairs, and purchased a copy of *The Post*. Oblivious to a beautiful spring morning, he read the article as he walked to the Dunkin' Donuts on Second Avenue and 33rd Street.

He read the article a second and third time as he inhaled glazed donuts and washed them down with coffee. It appeared to him that Lois had done her research, having accurately outlined the history of "The Dan." The article had included his plea to Fagen and Becker, and he personally seemed to come across as law-abiding, sincere, and intelligent. *Nice job, Lois.*

Just before ten, he walked down the block, crossed the street, and went into Borders, where his co-workers hooted, hollered, high-fived him, and accused him of trying to parlay his fifteen minutes of fame into "minor celebrity" status. Speculation flew that he would soon leave the bookstore for a higher paying position. But they quickly lost interest, and soon everyone had settled back into their normal work routine.

At noon, Eddie's cell phone buzzed. The display showed a familiar number.

"Hello?"

"Eddie, it's Alison."

"I know. I saw your number on the caller ID." He walked quickly toward the front entrance. He'd need some privacy for this conversation. He began tentatively. "How are you?"

"How am I? Let's see . . . my husband, who was, in his own words, trying to save his marriage—our marriage—is now focusing his attention on meeting a couple of burned-out guitar pickers."

He could hear her breathing fire into the phone. *She's seen the article.* "Look, Alison, I can explain . . ."

"Go ahead, explain."

"Well, first, let me assure you that I'm no longer parading up and down the sidewalks."

"I read that in the article."

"Right."

"What's the matter? Was jail too scary for you?"

"Do you want to hear this?"

"Go on."

"Well, there were two reasons why I agreed to be interviewed for a third article. First, it gave me a chance to explain, in print, why I want to meet Fagen and Becker. And second, I had a chance to meet one of the editors of *Rolling Stone* magazine."

"That must have been a thrill."

"Not exactly a thrill, but I wasn't going to pass up the chance, either." *How can I take control of this conversation?* "Look, Alison, don't you think I regained some of my credibility in that article?"

"Your credibility?"

"Yeah. I thought I came across as a reasonable person, don't you think?"

"As opposed to an immature hero-worshipper?"

"Look, Alison, I'm trying to make the best I can out of a bad situation." *A bad situation of my own making.* "That reporter," he pictured Lois as she walked toward him that first day on the street, "was going to write the story about my arrest with or without my help. The police tipped her off. There was nothing I could do about it."

"So?"

"So I agreed to be interviewed for a third article, to try to put the thing to bed, once and for all."

"Whatever."

We can't talk at all . . . He didn't know what to say. Reaching the end of the block, he turned and started back toward the store.

"Eddie, look, I hate to tell you this on the phone . . ." He heard her clear her throat. "I'm filing for divorce as soon as I can."

He watched as mothers strolled by, pushing baby carriages. Trucks and taxicabs cruised along Second Avenue in slow-motion. He tried to think of an argument that made sense, or would make sense to Alison, but nothing came to him except for the nagging thought that perhaps, just perhaps, divorce was the inevitable outcome of this situation he had created.

"Why?" he asked her.

"Why? I shouldn't have to explain it to you."

Dead silence on the line. "Alison," he ventured, "I know how you must feel. But I'm trying to put all of this behind me. Behind us. We should talk."

"I'm tired of talking to a fool."

That hurt. "I'm sorry you feel that way."

"It's a little late to be sorry."

The inevitable outcome . . . "Alison, if that's how you feel, then go ahead and file."

"That's what I plan to do."

"Well, go ahead, then."

"Fine."

"Fine. Good-bye, Eddie."

"Bye." He listened to her disconnect.

*****

Not wanting to be around his co-workers, or people in general, Eddie went back into Borders, quickly purchased a ham-and-cheese sandwich and a Coke at the Dean & DeLuca counter, and retreated into a far corner of the storeroom.

Half an hour later, having licked his wounds and finished his lunch, he went back into the store and occupied himself with whatever dog work he could find—opening boxes, unpacking books, rearranging displays, and making order out of chaos at the magazine rack—anything to keep the clock moving. By mid-afternoon he was itching to just get the hell out of there.

His cell phone buzzed again. He recognized the number, thought about letting it ring through to the message center, and then decided to take the call. *How much worse can it get?* He again walked toward the front entrance.

"Hello?"

"Hello, schmuck. It's—in your own words—your typical New Jersey suburban Jewish mother."

"How are you, Ma?"

"How am I? What do you think?"

Déjà vu all over again. "Mom, I can explain the newspaper article."

"I'm listening."

"I agreed to do the interview for a third article so I could put this whole thing behind me. And I have . . . put it behind me . . . now."

"How so?"

"Well, I'm not going to be demonstrating on the sidewalk anymore."

"Your father told me that. Let's see . . . that was when you got arrested."

"He explained that to you, right?"

"Right."

"How's he doing, by the way?"

"He's fine, he's at work, and he's not happy with you, either. And don't change the subject."

"Where was I?" Eddie backtracked, trying to figure out a better way to explain this. "Ma, give me a chance, will ya?"

"I'm listening."

"When I was arrested, it was a misunderstanding. The police dropped the charges and released me. Dad told you that, right?"

"Right."

"But that reporter got wind of my arrest, and wrote the second article."

"That I understand. So why the third article?"

He hesitated. "The reporter asked to interview me again, so she could write the third article. She asked me, I didn't ask her. She said it was a chance for me to come across as a reasonable, law-abiding, intelligent person."

"Well, you got halfway there."

He smiled. "Nice that you still have your sense of humor."

"I'm not laughing."

"I'm not, either. Plus, I got a chance to meet an editor from *Rolling Stone* magazine."

"How wonderful."

"He knew a lot about Steely Dan."

"Don't start in with that again."

"Mom, I assure you, all of this is behind me."

"Eddie . . ."

"Yeah?"

"I want you to call Alison, today, and explain this to her. Otherwise, your marriage is in the toilet."

"Ma—"

"Do you want to save your marriage?"

He would have to finesse that question. He knew what his mother wanted to hear. "Yes, I think so, but . . ." He cleared his throat. "I don't really know at this point."

"When did you last speak to Alison?"

Time for the truth, with a little sugar-coating. "We saw each other last week. She was in Manhattan for the day." *All true, it just wasn't the answer to his mother's question.*

"And . . ."

"And, it didn't go very well."

"Eddie, listen to me. Don't you want to save your marriage?"

He could feel his mother's intensity. He served up a waffle: "Ma, like I said, I don't know."

"Eddie, listen to me. You call Alison today and explain this whole thing to her. Will you do that? Your father and I don't want you throwing your marriage away."

"Mom, I need to think about it for a day or two."

"Think fast. Don't be stupid."

"Yeah."

"You call us tomorrow, and let us know what's going on. Okay?"

"Okay, Mom."

"Don't forget."

How could I forget? He heard his mother hang up.

30

Saturday, March 25, 2000

letters@nypost.com

Searching For Steely Dan

The Issue: Eddie Zittner's quest to meet two of rock's most reclusive stars.

I have mixed feelings about Mr. Zittner's escapades.

I congratulate him for drawing attention to Steely Dan, a wonderful rock band that has produced some outstanding music over the years. They are, as your article stated ("Steely Dan, Where Are You?" March 23), under-appreciated by many fans of rock and roll.

On the other hand, we should respect everyone's right to privacy, even that of celebrities. If Fagen and Becker want to stay out of the public spotlight, then so be it. I do not think of Mr. Zittner as a stalker—he seems to mean no harm to anyone. Maybe he could find some more productive things to do with his time.

Mitch Grudiniser, Manhattan

****

I'm a big fan of "The Dan" and can understand Zittner's frustration. It would be nice to be able to purchase some sheet music or a T-Shirt signed by Fagen and Becker, but that wouldn't be "The Dan" now, would it?

With apologies to fans of the Beatles, the Eagles, the Grateful Dead, and many other rock groups, there is no better music than that of Steely Dan. Mr. Sterling's comment that Steely Dan combines "extraordinary music and lyrics laced with dark humor" was right on!

Tisha Bovadt, Brooklyn

****

Don't the police have better things to do than arrest an "ordinary guy" demonstrating on the sidewalk?

The Constitution says that all of us have the right to freedom of speech, and the right to demonstrate peacefully. Isn't that what Zittner was doing? If the police couldn't make the charges stick, then he should have never been arrested in the first place.

Mayor Guiliani, please instruct the fine officers of the NYPD that the streets do not need to be protected from the likes of Eddie Zittner. There are real criminals out there!

Peter Collzig, Washington Heights

****

Eddie Zittner should have his head examined.

Sure, Steely Dan is a good band. But I would rate the Beatles, Led Zeppelin, the Stones, Aerosmith, the Who, the Eagles, the Beach Boys and a bunch of others ahead of them.

Get real, Zittner.

Andre Chaitivio, Queens

****

Zittner's story proves once again that there's a nut case around every corner. Why would an "ordinary guy" march around with a sign exhorting rock and roll stars to "come on down and pay attention to me." Because he's not an ordinary guy, he's a wacko.

Zittner should go back to New Jersey, beg forgiveness from his wife, and find a real job.

Perhaps he didn't get enough breast feeding as a child.

Sonya Stribbles, Jericho

31

Sunday, March 26, 2000

  Lois Lane Smith glanced out the window as the bus glided north on Third Avenue. *The end of another clear, sunny, just 'outright beautiful' day.* She had left her tiny studio apartment in mid-morning and spent the better part of the day window-shopping, working her way through the West Village, then east to Washington Square, and finally north along Fifth Avenue. Stopping at City Market for a late lunch, she had watched what seemed to be an epidemic of young families eating soup, salad, and grilled cheese sandwiches—a favorite of the elementary school set, she noted—and then gorging on a variety of pastries and chocolates.

  Now, hours later, she was confronted with yet another young family, this one sitting directly opposite her. A husband and wife, in their thirties, it appeared, leaned haphazardly against each other, both zonked from the day's activities. The husband clung to a toddler, a young boy dressed in a denim shirt, green OshKosh B'Gosh overalls, and a cute pair of silver and white Nike sneakers. Every so often the child pulled on his father's shirt, or squirmed, or cried out, with little effect.

  Is that what married life is all about?

  Her thoughts drifted to Eddie Zittner. He was flaky, sure, but he also seemed to be a nice guy—sweet, in a nebbishy kind of way. She had made him a minor celebrity, stretching his fifteen minutes of fame into perhaps thirty, and had received a "good job" from her boss, who didn't hand those out very often. She smiled as she recalled the moment.

  On the negative side, Zittner was married. *Big negative . . .* He said he was separated from his wife. She wondered how she might check that out.

  She got off the bus near the corner of 32nd Street, and made her way to the lighted entrance of The Future Condominiums.

*****

  Eddie Zittner was sweating as he listened for the chime of the elevator doors. He sat down, got up, and sat down again. The clock crept past eight p.m., then five after, then ten after. He took another sip of wine and realized that he'd nearly finished off the glass.

  She was making him wait.

  Finally, he heard the doors chime, took a deep breath, strolled to the door, opened it, and took a step into the hallway.

Lois walked toward him, smiling. She wore a blue pullover sweater and grey slacks. *Simple and elegant.* He remembered her walk, and the way her hips moved, and the confident way she carried herself. *Perfection and grace.* He smiled and said hello. *Should I kiss her? Will she try to kiss me?*

She walked up to him, they embraced awkwardly, and she brushed a kiss across his cheek.

"Nice building," she said.

"Come on inside. Can I take your coat?" He escorted her into the apartment and hung her coat in the entry closet. She walked past him and scanned the living room, taking in the expensive furniture, the entertainment center, and the lithographs that lined the walls. Then she moved to the window and looked out over the twinkling lights.

"This is magnificent. Brooklyn never looked so good."

Eddie basked in the reflected glow of his brother's good fortune. "I told you so."

"How does your brother afford this place?"

"He rents it from a friend. He got a really good deal on it."

"I'll bet. This place must go for at least a million. What does your brother do?"

"He's in investment banking." *Let's not get started on my brother's career.* "You must be hungry. I've got dinner all set up."

They adjourned to the kitchen. Five minutes later, after some cautious zapping in the microwave, the food was ready. They sat down at the kitchen counter and dug into containers of cashew chicken, sugar snap peas, noodles fragrant with garlic and onions, and, of course, sizzling black pepper shrimp.

Lois picked up a shrimp with her chopsticks. "Eddie, you are so predictable."

He gulped a mouthful of noodles and looked up. "How so?"

"How so?" She held the shrimp in front of his face. He leaned forward and tried to grab it with his teeth, but she pulled it back and popped it into her mouth.

"Predictable . . ." He smiled, mischief on his mind. "Well, maybe I can surprise you later on."

"I don't think so." She put down her chopsticks. "Hey, I meant to ask you . . ."

"What?"

"A serious question." She put on her best poker-face. "Have you had your head examined yet?"

He grinned at her. *I should have seen that coming.*

"And one more question . . . Were you breast fed as a child?"

He watched as she totally lost control. *That was too easy for her . . . like shooting fish in a barrel.* "Oh, that's funny . . ." He smiled and sipped his wine as he waited for her to stop gasping. "Okay, now that you've had your fun, can I ask you something?"

"Oh, God . . ." She caught her breath. "Sure."

He gave her his most sincere look. "I want to go out and visit some jazz clubs. You know, ask some questions about Fagen and Becker? Maybe I can get a line on them. Will you go with me?"

*****

"Hmm." She took a deep breath. *Probably no harm in it, except that it proves he's still on his noble quest to find "The Dan."*

He played for sympathy. "I really don't know my way around Manhattan very well."

Oh, please! And I'm supposed to be your tour guide? She smiled tentatively. "Okay. Yeah, that might be fun."

By nine, they had finished dinner, cleared the dishes, and moved back into the living room. Eddie set two glasses of wine on the coffee table, grabbed the remote, and switched on the television just as Billy Crystal danced across the stage.

"So," he asked, "who's gonna win?"

"I've got my money on *American Beauty*."

"For Best Picture?"

"For Best Picture, and Kevin Spacey for Best Actor."

"No way. Denzel will win Best Actor."

"You're kidding."

"No. He'll win for *Hurricane*." He stood and shadow-boxed to emphasize his point.

She shook her head in amazement. "You're not kidding, you're just crazy."

"Crazy like a fox." He sat back down.

"And who do you like for Best Actress?" she asked.

"Decisions, decisions." He smiled at her. "I'll go with Meryl Streep."

She looked astonished. "You're a lunatic. Soft in the head. That movie stunk."

"*Music of the Heart*?"

"Yes. It reeked."

"You actually went to see it?"

"Yes." She raised her eyebrows. "Didn't you?"

He grinned broadly. "No."

"Then how can you say . . .?" She punched him on the arm.

"Hey," he cried, "Meryl Streep always wins!" She pummeled him lightly about the head and shoulders. "Okay, okay, stop . . . you're messing me up." He rearranged his shirt. "Seriously, I like Annette Bening for Best Actress."

She smiled. "You're still crazy. Hilary Swank will win."

An hour later, as the ceremony dragged through Best Foreign Film and Best Cinematography and Best Who-knew-what, Eddie, feeling comfortable, steered the discussion to more personal matters.

"Do you have a steady boyfriend?" he ventured.

A steady boyfriend? She grinned. "What are we, teenagers?"

He raised his hands as if to surrender. "It was an innocent question."

"You might say I have an unsteady boyfriend."

"Unsteady. Does that mean he drinks a lot?"

Ouch. Was that a Freudian slip? Phil, "The Wine Merchant," as he sometimes referred to himself, had been known to have a few too many. On a couple of occasions, pissed off with his devil-may-care attitude, she had declined to accompany him to a hotel. Denied sex, he would drink until he could hardly stand.

"Yes, he does drink too much on occasion. But he's not what you'd call a boyfriend. We just date occasionally." *Let's get off this subject.* "Tell me about your situation. You said you were separated?" She watched as he shifted on the sofa.

*****

"Yeah, we're separated. Have been for a few weeks." *I might as well be honest about it.*

"What's your wife's name?" she asked.

"Alison."

"Nice name. How long have you been married?"

The reporter never sleeps. "Can I just give you the condensed version of my marriage?"

"I'm sorry, I didn't mean to pry."

"No, I want to be upfront with you. No secrets." *No big ones, anyway.*

"Okay . . ." She leaned back on the sofa. "Give me the condensed version."

He took a deep breath. "We met at Rutgers during our senior year. We got married right after we graduated. We've been married, uh, seven years. We live in an apartment near Rutgers. We separated almost a month ago. That's about it."

"That's it?"

"That's it. We've just grown apart in the last few months."

"What kind of work does she do?"

"She's in advertising."

"Oh. And no rugrats crawling around the apartment?"

"No. No kids." He seemed to cringe as he said it.

"I'm sorry. I didn't mean to make you uncomfortable." She extended her hand to him in a gesture of reconciliation.

Me, uncomfortable? "No, it's all right." He took her hand.

She slid over to him and glanced at the television. Kevin Spacey had just won for Best Actor. "I told you so." She smiled.

He leaned over, touched her cheek, and kissed her lightly on the lips. "I still liked Denzel better."

"You're entitled to your opinion." She kissed him back. "It's not your fault that no one agrees with you."

Soon he was nuzzling her neck, and his hand was under her sweater. He felt her nipples harden as he worked his fingers under her bra.

She pulled away. "Let's take it a little slower." She removed his hand and slid back across the sofa.

A little slower. "What's the matter?"

"Nothing. It's just that, well, we hardly know each other."

We hardly know each other. He shrunk into the opposite corner of the sofa.

"Hey, don't be hurt," she said.

"I'm not."

"I do like you." She smiled at him.

"Well, that's encouraging."

She slid back next to him, snuggled close, and took his hand. "I wouldn't have agreed to come here if I didn't like you."

He put his arm around her, leaned down, and kissed her lightly on the cheek.

She kissed him back. "I'll behave if you behave."

"Such a deal." He smiled.

They watched as Hilary Swank won for Best Actress.

"I told you so," she said.

32

Monday, March 27, 2000

From: MarKau55@nyc.rr.com

To: EZEddie32@nyc.rr.com

Subject: Return of the Dark Brothers!

     Eddie, did you see the article about Fagen and Becker in Rolling Stone Magazine? It's terrific. I can't remember the last time I saw such a good article about them.
     I've been following your exploits in The New York Post. Are you more clever than you appear to be? Did you have this Steely Dan thing all planned out in advance? I mean, I know you're a smart guy and all (and good looking, let's not forget that!) Did you plan it, or did things just fall into place? Someone must be watching out for you.
     I still feel guilty about what happened between me and Mark. We (you and I) didn't have a committed relationship or anything, but still. I keep telling myself that chemistry between two people "just happens," but I still feel bad. I don't know what else to say. It's just how I feel.
     Did you see the Academy Awards last night?
     .....Marcie

****

From: EZEddie32@nyc.rr.com

To: MarKau55@nyc.rr.com

Subject: Feeling guilty

     Marcie, stop feeling guilty about what happened. Things happen. It hurts, but you get over it, eventually. You are 100% right about chemistry. Some people just hit it off, and others just don't. I'm okay, and I'm truly happy for you and Mark. Please don't worry about me.
     I read the article in Rolling Stone! I agree, it's fantastic. The description of how Fagen walks and sits is priceless. And it says Becker is the sarcastic one. Who would have known?
     Funny thing about the magazine: I had "borrowed" a copy from the store's magazine rack, which is a "technical" violation of policy. So I'm sitting in the storeroom, reading and eating my lunch, when my boss wanders in. I figure he's gonna chew my ass out, but all he says is: "Eddie, you work

here, right? Why don't you use your employee discount and buy the damned magazine. It's cheap, but it's not free." Can you believe it?

Thank you very much for calling me smart and good looking! Not many people have called me that lately—or ever!

This thing with The Post newspaper articles just kind of happened. I am clever, but not clever enough to engineer that whole thing. You're right, someone may be watching over me. But who?

I did watch the Academy Awards. Hilary Swank over Meryl Streep? Please!

…EZEddie

33

Tuesday, March 28, 2000

They had agreed to "dress up" for this, their second "not-a-date," or their third "not-a-date" if you counted the dinner at Friend of a Farmer.

Eddie admired his reflection in the storefront windows as he hurried along Eighth Avenue toward 63rd Street. He was wearing a white button-down shirt, black slacks, black loafers, and a charcoal grey sport jacket that his brother had graciously loaned him. As he approached the entrance to Iridium, he spotted Lois standing outside, her arms crossed, and one foot tapping impatiently on the sidewalk. She was wearing a black dress that had a pattern of silver swirls, a black leather coat draped over her shoulders, and an outrageous pair of high heels.

She heard his footsteps and turned. *A flash of spectacular thigh.* "You're late." She frowned at him.

He glanced at his watch. "I'm five minutes late."

They stared at each other for a few seconds before she broke down and pecked his cheek. "You clean up nice, anyway."

"That's why I'm late." He spread his arms and spun around. "This takes a while."

"Really!"

"Hey." He grabbed her and gave her a proper kiss. "You look fabulous." Her eyes twinkled.

Soon they were escorted down a flight of stairs, and seated at a tiny table in what was a converted basement. A waitress took their drink orders.

"So why did you pick this place?" she asked.

He thought for a few seconds. Lois had suggested they meet in front of the Village Vanguard, which was near her apartment, and wander around, checking out the dozen or so jazz clubs that were sprinkled around the Village. But he had done his research, and wanted to start at Iridium.

"A number of reasons. First, it's near River Sound, and what I thought was Fagen's apartment. If they sit in anywhere, this might be the place they'd do it."

"Okay. That makes sense, for someone who thinks like you."

He smiled. "Second, the Pharoah Sanders Quartet is playing here tonight. See the piano up there?" He gestured toward the stage. "Fagen's instrument. Guitars? Becker's instrument."

"Along with thousands of other musicians, I would guess." She looked doubtful.

"And third, a couple of fans told me this would be a good place to look, in emails they sent me. And it's mentioned in a couple of chat rooms."

"Oh, well, that clinches it."

The waitress arrived with a glass of chardonnay and a mug of Sam Adams. Starving, Eddie asked if there were any snacks. The waitress said she would see what she could find.

Lois sipped her wine. "What do you think the chances are of those two guys showing up, on this particular night, at this particular club?"

He thought for a moment. "It's worth a shot."

"Uh, huh."

"We'll catch the first set. If they don't show, we'll head down to The Village."

"Eddie. This is a useless exercise."

He smiled and mouthed the words "trust me."

The lights dimmed, the Pharoah Sanders Quartet was introduced, and they began with a subdued version of "You Don't Know What Love Is." But after a few numbers, it became obvious that Sanders was going to focus on more experimental stuff, and that no one was going to be sitting in with them.

He whispered to her, "No Fagen, no Becker. Let's go."

She hissed back. "Are you crazy? We paid the cover. Anyway, this is too good to walk out on."

She's right. He grabbed a handful of peanuts and signaled the waitress for another round.

When the set was over, he stood and put on his jacket. "Let's go," he said.

Lois didn't move a muscle. "That's it? That's all you're gonna do?"

"What else is there?"

"I thought you were going to *ask around?*"

He gestured around the room, which was emptying rapidly. "Who am I gonna ask?"

Lois signaled for the waitress, who dragged herself away from a conversation with a bartender and strolled over to their table. She looked puzzled; she'd already cashed them out. "Need something else?"

Lois took charge. "Is there a manager or someone else I can speak to?"

The waitress looked concerned. "Was everything all right?"

"Yes, fine," Lois reassured her, "you were wonderful. I'm a reporter from The New York Post. I just want to ask a few questions."

The waitress popped her gum. "Just a minute." She walked away and soon disappeared into the kitchen. A minute later she returned with a tall black man in tow.

The man was gleaming with jewelry and dressed to kill. He glanced at Eddie, took a good, long look at Lois, and smiled. "How may I help you?" The waitress made herself scarce.

Eddie guessed that the man was in his mid-thirties. *This guy makes Puff Daddy look shabby.*

Lois was all business. "Are you the manager?"

"I'm one of the managers."

"Good. I'm Lois Lane Smith of The New York Post. Could you join us for a few minutes?"

The man turned, grabbed a chair from the next table, and sat down. "Wonderful to meet you, Ms. Smith. I'm Darius Williams." He turned to Eddie. "And you are?"

"Eddie Zittner."

"Nice to meet you, Mr. Zittner." Williams turned his attention back to Lois. "The Post? Is this official business?"

"Oh, no," she replied coyly, "we're just out socially."

"On a date," Eddie chimed in.

Lois ignored him. Williams continued, "Did you catch the first set?"

"Oh, yes, we did," she replied. "It was terrific."

"Cool," Eddie added, trying to get a rise out of her. All he got was a withering glance. *I'll be on my knees tomorrow.*

"Well." Williams's eyes flicked from Lois to Eddie and then back to Lois. "I'm glad you enjoyed it."

Lois continued, "Mr. Williams . . ."

"Call me Darius." He smiled.

"Darius. Can we ask you a few questions?" She glanced at Eddie for support.

"Certainly," Williams said.

She continued, "First, how long have you been at Iridium?"

"Oh, six or seven years now."

"So you've seen lots of acts."

"Yes."

"Lots of musicians."

"Yes."

"Have you ever heard of the group 'Steely Dan'?"

Williams smiled. "Yes, absolutely. Great music."

"We agree," Eddie said. Everyone was smiling.

"But as far as I know," Williams continued, "they've never played here."

"We assumed that," Lois said. "They don't usually play clubs like this one. Have you ever heard the names Donald Fagen or Walter Becker?"

Williams looked thoughtful. "No. Who are they?"

"Steely Dan," she replied. "Fagen and Becker are the two men that founded the band. They just released a new CD."

Williams searched his memory, but came up empty. "The names don't ring a bell."

"Do you think it's possible one of them came in to sit in with one of your acts?"

"No. I would have remembered that."

"How so?"

"I meet all the musicians. We hang out after the sets."

She smiled. "Smokin' and jokin'?"

Williams grinned. "Yeah, somethin' like that." He looked around the room, which was beginning to fill up for the second set. "Hey, Lois Lane Smith from The Post, I've got to get busy." He winked at her, then stood and offered his hand to Eddie. "Mr. Zittner?"

Eddie extended his hand and had it crushed in a vice-like grip. Williams smiled, turned, and worked his way toward the bar.

"Some journalist you are!" Lois gave him another withering glance.

Minutes later, they were riding a southbound subway, heading for Greenwich Village. They watched with amusement as two guys in Yankee caps argued about how loud one of them was playing his Walkman.

Yankee fans everywhere. "Did you ever play baseball?" he asked her.

"Baseball?" She looked confused.

"Yeah. I'm wondering if I'll get to second base tonight."

She elbowed him in the ribs. "You'll be lucky if I kiss you goodnight."

34

Working title: <u>Yankee Fans</u>

An unpublished short story
by Eddie Zittner

<u>Black Boots</u>

     So I get on the A train heading south toward Sheridan Square. It's after eleven, so it's not the express anymore, it's the local, which is a big pain in the ass for me. This is what I get for helping Julio, my brother-in-law, fix up the store he rented. We're installing new display cases and light fixtures, and I'm getting filthy—dust and insulation shit inside my clothes—and the son-of-a-bitch won't give me a ride home. No, he's got to drive to Washington Heights to get more supplies out of the storage locker he's got up there. I say, what do you need with more supplies this late at night? He says he wants to get the stuff tonight. Load up his car. It will save him time tomorrow. Okay, so I take the subway. But he's a slimy bastard. If I find out he's fooling around on my sister, in Washington Heights or anywhere else, he's a dead man.

     I'm waiting for the doors to close, so we can start the slow trip down the West Side. I'm sitting in my usual seat, right next to the middle door, so I can stretch my legs and show off my black boots a little. These were my father's boots for as long as I can remember. My father loved westerns. He always took me to the movies when I was a kid. John Wayne was his favorite, but any western movie was okay with him. He always wanted to take a trip out west, to see what it was really like out there. But he never made it, never got farther than Chicago. My mom gave me the boots when he died two years ago. I know he wanted me to have them. They're old, really old, but still in good shape, new soles and all, and I keep them shined up pretty good.

     I can look out the window across the car, not that there's much to see, just an empty platform. I've got my player on, earphones on, listening to music. There's only one other person in this car, an old guy, not very big, dressed like he just walked off a golf course. Mr. Khaki. He reminds me of Rabbit Angstrom. Run, Rabbit, run. But he's not running anywhere, he's already half asleep.

     Just as the doors are about to close, another guy runs up to the train and jumps into the car, right in front of me. He shouts "Made it!" and sits down, just to my left, not next to me, but on the seats facing forward. He stretches his legs out right in front of him, as far as he can, blocking my foot space. Grey overcoat. Yankee cap, just like mine. He's not carrying anything, no briefcase, nothing. Ordinary looking guy, maybe forty, big, maybe 6'1", 220. A little soft in the middle, but big. Huge hands. His eyes look a little red, bloodshot, whatever.

The doors close. The train jerks a couple of times, and then begins to roll south, slowly gathering speed. Grey Overcoat still has his legs out, stretched straight out, still blocking my foot space. His arms are behind his head, eyes closed, butt balanced on the edge of his seat.

96th Street Station. We stop, but no one gets on, no one gets off, this car anyway. Soon we're rolling again. Just the three of us.

All of a sudden, Grey Overcoat opens his eyes, looks at me, and says, "Is that Celine Dion you're listening to?"

<u>Grey Overcoat</u>

I've had a goddamned bad day, bad week, bad month, bad year. Nothing is selling. I'm in the office way after regular hours, making cold calls to the West Coast, Midwest, Texas, wherever. I'm jumping from list to list, but no hits, no success. No one wants to open an account, no one wants to buy bonds, mutual funds, insurance, anything. Some slam-downs, which piss me off. At least hear what I have to say. My regulars, my daytime clients, locals, aren't buying anything either. And now, this morning, my wife is on my case to go on vacation, a cruise to the Bahamas out of Fort Lauderdale. Just what I need, a week in the sun. I guarantee that if I take a week off, my boss will have someone else at my desk when I get back, and a pink slip for me.

So I barely make the train, and sit down next to this monster wearing a Yankee cap, just like mine. Bald; looks like he shaves his head. Earphones, too; he's listening to some kind of music, but I can't tell what. Must be 6'6", over 300 pounds, maybe thirty years old, mustache, goatee, jeans, and stupid looking cowboy boots—must have been worn by Roy Rogers, as old as they look. A little soft in the belly, but huge. Dark eyes, dark hair, dark skin. Looks a little bit Latino to me.

Another guy across the way, an old guy, maybe fifty-five, no, closer to sixty, small, wearing what looks like a golf outfit, white polo shirt, khaki pants, brown loafers. The Golfer. Who wears white polo shirts? He's bald, too, but at least it's a natural bald, not shaved bald like the giant. He has some hair around his ears and in the back, going grey, no, already grey. Hey, something to be thankful for—at least I've got my hair.

The Steel Cadillac begins to move. I'm stretched out on my seat, eyes closed, trying to relax, trying to unwind, when I hear music leaking out from around the monster's earphones. I can barely hear it over the rumble of the train.

We stop at 96th Street. Now I can hear it clearly—it's music all right—Celine Dion. I hate Celine Dion. Why? Because my wife loves her and can't get enough of her. I don't know how many times I've been sitting at home, waiting for dinner, reading, while my wife is listening to Celine

Dion. And it's worse when Jennifer, our fourteen year old, comes in to set the table, and starts singing along, doing the back-up vocals. So, for a minute or two, I'm listening to Celine Dion leaking out from this guy's earphones, trying to tolerate it, trying to ignore it.

I can't fucking believe it. Why is this monster, this Latino, this gorilla, listening to Celine Dion? So as soon as we're moving again, I ask him: "Is that Celine Dion you're listening to?" as if I didn't know damn well that it was.

He says, "Yeah, what of it?"
I say, "She sucks."
He says, "Huh?"
I repeat, "She sucks."
He says, "What of it? What's it to you?"
I say, "I don't like her," close my eyes again, and try to relax. But it's not easy. I think to myself, what's with this guy? Why is he so belligerent?

(to be continued)

35

Thursday, March 30, 2000

Eddie Zittner had his eyes closed, his earphones on, and was using a spoon to tap out a rhythm on a half-empty bottle of Kingfisher beer. *The Curry Leaf, yet another scintillating stop on the never-ending tour of "Mark's favorite restaurants."*

He opened his eyes and gazed through the maze of lights that dangled from the ceiling. He checked his watch: five minutes after seven. *His brother was now officially late.* He closed his eyes and went back to his tapping.

A few seconds later, someone touched his shoulder and whispered, "Steely Dan, I presume?"

Eddie's eyes opened, and he looked up as his brother slid into the chair opposite him. He pulled out his earphones and switched off his Walkman. "No, Matchbox Twenty."

"Good stuff." Mark signaled the waiter for another beer. "Nice to see you're varying your musical selections."

"Well, I can't listen to Steely Dan all the time."

Mark looked stunned by the remark. "Did I just step into some alternate universe?"

Eddie watched with amusement as his brother looked around the restaurant, as if re-familiarizing himself with suddenly "unfamiliar" surroundings. Now his brother was making a big show of looking under the table. *Enough already.* "Hey, everyone needs a little variety in life."

The waiter appeared with another Kingfisher, and then took their dinner order.

Mark took a swig of beer. "Speaking of variety, does this so-called 'broadening of your interests' include women? Like that reporter?"

"Why not?" In the last few days, Eddie had done a lot of thinking, about women in general, and his wife in particular. *Why should I grovel at Alison's feet, just to win her back?* They'd been separated a month now, and all he'd gotten from her was "I'm not sure I'm still in love with you" at Denny's, and that one phone call a week ago. She seemed intent on filing for divorce, although he hadn't been served with any papers yet. Sure, those newspaper articles hadn't helped, but still, seven years of marriage, and she wouldn't spare him an hour to sit down and discuss things?

And Marcie. He tried to be philosophical about her. He never had any real claim on her, did he? *No, he didn't.* And he had to be happy for his brother, didn't he? *Yes, he did.* Mark had done a lot for him in the last month. Hey, if they were made for each other, then so be it. But he couldn't bring himself to ask his brother about her—not just yet. Deep down, he knew he'd get over her eventually. But it still hurt to think about her.

And now there was Lois.

As if reading his mind, Mark asked, "Are you getting hung up on . . . what was her name again? Lois?"

"I don't know. Maybe I am." *Has she finally gotten to me?* He occupied himself by breaking a sheet of poppadum into tiny pieces. He had to admit, at least to himself, that he was attracted to her.

"Have you told anyone else about what Alison said? I mean, besides me?"

"No. Why rush the inevitable?"

Mark made clucking sounds and flapped his arms like a rooster. "What's inevitable, bro, you telling Mom and Dad, or a divorce?"

"Good question."

"You're going to have to tell them at some point."

"I know."

"Better do it soon. You know how the New Jersey grapevine works." An idea seemed to flash into Mark's head. "Hey, this would be a great time to get Dad on the phone and tell him."

"Why?"

"The Dow's at 11,000. He's probably happy as a clam." Mark covered a piece of poppadum with chutney and began crunching through it. "On the other hand, the Mets just lost their opener—in Tokyo, of all places."

Eddie smiled. "That'll piss him off. Who's kakamamie idea was it to open the season in Tokyo?"

"I don't know, the Commissioner?" Mark grabbed another piece of poppadum. "So you figure you'll play Alison a little while longer? See if she goes through with it?"

"I'm not playing her, she's playing me." *Like a yoyo . . .*

The waiter arrived with a tray full of plates and bowls, which he arranged on the table. A mountain of tandoori shrimp and grilled vegetables sputtered on a blackened steel platter. Clouds of steam floated toward the ceiling. The smell of pungent spices was overwhelming.

Mark tore himself a piece of onion naan, and started in on the shrimp. Eddie surveyed the table and decided to start with the curry. First, he spooned basmati rice onto his plate, and then covered it with a heaping portion of lamb dripping with brick-red sauce. Starving, he stabbed a chunk of the meat, popped it into his mouth, chewed for a few seconds, and grabbed for his beer.

"Oh Lord that's hot!"

Mark swallowed a shrimp. "You said you liked vindaloo." He grabbed a bowl of raita and spooned some onto his brother's plate. "Here, this'll cool you off."

Using a combination of raita, beer, and ice-water, Eddie put out the fire in his mouth. Then, proceeding cautiously, he mixed the curry with generous amounts of rice before his next bite.

"By the way," Mark raised his bottle of beer, "congrats on your promotion."

After lunch, he had called Mark, telling him that he was now a full-time employee of Borders, and, surprise, in charge of the fiction department. Mark had congratulated him and suggested a dinner celebration. But he wondered if Mark thought that his taking a full time job was yet another nail in the coffin of his marriage.

"Thanks." Eddie smiled, then turned serious. "Mark, now that I'll be working full time, I can afford my own place."

"Why move out, bro? I've got plenty of room."

"You know. I don't want to impose."

"Look, Eddie." Mark speared another shrimp. "I can understand how you feel. But it's really not a problem. And I've got two trips coming up in April. I won't be there half the time."

Eddie knew that was an exaggeration, but appreciated it anyway. "You sure?"

"Yeah. No point in you moving again. Maybe things will work out with Alison."

Eddie finished his beer and signaled the waiter for two more. *Yeah, let's see how things work out with Alison . . . and Lois.*

<u>36</u>

Friday, March 31, 2000

"Lois Lane Smith."
"Lois, it's Eddie."
"Eddie Zittner, noted writer of short stories."
"You liked it?"
"Yeah. I thought you captured 'Black Boots' perfectly."
"Well, thank you."
"So when are you gonna finish it?"
"Finish it?"
"Yes, that's what writers usually do."
"I'm working on it."
"Oh."
"Yeah. It's what we writers call 'a work in progress.'"
"I wish I had that luxury."
"I guess you work against deadlines, huh?"
"Yeah."
"What are you working on now?"
"Right this minute? I'm way deep into nothing special."
"Nothing special?"
"Finishing a story. And eating lunch."
"What are you having?"
"Chicken Caesar salad."
"Not very exciting."
"No, but I've got a piece of cheesecake here with my name on it."
"Now *that* sounds good."
"I'm sure it will be. So where are you?"
"I'm in the deepest, darkest recesses of the Borders' storeroom, eating turkey on whole wheat."
"*That* sounds dull and dry."
"It is."
"So to what do I owe the pleasure of this call?"
"The reason I called . . ."
"I'm listening."
"Would you like to go out Saturday night?"
"Saturday night? Isn't that a big step?"
"I don't know about a big step. I just thought we might take in a movie."
"That sounds dull . . . like your sandwich."

"You *like* movies!"

"I know. I'm just not in the mood to sit in a dark theatre this weekend."

"Okay, how about the circus? It's still at The Garden. Plenty of bright lights."

"You've got tickets?"

"I haven't tried yet."

"Jesus, do you know what that'll cost?"

"No idea."

"Well . . . I don't really want to go to the circus, either."

"Hard to please, aren't you? How about dinner?"

"It's spring! Let's do something fun!"

"Just being together would be fun."

"Why don't we go skating?"

"Skating? Where?"

"Central Park."

"Outdoors?"

"Yes, outdoors!"

"You mean ice skating?"

"What other kind of skating is there?"

"Roller skating."

"Roller skating?"

"Yeah, you know, where you clamp your skates onto your shoes and then tighten them with a church key."

"Who does *that* anymore?"

"I did, when I was a kid."

"You're not that old."

"I think my skates were hand-me-downs."

"From your great-grandfather?"

"From my father."

"Well, are you interested?"

"Yeah. I guess I could stumble around a skating rink a few times."

"Such enthusiasm."

"No, really, let's do it."

"Do you know how to ice skate?"

"I can roller skate. How difficult could it be?"

"Oh, boy."

"Danger is my middle name."

"Right . . ."

"Edward Danger Zittner."

"Seriously, do you want to go?"

"Yes!"

"You working tomorrow?"

"Yeah, nine to four."

"Okay. I'll be out most of the afternoon. How about we meet at the rink at six?"

"Sure, six works for me. What about skates?"

"We can rent them there."

"Okay. Now exactly where is this place?"

"Wollman's Skating Rink. It's at the south end of Central Park, just north of 59th Street. You know the Plaza Hotel? It's a couple of hundred yards north of there."

"I'll find it."

"And Eddie . . ."

"What?"

"Be sure to pack a lot of padding around your butt."

"Right. I'll try to remember."

"Okay. See you tomorrow. My cheesecake awaits."

"Bye."

37

Saturday, April 1, 2000

    Lois arrived at Wollman's a few minutes before six. Not spotting her "date," she found a vacant bench on the upper viewing terrace and sat down. It had been another beautiful early-spring day, but now the sun was setting behind the unbroken wall of concrete along Central Park West. *There's a chill in the air . . .*

    She gazed out over pathways that were still crowded, with teenagers walking dogs, commuters taking the shortest route home, and, of course, mothers pushing baby carriages. Sighing, she turned her attention back to the rink, which was filling up with skaters. *Fat ones, small ones, short ones . . . skinny ones. What song was that from?*

    Then, looking south again, she spotted Eddie walking along one of the pathways. *Am I a fool to keep going out with this guy?*

*****

    Having fought his way through crowds of vendors, joggers, shoppers, and who-knew-who-else, Eddie broke free of the 59th Street entrance and started up the pathway that led north. Two minutes later, he spotted the skating rink a few hundred feet ahead. *Relax, Eddie, you found it.* And it hadn't been that hard; it was right where Lois had said it would be.

    Approaching the rink, he spotted her on the upper level and waived to her. She stood, waived back, and started walking toward the enormous granite steps that led down to the entrance.

*****

    "You found it." She smiled at him.
    "Your directions were perfect."
    They embraced and pecked each other on the cheek. She looked him over. "Aren't you colorful today?" He was wearing a scarlet and white sweater with his usual black corduroys, black shoes, and black leather waistcoat.
    "I thought I'd show off my Rutgers colors. And you . . ." He embraced her again. "You look sensational, as always." He tried to kiss her, but she resisted and broke free of his grip.
    "These old things?" She stepped back and vogued for him. She was wearing a knit wool cap, cowl-neck sweater, and fuzzy tights, all in

matching forest green with gold trim. A black leather jacket, gloves, and boots completed her outfit.

Minutes later, they had paid the entry fee and rented skates. She watched as Eddie stood at the edge of the rink and tried a few tentative steps.

"Okay, Mr. Ice-Skater," she said, "let's see what you've got."

Eddie balanced himself on his left foot and slid his right foot forward, gliding perhaps eighteen inches. Having successfully accomplished what he called "one small step for Easy Eddie," he then extended his left skate, pushed off with his right foot, lost his balance, tilted backwards, did a breaching-whale-like half twist, and fell in a heap. In the corner of his eye, small children glided past him. He groaned and looked up at her.

She chuckled. *Easy Eddie?* "I'd call that one giant leap into mediocrity."

Lois, a competent skater, helped him up and held his hand as they bumped along, Eddie slowly getting the hang of it. In minutes, he was able to skate on his own, and snow-plow to an unsteady stop—that is, when he didn't just ram into the nearest soft object. Soon they were holding hands and gliding smoothly around the rink. As the sun set, overhead lights came on, casting long shadows over the ice. The rink became a shining silver dollar, surrounded by deep grey slopes, and in the distance, Manhattan became a city of lights.

*****

At seven-thirty, tired and hungry, they returned the skates and bought pizza, bottled water, and coffee at the snack bar.

"Where'd you learn to skate like that?" he asked.

"My parents taught me. Or, rather, my mother taught me. My father wasn't much of a skater."

Neither was mine. "You never told me where you grew up."

"Queens. My parents still live there."

Having inhaled one piece of pizza, he reached for another. "Any brothers and sisters?"

"No, I'm an only-child. They broke the mold with me."

"What was it like for you growing up?"

He watched as she chewed thoughtfully. "I guess I had a normal childhood. Lots of relatives around, that sort of thing."

"Were you raised Jewish?"

"No, not really, my parents aren't very religious."

"So you played both sides of the street?"

"Absolutely. I celebrated every holiday . . . when I could get away with it."

"What are your parents like?"

"My parents? Let's see . . ." She settled back in her chair. "My mother is the classic 'earth mother.' You know, braided hair, flowered dresses, herb garden, tea brewing on the porch . . . that kind of thing."

"And does she work?"

"Yeah, she's a school teacher. Elementary school. I think it satisfies her need to have children around."

"You weren't enough?"

"Oh, I was a handful, but yeah, I always sensed that she wanted more children."

Having wolfed down half the pizza, he reached for his coffee. "What about your Dad?"

"My dad was a pot-smoking hippie—back in the sixties, of course—with an afro, the weakest afro you'll ever see. I'll show you a picture sometime."

"Hmm . . . what's he like now?"

"Now? He's changed a lot. He got his degree in accounting. He became a 'God-forbid CPA' as my mother likes to call him."

"No kidding. Just like my dad."

"He's a CPA, too?"

"That's how he got started. He runs an H&R Block office in Jersey."

She looked surprised. "Shit, it's tax time, isn't it?"

"Yeah." *Shit is right. I need to call Alison and figure out how we're gonna do them.* Noting that Lois had started on her coffee, he picked up the last piece of pizza. "So where does your father work?"

"Oh. He runs a back office for American Express. Tie and jacket every day. He's a complete sell-out."

"And your folks, do they get along?"

"Oh, yeah, as long as they stay out of each other's way. They've been married thirty years now."

"Did you ever want brothers and sisters?"

*****

He's interviewing me and I didn't even realize it. "Yeah, there were times when I did. Mostly I had to make-do with my cousins from Brooklyn." She sipped her coffee. "But enough about me—I'll bore you to death."

"On the contrary," he replied.

Eddie had a strange look on his face, and she suddenly felt uncomfortable. *He's leading up to something. What should I say next?* "So . . . the night is young." *Did I actually say that?*

He seemed to gather up his courage. "Look, there is something I wanted to tell you. Remember I told you I was separated from my wife?"

"I remember." *Here it comes. He's going back to her, and he's telling me here? In the middle of a date?*

"Well . . ." He took a deep breath. "She's filing for divorce."

She looked at him. *Is this an April Fools joke?* "Are you serious?"

"Yes."

He looked serious . . . Oh my God. "I'm sorry."

"I don't know whether to be sorry or not."

Neither do I. "When did she tell you?"

"A few days ago."

Her mind raced. *Do you still love her?* "Do you—" She stopped herself. "I'm sorry. Sometimes I can't turn off the reporter in me."

"It's okay."

"Are you okay?"

"Yeah."

What should I say next? "It must be hard."

"No," he smiled, "not as hard as I thought it would be. I think I'm beginning to accept it."

"Still," she fumbled for the right words, "it takes a while."

They fell into an uncertain silence. The snack bar was still crowded, but it seemed like the people around them were frozen in place. Finally, he spoke. "I guess I've totally screwed up our date."

"No, you haven't."

He glanced at his watch. "Eight-thirty and I've thrown a wet blanket over the entire evening."

"On the contrary." She forced a smile. "The night is still young . . . we could go to a movie."

He looked skeptical. "After all that exercise? I'd be asleep in fifteen minutes."

"What an old fart. Why don't we go back to my place? There's probably something good on the cable."

*****

She's trying to salvage the evening. Is it worth it? "Do you have any wine there?"

She grinned. "I might be able to scare up a bottle."

An hour later, he sat on the sofa, feet propped on the coffee table, watching Obe-Wan Kenobi match wits with Darth Vader. They hadn't spoken much on the trip downtown. Not much privacy on the bus—or maybe they both sensed the need to shut up and think about what was happening. The apartment was tiny, and it appeared to him that Lois had decorated it with whatever she could beg, scrounge, or buy on-the-cheap. But it was clean, and quiet, and she had made it "comfortable." *And she'd picked the least romantic movie of all time. I guess I deserved that.*

*****

She stared at the television screen. *Why did I pick this movie?* But she knew why: her subconscious was throwing up roadblocks wherever it could. Instead of a nice, fast, convenient taxi, she had chosen a long bus ride home—cheaper, yeah, and a lot less private, too. Not much chance for intimate conversation. And the yawning gap between them on the sofa? You could drive a truck through it. If she'd had a dog, it would be up here on her lap, growling every time Eddie glanced her way, which wasn't very often. He was probably trying to think of a way to dig himself out of the hole he was in, or a way to just get the hell out of her apartment.

She was attracted to him. Most of the time he seemed earnest and sincere. On the other hand, he could be a bit stubborn. And he was a flake. Who pursues a couple of old rock stars? And gets himself arrested in the process? Outrageous thoughts flashed through her brain: *Was he setting her up? Was he clever enough to be trying for a pity-fuck?* She decided to take her chances. She moved closer.

*****

He could feel her thigh against his. Did this mean she wasn't angry? Was she making a move on him? Did she sense that he was vulnerable? Was he vulnerable? Or just pathetic?

He took a deep breath, turned his head, and began nibbling on her ear.

*****

She felt him turn his head and nuzzle against her. She closed her eyes and leaned back. *Try to enjoy the moment, Lois.* But then her body reacted, and she felt her nipples start to tingle, and she started to sweat. She sighed, leaned forward, turned toward him, closed her eyes, and kissed him. Her hand brushed against his thigh.

*****

Her tongue flicked into his mouth. He sucked it gently, and touched her tongue with his. He felt her hand on his thigh. He was getting hard. He reached under her sweater and touched her breasts. He felt her nipples. *This will not be like the last time, with Marcie.*

*****

She thought about Phil, and the last time they had been together. She wondered where he was tonight. She wondered who he was with tonight. She wondered who he was screwing tonight.

Then she wondered what, this very minute, was going through Eddie's mind.

She pulled away and took a deep breath. "Let's go to the bedroom, Easy Eddie."

"Easy Eddie?" He smiled and took her hand.

38

Sunday, April 2, 2000

    Lois sprawled across the sofa, feet propped on the coffee table, and stared out the half-open window. It was overcast, and her flannel pajamas and "Bugs Bunny" slippers were losing the battle against the cool air that drifted in. She thought about getting her robe, but instead reached down and grabbed the quilt that was placed strategically at her feet. Once settled under the quilt—a gift her mother had given her the day she had moved into this very apartment—she realized that her coffee cup was empty.
    Forget coffee . . . why did I sleep with him?
    She was unhappy with how last night had ended. They'd made love, slowly and tenderly, draining all of their energies, and then fallen asleep. An hour later, she'd woken with a start, fearful with thoughts that they'd started something that was spinning out of control. Afraid of waking him, she'd laid there in his arms and listened to his breathing.
    He'd woken a few minutes later, subdued and tentative, and maybe even a little embarrassed. He'd gotten up and dressed quickly. She'd put on a robe, and, uncertain of what to say, offered him a cup of coffee. He'd refused. Too late for coffee, he'd said, and he thought he'd better get going. She hadn't argued with him. They hadn't said much. After a quick good-night kiss, he promised to call, and slipped quietly out the door. She'd gone back to bed, tossed and turned for a while, and finally fallen into a troubled sleep.
    Why did I sleep with him?
    She picked up her cell phone and punched in his number.

*****

    Eddie lay in bed, listening to the soft music of the city waking up on Sunday morning. Paralyzed by his own doubts, he was unable—or unwilling—to move an arm, a leg, a finger, or even a toe. He'd been that way most of the night, he thought.
    Why did I sleep with her?
    He didn't know the answer. *Yes he did.* She was attractive. And smart. He was attracted to her. He'd wanted to sleep with her. He'd fallen for her, just like he'd fallen for Marcie a couple of weeks ago. What was happening to him? First Alison, then Marcie, then Lois, then the newspaper article, then getting arrested, then more newspaper articles, then Alison again—her phone call—and then, finally, last night.

He remembered making love, and waking up, and feeling uncomfortable, like he was standing naked in a storefront window. He remembered kissing Lois good-night, and the taxi ride, and then climbing into this bed. And then nothing, nothing else, until he'd woken up an uncountable number of minutes ago.

His stomach growled. He needed to eat and get ready for work. He got up and looked out the window. *It's gonna rain for sure . . .* He put on a pair of pants and walked into the kitchen. Ten-thirty, and no sign of his brother, but there was a copy of the *Times* on the counter. His brother had slept here last night, or he'd slept somewhere else—Marcie's?—came back to get something, and had gone out again.

He brewed a pot of coffee, and toasted an onion bagel. Not finding any cream cheese, he sliced some cheddar, layered it on the bagel halves, and zapped it in the microwave, watching as the cheese slowly melted. Then he sat at the kitchen table and ate, drank, and glanced at the front page. *The last day of the Circus.*

His cell phone buzzed. He picked it up and looked at the display: Lois, calling him. He smiled. *Rescue me from a dreary Sunday.* "Hello?"

"Hi, Eddie. It's me, Lois."

She sounded good . . . maybe a bit restrained. "I know. I saw the caller ID."

"Did you get home all right? I mean, I assume you got home all right?"

"Yeah, no problem."

"Where are you now? I mean, are you at the apartment? Your brother's apartment?"

"Yeah, I'm eating breakfast."

*****

Lois, you're all over the place. "Mmm." *What do I say next?* "I just had coffee." *Buy some time.* "Eddie, can you hold just a minute?"

"Sure."

She put the phone down, tossed the quilt aside, stood up, picked up her cup, walked into the kitchen, and poured herself more coffee. *He didn't even ask if I was all right.* She walked back into the living room, placed the cup on the coffee table, turned, and walked into the bathroom. *On the other hand, what would he have said? I had a good time? Was it good for you?* She looked in the mirror. *I knew he was lying about his wife.* She thought about slapping herself a few times, and then thought better of it. *Grow up, Lois.* She played with her hair, which was still mashed flat with sleep. *Act your age.* She went back to the living room, flopped back onto the sofa, and picked up the phone.

"Sorry, someone at the door."

"Sunday morning?"

I'm wallowing in pity and lies. "One of those Jehovah's Witnesses." *What? He'll never believe that.*

"They can be a nuisance."

She took a breath. "Look, Eddie, I think we should talk."

*****

We should talk? Warning lights flashed in Eddie's head.

"Are you all right?"

"Yes . . . no . . . no, I'm not all right."

"Can we meet somewhere?"

*****

Can we meet? "Yes . . . I mean, no, I just wanted to talk on the phone."

"What's wrong?"

"What's wrong?" *Funny you should ask.* "Nothing, really, it's just that, well, I think we're moving a bit too fast."

*****

"A bit too fast?" He set his bagel down on a napkin, and pushed it aside.

"Yeah, Eddie, don't you think so? Don't you think things are moving too fast?"

Yeah. The view is getting blurry in the rear-view mirror of my life.

"Eddie? Are you still there?"

"Yeah, I'm still here." *Hanging on your every word.* "Lois, are you breaking up with me?"

*****

"Breaking up?" *Hold it together, girl.* "I didn't realize we were a couple."

"Well, we've had a few dates . . ."

"Look, Eddie, I like you . . . but this thing has caught me off guard." *And I'm already having an affair with a married man.*

*****

She wants to slow things down . . . life can be very strange. "I didn't mean to rush things, Lois."

"Well, you didn't, not really. I mean, I rushed things, too . . . we both rushed things."

A familiar narrow blade started to work its way into his belly. *Was this just a one-night stand?* "Do you want to let things cool off for a while?"

"Yeah, that would be good. I need some time to think."

"Can I call you again? I mean, *when* can I call you again?"

"In a week? How about a week?"

Time to think. "A week . . . I guess I can struggle through a week without you." He picked cold cheddar cheese off what remained of his bagel.

"Thanks, Eddie."

"Don't mention it."

"Easy Eddie . . . I can hear you smiling."

"I don't feel happy."

"I don't either, but we need some time apart."

She says that like we're an old married couple. "Don't say it that way. We've only known each other, what, three weeks?"

"Yeah, that's about right . . . three weeks."

"I'll call you in a week."

"Okay, Eddie." He heard her disconnect.

*****

She put down the phone. *Why did I call him Easy Eddie?*

39

Monday, April 3, 2000

Ten minutes late, Lois tiptoed into the conference room and eased into an empty chair in the back. A couple of friends, reporters she'd worked with many times, nodded to her and rolled their eyes. The city editor—an obese man in a wrinkled suit who liked to be called "The Boss"—was well into his weekly speech, exhorting the troops to greater and greater achievement. *Blood and Guts* was what he wanted; the *bloodier* and *guttier*, the better. *Guttier?* And don't forget that sex sells. *Who could forget that?* Even better: deviant sex, as long as it wasn't "too gross." *Too gross for The Post . . . what a concept.* And don't forget human interest stories: little old ladies, cats, dogs . . . babies! Those bastards at *The News* were still far ahead, circulation-wise and advertising-revenue-wise. Pound that pavement! Punch up those stories!

It was pretty much the same speech she'd heard every Monday morning for as long as she could remember. There were perhaps twenty reporters in the room. Maybe five were paying attention; the rest stared out the window or sipped coffee. Lois wished she'd picked up something at the Starbuck's downstairs.

She heard a faint buzzing, looked into her handbag, and saw her cell phone flashing. She picked up the phone, slung her handbag over her shoulder, stood, and headed for the door.

"Lois Lane Smith."

"Lois, Phil! Top o' the mornin' to ya!"

Funny you should call today. "Just a minute, Phil." She walked down the hallway, past restrooms and vending machines, looking for privacy and better reception. She found both next to a window that overlooked West 47th Street. "St. Patrick's Day was last month, Phil."

"That's right, it was!"

"Haven't heard from you in a while . . ."

"It hasn't been that long, has it?"

"It's been a month, Phil."

"Guilty as charged. I fall on my sword."

She smiled. "Well, be careful . . . you don't want to bend it."

"What?"

"You don't want to bend it? Your sword?" *We're not talking about the same thing.*

She visualized wrinkles on Phil's forehead as he tried to figure it out. After a few seconds, he blurted, "Oh, *that* sword!"

"Yeah, Phil, *that* sword. If you break it, you'll need a splint. But don't worry, you can make one out of tongue depressors. Or, in your case, toothpicks."

"I detect hostility."

"Me hostile? Just because you haven't called in a month?"

"Let me make it up to you. I'll buy you lunch."

"Just a minute, I've got company." Her co-workers, fully energized for another week's "news-wars," filed out of the conference room and paraded past her. "The Boss" gave her a glance that said "See me in my office." She smiled and mouthed the words "Five minutes?" He nodded and walked on. "What were you saying, Phil?"

"How about lunch?"

She had thought about Phil, on and off, since they'd last had lunch, which had included his usual proposition, her surprising refusal, his displeasure, his anger, his getting plastered, and her helping him to the sidewalk and pouring him into a cab. She didn't know if her "relationship" with Eddie Zittner would amount to anything. She didn't know if it could be called a "relationship." It was a business transaction turned strange friendship turned affair? Fling? One night stand? But she knew she was fed up with Phil.

"Phil, no . . . I think I've had it."

"What do you mean, had it?"

"I've had it, Phil. No more lunches that end up in hotel rooms."

"Okay, then, how about dinner?"

"Phil, you're not getting the message. It's over. I don't want to see you anymore."

"That's kind of abrupt."

"Abrupt? You haven't called me in a month, and you want to pick up right where we left off?"

"This is not like you, Lois. Did you meet someone?"

"I meet a lot of people, Phil."

"You know what I mean."

Yes, I know what you mean. "I don't know. Yes, I met someone, but we're not serious . . . yet."

"Not serious?"

"Not serious."

"Who is it?"

"It's none of your business, Phil."

"I'll bet it's that lunatic you've been writing about. The Steely Dan guy."

She could hear the anger in his voice. "It's none of your business, Phil."

"Bullshit, Lois, it must be him. Who else would it be?"

Thanks for stroking my ego, Phil.

"You wrote three articles about him. Did you bail him out of jail?"

"Phil, you think you know me so well." *Keep your cool, girl.*

"I do know you, Lois. What else did you do for him? Did you sleep with him?"

"Fuck you, Phil."

"You've slept with him. I can hear it in your voice."

"Look, Phil, I don't have time for this."

"And he's married, too. You have a real 'thing' for married men, don't you?"

She stared out the window.

"One drink, Lois? A drink and a little sword-play?"

No, Phil, you won't suck me in this time. She disconnected, dropped the phone into her handbag, and walked toward "The Boss's" office.

40

Wednesday, April 5, 2000

Eddie opened his eyes, rolled over, and turned on the bedside lamp. *Nine o'clock.* He needed to be at work by one. He could sleep for another hour, maybe two.

But sleep wouldn't come. He thought about last night, drinking with his friends, or, to be more precise, some of his co-workers from Borders.

John Russell: "J.R.," married, with a brand new baby boy, rambling on about the happiness of married life and fatherhood—but he never seemed particularly interested in getting up and going home. A man with roving eyes. Left at eleven.

Sarah Park: Korean. Wonderful body. Hot. Hotter than hot. Has a boyfriend but likes her independence. Runs the magazine rack and has a nice rack of her own. Untouchable. Left at eleven-thirty.

Thomas something, never could remember his last name. Single, nerdy, and totally dedicated to his job. He'd work eighty hours a week if they'd let him. A science fiction nut. Left at eleven-thirty with Sarah. *I wonder if he's poking the Korean barbeque?*

Raymond Obenjaya: immigrant from Kenya. A tree-stump of a man. No personality. Didn't see him leave . . . perhaps he just disappeared into thin air.

Wendy McGill: Referred to as "The Thrill" by her co-workers. Bleached blond, semi-attractive, too much make-up. Had been known to flirt blatantly with male customers. Smoked like a chimney, and pestered Eddie to "step outside and keep me company" while she smoked. He figured he could have her if he wanted her—but he didn't want her. Probably carrying STDs. She stayed till the bitter end, twelve-thirty, and then headed downtown in a taxi.

And yours truly, Eddie Zittner: Separated from his wife. Treading water. Drifting aimlessly. Another one who stayed to the bitter end.

He got out of bed, shaved, showered, dressed, and strolled into the kitchen. *No coffee and no note . . .*

An hour later, he'd eaten two heaping bowls of cereal—Cheerios mixed with Raisin Bran—and had moved into the living room, where he sipped coffee and plowed through a paperback copy of *The Concrete Blonde* by Michael Connelly. A random mix of Steely Dan, U2, REM, and Sting played softly in the background. Halfway through "Roxanne" his cell phone buzzed—a familiar number on the display. *Why is she calling?*

He muted the stereo and picked up. "Hello?"

"Eddie, it's Alison."

"Hi."

"Hi. I need to talk to you."

Neutral tone of voice, Eddie. "About what?"

"Where are you?"

"I'm at my brother's apartment."

"Where is that? The East Side?"

She'd never been to his brother's apartment. "Yeah, Third Avenue and 32nd Street."

"I'm ten minutes away. Can I just come over there? It'll save time."

She must have the divorce papers with her. "Uh, yeah, but what is it you want to talk about?"

"Us. Our relationship. What else would we talk about?"

Our relationship? He gave her the address, disconnected, and then called downstairs, instructing the doorman to send her up when she arrived.

He went into the kitchen and put on a fresh pot of coffee. He sweated through his t-shirt, hurried into the bedroom, stripped it off, and put on a nicer one. He brushed his teeth, again, and did some minor touch-ups on his hair. He sat back down and tried to read, with little success.

Minutes later, the elevator door chimed, and he stepped into the hallway. He watched as his wife strolled toward him wearing a black raincoat—glistening wet, he noted—and a pair of high heels. She carried her black leather briefcase, and . . . *Her hair was all over the place.*

She embraced him, backed him into the apartment, pushed the door shut, dropped her briefcase, and kissed him, hard, on the lips.

He didn't resist.

Seconds later, she was on her knees, and his pants were around his ankles, and his penis was in her mouth. She stopped and looked up at him. "This is what you like, isn't it?"

Close your eyes and you'll be there.

They moved quickly to the bedroom, where they stripped each other's clothes off, and, for the first time in months, consummated their marriage.

*****

They lay together, spooned together, his penis pressed against her thigh. The sound of thunder . . . and he remembered the first time they'd met, when they were juniors at Rutgers. *April of 1992? Or had it been May?* They had been between classes. A mutual friend—long forgotten—had called him over and introduced him to Alison. And as they were talking, just the two of them, it had started to rain. Without missing a beat, she had opened her umbrella, and they had huddled together and talked for more than two hours.

He felt her shoulders begin to shake. He leaned back, and then raised himself on one arm. Tears were rolling down her cheeks.

"What's the matter, Alison?"

She didn't speak for a long time. She wiped the tears away, and more came. He tried to embrace her, pull her back into his arms, but she pulled away, and then she stood, pulling the sheet off the bed and holding it in front of her. He covered himself with the blanket.

"What's the matter, Eddie? You. You're what's the matter."

He stared at her, not knowing what to say. He watched as she put on her bra, and then sat on the edge of the bed and pulled her pantyhose on. He started to get hard again. She stood and reached for her blouse.

"I thought you wanted to talk."

She stared back at him as she buttoned her blouse. Finished, she reached for her skirt. "I thought I did, too. I guess I didn't."

"So what does this mean?"

"I don't know." She put her jacket on.

"You don't know?"

She picked up her high heels. "I'm confused, Eddie."

"You're confused about what?"

Leaning against the dresser, she slipped her high-heels on. "You, Eddie. This whole thing." She moved to the bedroom door, stopped, and turned toward him. "You know, when I married you, I thought you were Russell Crowe. But you turned out to be . . . Jason Biggs."

Jason Biggs? From American Pie? "I don't know whether to be flattered or offended."

"Bye, Eddie."

He listened as her high-heels clicked along the hallway. Seconds later, he heard the apartment door close.

****

<u>To</u>: EZEddie32@nyc.rr.com

<u>From</u>: AlisonZ@jacobsagency.com

<u>Subject</u>: (no subject)

    Eddie, I'm writing this at work. It's after seven and I'm the only one here. I've been thinking about what happened this morning. But more than that, our problems have forced me to think hard about our marriage, our feelings for each other, and what I want to do with my life (I hope that doesn't sound totally like something from *Cosmopolitan*.)
    I said I was confused. I guess, in some ways, I still am, but in other ways, I'm not. Not anymore.
    Remember how we used to drive in the country, looking at houses? Pretty houses, with flower beds, and green lawns, and white picket fences? And we'd talk about having children? I think I wanted that, once. I wanted to be a housewife. I wanted a couple of kids. I wanted to kiss you goodbye and wave to you as you pulled out of the driveway and headed for work. But I'm not so sure that's what I want anymore.
    I am sure I loved you, Eddie. I was head over heels for you in college, and the first few years we were together were wonderful. But I just got tired of it, Eddie. Not tired of you, specifically. I think I just got tired of "being married" and living as a couple. It's gotten to be a chore.
    You know I'm good at my job. The more I work at it, the more I like it. I'm going to focus on that for a while, and see how far I can go.
    I'm still confused about some things, but I know that I need to get on with my life. And you need to get on with your life. That's why I've decided to go ahead with the divorce. I'm going to call my lawyer this evening and tell him to file the papers.
    I still have feelings for you, Eddie. We were together for a long time.

    …..Alison

41

Friday, April 7, 2000

Lois Lane Smith hurried across the street, scanning the opposite sidewalk for any sign of her mother. *One minute from my office and I'm five minutes late!* She approached the nondescript wine bar where they were to meet. The few tables scattered about the sidewalk were empty. *Too cold to sit outside.* She strolled through French doors and spotted her mother just sitting down.

She approached the table. "Hi, Ma."

Having just settled into her chair, Rachael Smith looked up, saw her daughter, smiled, and pushed herself back to her feet. They embraced and kissed. Lois looked at her mother for the first time in weeks. Yeah, she'd put on a few pounds over the years, but who hadn't? She still looked great. And what a beautiful dress—midnight blue!

"Ma, you look lovely!"

"Oh, please!" her mother's smile grew wider.

"Where'd you buy that dress?"

"Bloomie's . . . where else?"

They sat down and ordered glasses of wine.

"So, Ma, your first time in the city in what, a month?"

"Yes." Her mother put on her best 'sad face,' the one she used at school. "My only child never visits me in the country, so I guess I have to come to the city."

Lay some more Jewish guilt on me, Ma. "Since when is Queens the country?"

Her mother smiled. "I already told you why I'm here. Your father's having dinner with the big shots. Wives are invited . . . spouses, I guess I should say."

You go, girl! Equal opportunity! "How wonderful. Where?"

"I don't know yet. We're meeting at his office. But he told me to dress up, so, I'm dressed up."

"Mmm . . ."

"I have an hour and then I have to run."

"So, how's school?"

"Wonderful. Third graders; so grown up these days. The girls are wearing lipstick and eye-shadow. Little 'Britney Spears' look-alikes."

"Really?"

"And the boys . . . I think some of them are already shaving."

"Third grade? What are they, eight? Nine?"

"Maybe I exaggerate a little."

The waitress returned with the wine: a dry chardonnay for her, and a sweet chablis for her mother.

"So, what's new with you, doll?" Rachel Smith sipped her wine. "You sounded terrible on the phone last night."

She made a face. "Man trouble."

"So tell me about it . . ."

"Remember the guy I've been dating? Phil?" Talking to her parents, she'd mentioned Phil a number of times, but, prudently, had never mentioned that he was married.

"Yes, I remember you talking about him . . . the latest in a long line of disposable men."

Disposable? "Well, we split up, finally."

"I told you: disposable. So what happened?"

"He was a piece of shit, that's what happened."

"Such language!"

"Then I started up with a new guy."

"Another disposable one?"

She ignored the remark. "Remember my Steely Dan articles? From last month?" She knew her mother always scanned *The Post* for her stuff, clipped the articles out with her sewing scissors, and filed them away.

"How could I forget such memorable reporting."

"Remember the guy in the stories? Eddie Zittner?"

"I remember the name."

"That's the guy I started up with."

Her mother thought for a moment. "He's married, isn't he?"

"Separated."

"Still, a bad habit, going out with married men." With as much dramatic effect as possible, Rachael Smith raised her glass, slowly sipped her wine, and majestically put the glass back down.

Lois avoided her mother's eyes. *Had she somehow caught on that Phil was married?*

"And you have enough bad habits, doll."

"What bad habits?" She couldn't tell if her mother was being serious or not.

Her mother smiled and thoughtfully tapped her chin. "Well . . . for one thing, you eat too much cheesecake."

"Oh, really?" She stood and struck a seductive pose. She worked hard to keep her figure, and was damned proud of it. "Is all that cheesecake showing?"

Her mother hissed at her. "Sit down . . . you'll make a scene." She sat. "Okay," her mother continued, "you can afford a piece of cheesecake every now and then. But wait until you get older."

"I can wait." She smiled. "What other bad habits do I have?"

"Pish!" Her mother brushed her off. "So tell me about this Zittner fellow."

Lois explained: At first, she thought he might be some kind of crazy stalker. Then she thought he was just a harmless flake . . . but he turned out, finally, to be a nice guy. He had a certain charm: he was funny, he was smart, and he was reasonably good-looking. He kind of grew on you. They had some things, some interests, in common. And he didn't give up easily: he was low-key, but persistent. On the other hand, he could be a bit of a doofus at times. And he was stubborn: he wouldn't give up on his obsession to get Fagen and Becker's autographs. She wondered if he was really worth investing her time in, or should she just write him off?

"Invest? Write-off? You've been listening to your father too long."

"You know what I mean, Ma."

"I know what you mean, doll. I read all the articles. I have a photographic memory, remember?"

"Right, Ma." Lois smiled at her mother. This was a running joke in the family. Rachael Smith was a wonderful teacher who never missed a beat in the classroom, and could make a lesson plan appear out of thin air. But around the house, she was a disaster. Her husband was still trying, without much success, to get her to make a "things to do" list. "So," Lois continued, "what do you think?"

"What do I think? Well, from what I read in your articles, and what you just told me . . ." Her mother thought for a long moment. "Follow my logic: How did you first meet him? Demonstrating on the sidewalk, right? Doesn't that tell you something about him? For some people, that takes guts. For others, they just have to be a little *meshugenah*. So, if he can give up his obsession, then maybe, just maybe, he *might* be salvageable."

Salvageable. "What about his wife? He said she's already filed for divorce."

"But there's no proof, is there? You're a reporter, doll. Keep digging."

Keep digging . . . what a reporter I am. Three articles, and three dates, and I still can't figure this guy out. I'm way too dumb sometimes . . .

42

Sunday, April 9, 2000

Eddie rang the bell. A few seconds later the door opened.

"Well, if it isn't my long lost son." Elaine Zittner—again wearing an apron!—stepped outside and gave him a hug.

"What's with the 'long lost,' Ma?"

"It's been a month."

A month? It couldn't be that long. They walked through the living room. "How's Dad?"

"Tired. Tax time, remember?"

Shit! He followed his mother into the kitchen, where a cornucopia of vegetables sat draining in the sink. "Where is he?"

"In the back."

He glanced out the kitchen window. *Is that my father, grilling steaks?* "He's cooking?"

"He insisted. He got home an hour ago."

Eddie checked his watch: six-thirty. It wasn't that unusual for his father to work on the weekends. *But a full day at the office? On Sunday?*

His mother picked up a chopping block. "Look, I'm going to make a salad. Why don't you go out and join him? Take a beer with you."

He took a beer out of the refrigerator, twisted the cap off, stepped outside, and started down the walkway. *Oleanders, growing outside my door.*

His father spotted him and waved. "Hey, Easy."

Eddie saw his father smile, and his eyes dance, just like he'd seen them dance a thousand times before. But his father looked dead tired. "Hey, Dad." They hugged. "How are you?"

"I'm fine. Just busy as hell at the office."

"Yeah, Mom told me."

Harry Zittner turned his attention back to the grille. The steaks needed another five minutes or so, he said. He picked up a pair of tongs and turned the thick, well-marbled rib eyes, sending bright tongues of flame licking skyward. Stepping back, he grabbed a spray bottle and squirted a mist of water over the coals. Eddie watched as the flames gradually diminished. His father mopped his forehead with a towel.

"So, what's new, Dad?"

His father had a few well-chosen words for the Justice Department, and the damage they would do, to the economy as a whole, and the stock market in particular, if they filed an anti-trust suit against Microsoft. "The beginning of the end" was how he described it: "Time to start hedging your bets." Eddie nodded and chugged the last of his beer.

Moments later, declaring the steaks "done", Harry Zittner loaded them onto a stainless steel platter and headed for the kitchen door. Eddie followed, grabbing the tongs, the towel, and the empty beer bottle.

Soon, father, mother, and son were seated in the dining room, each with a steak, a split baked potato, a salad, and a glass of red wine. Eddie wedged butter into his potato, and covered it with black pepper and chives. He watched as his father sprayed his potato with a stream of golden something-or-other.

He nodded toward the squeeze bottle. "Is that stuff any good?"

"It's not bad," his mother said.

His father smiled. "A concession to the evils of cholesterol."

"And the steak?" Eddie asked.

"I'm entitled." Harry Zittner glanced at his wife.

Eddie saw the look that passed between his parents. "Once a month, Lovey," his mother said. "That's what we agreed on." She smiled, but Eddie could see the look of concern in her eyes. His father grunted as he sliced a piece of steak and dipped it in A-1 Sauce.

They concentrated on their food. Eddie noted that his parents had avoided the subject of his marriage since he'd arrived. Now his mother took yet another detour: "Mark tells us he and Marcie are getting serious."

Eddie felt a twinge of regret, and his father looked uncomfortable. "Maybe Eddie doesn't want to talk about Mark and Marcie."

"No, Dad, Mom, its okay." It had been a raw nerve for the first week or two, but now he was comfortable with it, even philosophical about it, and happy, genuinely happy, for his brother. *Ugly duckling blossoms into swan . . . and gets the girl.* "Mark and I have talked about her a couple of times. I'm happy for him . . . for both of them." Maybe the fact that he had gotten laid—twice in one week!—had something to do with his accepting the loss of Marcie. But he'd never really had any claim on her, had he?

He watched as his parents exchanged another glance. *I'm sure they're happy about Mark and Marcie . . . why wouldn't they be?* Now if he could just find a way to "win back" Alison, everything would be perfect.

"Has Mark told you much about Marcie?" *Let's make this conversation really uncomfortable!*

"A little," his mother replied. "She's in law school, right?"

His father swallowed a mouthful of food. "Mark said she was at N.Y.U. She graduates in December, right?"

"Right." Eddie smiled. "And she's Jewish. Did Mark mention that?"

"Yeah, Mark told us she's Jewish," his father said, and Eddie saw the grin on his mother's face, confirming the fact.

But Reformed or Conservative . . . isn't that the question? He was sliding into quicksand, but couldn't stop himself. "Pretty, too. She reminds me of Liv Tyler."

His mother looked puzzled. "Liv Tyler, the actress?"

"Yeah. She was in *Armageddon* . . . you know, with Bruce Willis?" He poured more wine for himself, ignoring his parents' half-empty glasses.

"The daughter?" Elaine Zittner looked concerned. "She looked so young in that movie."

"Make-up, Ma. She's in her mid-twenties."

"Liv Tyler? Or Marcie?"

"Both. I think they're both in their mid-twenties." Now thoroughly disgusted with himself, he picked up the bottle of A-1 Sauce and shook it with as much hostility as possible.

His father put down his knife and fork. "Eddie, take it easy. Look, let's talk about you and Alison."

He took a deep breath. *What was there to talk about?* He'd called his parents yesterday, and given them a highly edited version of his meeting with Alison, and her subsequent email. Both parents had insisted he come to dinner so they'd have more time to talk.

"Tell us again what happened," his mother asked.

He repeated the story, modifying the truth to protect his parent's fragile sensibilities: Alison had been in Manhattan and she'd wanted to talk. She came to Mark's apartment. They went to a nearby coffee shop. They'd had a good talk, but hadn't made any progress; they still disagreed on many things. Later that day, she had emailed him, telling him that she was filing for divorce.

His mother spoke first. "I still don't understand how a simple disagreement about a rock and roll band could break up a marriage."

Harry Zittner glanced at his wife. "That's an over-simplification, Ellie. You know there's more to it than that."

"That's right." Looking for courage, Eddie took a generous swallow of wine. "It's not just a simple disagreement. We've got lots of issues." *Jason Biggs?* "I think Alison and I are moving in different directions." *Assuming I'm going in some direction . . .* "She said she doesn't want to be part of a 'couple' any more. She wants to focus on her career."

His mother looked doubtful. "And she can't do that while she's married to you?"

He had no good answer to that question.

His father said, "Eddie, don't give up. I mean, you *shouldn't* give up."

"I don't know, Dad. To tell you the truth, I'm not so sure I want to go back to her."

His mother glanced at her husband, then back at him. "I don't understand."

"I don't expect you to, Mom. Not completely, anyway. Things happen in a marriage."

"Yes, things happen, and you talk about them, and you work them out, and you go on."

"It's a different generation, Mom."

"Yeah . . . the *Sex and the City* generation. Everyone wants to wear Prada, and Manolo Blahnik."

Yeah, maybe that's it. He remembered the sound of Alison's high heels as they clicked down the hallway.

His father jumped in. "Okay, Eddie, let's say, hypothetically, that you and Alison don't get back together." This earned him a sharp glance from his wife. "What will you do? You can't stay at your brother's place indefinitely."

"I don't know what I'll do. I'm a full-time employee at Borders now . . ." *Damn!* "Uh, didn't I mention that last week?" Quick glances at his parents' faces said no, he'd neglected to tell them. Lies and omissions were catching up with him—and there was no choice but to plunge on. "So, I'm earning enough money to afford my own place now."

"You'd stay in Manhattan?" his father asked. "I didn't think you were that crazy about Manhattan."

He took a deep breath and remembered how Lois had called him "Easy Eddie." "Manhattan's not that bad. It kind of grows on you."

43

Monday, April 10, 2000

Lois Lane Smith stared at the words that glowed on her computer screen. The words seemed to be staring back at her. *It's been a long day.*

Since the meeting with her mother, she'd talked to her friends, her co-workers, and her landlord. She'd had a long telephone conversation with her father. All had weighed in with advice, which had run the gamut from "everyone is different" to "sounds like a flake" to "you're scraping bottom, girl." She'd been told to use her head, follow her heart, go with her gut, and give him the boot. The advice was well intentioned, but, for the most part, useless. And sometimes unwelcome, she thought, remembering last week's phone call with Phil. Her mother had been the one voice of reason in a symphony of jibberish.

After covering yet another absurd story—a hot-dog-eating contest, of all things—she'd returned to the office at four. She'd been greeted by the flashing yellow light on her phone. There were two messages, both from Eddie, the first at noon, and the second at three. *His break times . . . he must be at work.* Both messages had said pretty much the same thing: a week had elapsed and he wanted to talk. He'd also called her cell phone at about the same times—she knew it was him from the Caller ID. She'd let those calls roll into her voicemail. *Probably the same message.* She wasn't ready to talk, not just yet, but she knew she'd have to, eventually. *And he'd call her, again, on his next break.*

Just after five, her cell phone buzzed. She saved her work, leaned back in her chair, and took the call.

"Hello?"

"Lois, it's me, Eddie."

"Hi."

"How are you?"

"I'm fine." *Lie number one.*

"Are you at work?"

"Yeah, I just walked in." *Lie number two.*

"Did you get my messages?"

"I see the message light flashing, but, no, I haven't listened to them yet." *Lie number three . . . he'll never believe that one.*

"You must be busy."

"I am." *Lie number four.*

"What are you working on?"

"You won't believe it if I tell you."

"Try me."

"Man bites dog . . . literally."

"I don't get it. Sounds like an inside joke."

"No joke. I just covered a hot-dog-eating contest."

"You're boss must really like you."

"Yeah. He told me I've really been cutting the mustard lately." Silence. *Did he miss that? Or is he playing with me?* "Anyway, I told him I didn't relish the idea of doing more human interest stories." *Still nothing . . .*

Eddie waited a beat before speaking. "So, how are you gonna spin it?"

He sounds so serious . . . "I'm writing it as a David and Goliath story: don't bet against the little guy, particularly if he's Japanese."

"No kidding."

"No kidding. The little bastard wolfed down forty-two of the suckers."

"My God!"

"Yeah, and he barfed them all up about five minutes later. Not something you'd want to see. I had to wait for him to get cleaned up before I could interview him."

They quickly ran out of conversation, and an uncomfortable silence descended.

Eddie broke the ice: "Well, it's been a week. I thought we might go out again."

"You mean just to talk?"

"Well, yeah, to talk and to have some fun. I thought we might go back to Iridium."

"Why Iridium?" *Red flag, girl!* She got up and walked toward the hallway.

"It was fun, wasn't it?"

"Yes. Who's playing there?"

"I believe it's the Mark Whitfield Trio."

"Mark Whitfield?"

"Yeah, he plays jazz guitar."

She arrived at the window overlooking West 47th Street. "Do you figure you'll spot Fagen or Becker this time?"

Silence. She figured Eddie was trying to come up with some kind of response.

Finally, he said, "No, Lois, it's not like that. I just thought we had a good time there, and we could do it again."

"Eddie, why is this so important to you?"

"It's not that important. If one of them is there, fine, if not, we'll have a good time anyway."

"Eddie, I don't think so. Not this time."

"Why? Because of the Steely Dan thing?"

"That's part of it."

"What else?"

"Eddie, it's just that, well, I've been thinking, and, to tell you the truth," *Lie number five?* "I'm just not totally comfortable with you. I don't know what to make of you. I don't know if I can trust you."

"Trust? What do you mean by trust?"

"Well, for one thing, you're still married . . ."

"I told you we'd split up. She's filed for divorce."

"I know you told me that."

"So you don't believe me?"

"I don't know what to believe."

"Okay, forget about Iridium. Let's just have dinner. We can talk over dinner."

She stared out the window. Rush hour traffic clogged the streets. She didn't know what to say.

"Or lunch," he continued.

"Eddie . . ."

"Or coffee . . . meet me for a cup of coffee."

"Eddie . . ."

"Lois, I thought we had something good going . . ."

"I don't know . . ."

"Lois, please? We should talk face-to-face, not on the phone."

Do I owe him that? Or am I just being stupid? "Okay, Eddie, I can meet you tomorrow morning. I have an appointment at ten."

"Can you meet me at eight?"

"Where?"

"The Café Indulge. It's right across the street from the Borders where I work."

I guess I could do that. "Give me that address again?"

"The Café Indulge, corner of Second Avenue and 31st Street."

She jotted the name and address into her day planner. "Okay, eight o'clock tomorrow morning."

She heard him say, "I'll be there," and disconnect.

44

Tuesday, April 11, 2000

It was Eddie's favorite table in his favorite corner of his favorite coffee shop.

The back of his chair almost touched the window overlooking 31st Street. Early morning sunlight flooded through the windows on his left, which overlooked Second Avenue. From there, he could watch customers—mostly pretty young students and nurses—file through the entryway and line up in front of glass display cases filled with delicious pastries. Or he could watch the Russian waitresses as they floated from table to table. When the restaurant wasn't crowded, the waitresses would gather on the sidewalk and smoke their cigarettes—*so close* he could almost reach through the windows and touch them.

He sipped his coffee. A pecan danish sat half-eaten on his plate. Across the street, Borders and the Loews theater complex were closed and dark. *Another beautiful spring day . . . perfect for screwing up yet another relationship.*

A cab rolled to a stop, and he saw her getting out. He watched as she got her bearings and started walking toward the entrance. She was wearing spring colors: a creamy blouse with flowers on it, and a blueprint blue pantsuit. Tan shoes. Her oversized handbag was slung over her shoulder. *And her hair was pinned up like the first time he'd seen her.*

He watched as she pushed through the doors, scanned the room, and spotted him. *A 'Mona Lisa' smile . . .* A minute later they'd given each other a polite hug, and were sitting, silent, trying to decide how much eye contact to make, or how they might begin a conversation. Eddie's favorite waitress, Katrina, glided up to the table with her customary "Das Vadanya," poured Lois some coffee, refilled Eddie's cup, and asked if they wanted anything else. Lois responded with a "Nyet," and Katrina smiled as she glided away.

Eddie finally broke the ice. "Thanks for coming."

"You were right," Lois replied, "serious discussions should always be face-to-face."

He smiled. "So this is going to be a 'serious discussion?'"

"I guess so. There are some things we should talk about."

"Well, then, let's get right to it." He stirred more sugar into his coffee.

"I don't want this to sound like the Spanish Inquisition."

"It's okay. Ask me anything you want."

"Eddie, I don't have a list of questions. I have . . . concerns."

"Concerns. My marriage obviously being first on your list?"

"Yes."

She looked very serious sipping her coffee. He decided to play it straight. "I already told you everything."

She looked up. "Everything? You've told me very little."

"I told you my wife filed for divorce. Or at least she said she did. I haven't seen any papers yet."

"How do I know that's true?"

"I don't know how I could prove it." He tried to keep from sounding annoyed.

"How do I know that you're not trying to reconcile?"

Stay in control, Eddie. "I live full-time in Manhattan, with my brother, in his apartment. Remember? I've seen my wife once in the last month."

"I've never met your brother. Maybe he's working overseas somewhere. Maybe he doesn't exist." Eddie watched her. She seemed to be getting agitated. "For all I know," she continued, "you could be leading a double life. Maybe you spend half your time with your wife in Jersey, and the other half chasing women in Manhattan. Or maybe you have one of those open marriages—screw who you want, when you want, just not in front of me."

"You sound like an article from *The Post*."

"What's that supposed to mean?" Anger flashed across her face.

"Lois, take it easy. I didn't mean anything; poor choice of words. But think about what you're saying. Do you think I'm really like that?"

She took a deep breath. "I don't know. How would I know?"

"Do you want to meet my brother?"

"That's not the point. Look how we met, Eddie; on the streets of New York, you demonstrating like . . . I don't know what."

"I explained all that to you."

"And then you got arrested."

"And they dropped the charges." He could feel anger creeping into his voice.

"Still," she said.

"So, you don't trust me."

"I have my doubts."

"But we've spent a lot of time together . . . since I got arrested." That sounded sarcastic, even to him. He needed to get the conversation going in a different direction. "Look, Lois, I'm an ordinary guy. You said so yourself in your newspaper article . . . articles."

"An ordinary guy with an obsession . . . who won't let go of it."

Who, like a jerk, asked her to go back to Iridium. He sat back and looked around the restaurant. The line at the pastry counter was gone. It was just the two of them, and a young couple eating breakfast. The waitresses had taken over one of the tables in the back. *On the other hand, why can't I pursue a couple of lousy autographs? What's so terrible? Why does it bug everyone so much?*

"What's wrong with having a hobby?"

"A hobby? Is that what you're calling it now?"

"Yes. A hobby. What's the harm?"

Lois finished her coffee. "It's not harmful, exactly. It just . . . tells me things about you."

"Things you don't like."

"Yeah, I guess you could say that . . . things I don't like."

He felt that familiar narrow blade starting to work its way into him. "Lois. I'm an ordinary guy. I'm normal."

"I don't know about normal. A normal person doesn't go to the lengths you do to get a couple of autographs."

"You know me better than that. I'm normal."

She thought for a few seconds. "Okay, let's take it on faith that you're normal. Then why are you doing this?"

"I told you, it's just a hobby."

"Why is this 'hobby' so important to you? I mean, I can understand why you love Steely Dan—at least on some level I can understand it—but why is meeting Fagen and Becker so damned important?"

He felt like he was inches from losing it. "Why does it bug you so much?" *I'll be what I want to be . . .*

They stared at each other for what seemed like an eternity. Finally she said, "Look, I've got to go."

"Then go." He waved her away with his hand.

She stood, picked up her handbag, and walked out the door. He watched as she walked along the sidewalk, looking for a taxi.

45

Thursday, April 14, 2000

Having finished his lunch—a soggy tuna-on-rye and a bag of Ruffles—Eddie Zittner sat in the far corner of the storeroom, trying to decide whether to flip through another magazine or just go back to work. His cell phone rang. He recognized the number immediately.

"Hi, Ma."

"Eddie . . ." He could hear his mother's voice cracking. "You father's had another heart attack."

Time became a trickle of sand falling through an hourglass. His stomach felt like it was full of stones. He stood, took a deep breath, and, unsteady, had to brace himself against the wall. "Mom, is he okay? Are you okay?"

"I don't know. They're taking him to the hospital."

"Which one?"

"Holy Name. It's near his office."

"I'll be there as soon as I can." *Find my coat, find the manager, find a taxi.* He walked toward the coat rack.

"Eddie, will you call your brother for me?"

He tried to remember what his brother had said that morning: Something about a meeting in Hartford. Was he taking the train, or sharing a limousine? It didn't matter; he was probably there already. "I will, Mom. Are you okay?"

He heard her sobbing and trying to catch her breath. "So far," she managed.

"Look, I'm gonna take a cab. I'll call Mark from the cab."

"Do you have enough money?"

Enough money? He tried to remember how much he had on him. *A hundred dollars?* "I think so, Ma. I'll be there as soon as I can."

He heard her disconnect. He grabbed his coat, pushed through double doors that led into the store, and quickly spotted the manager. Minutes later, he was in a taxi heading west on 34th Street.

The trip uptown was a blur. The taxi sped along the West Side Highway. To his left, sailboats floated on the Hudson, first coming toward him, then spinning, and then tacking away. Across the river, puffy clouds cast uncertain shadows across the cliffs of Edgewater and Fort Lee.

Every five minutes or so, he tried to reach his brother, with no success. Finally, as the taxi crossed the George Washington Bridge, Mark picked up. Eddie quickly told him what had happened. Mark thought it would take him at least two hours to get to the hospital, assuming he could contact the limo driver right away. He said he would leave as soon as possible.

Just after two, Eddie walked into the Cardiac Emergency Center at Holy Name. He spotted his mother sitting, staring out a window overlooking Teaneck Road. He rushed to her side, and she stood, and they embraced. Her eye make-up was pretty much gone, he saw, but otherwise, she seemed to be all right.

"I spoke to Mark," he said. "He was in Hartford. He said he'd leave as soon as he could find his limo."

"I know," his mother replied. "He called me after he spoke to you."

"What did the doctors say?"

"They don't know yet. They shot him full of blood thinners. Eddie . . . he may need a bypass."

He thought of all the times his mother had nagged his father: about working too hard, about watching his weight, about a hundred other "little things" that didn't seem like "little things" any more. He thought about his father grilling steaks in the back yard. *Well-marbled rib eyes . . .*

"A bypass? How many?"

"They won't know until they go in."

"When? Tonight?"

"No, they want to stabilize him first. If they operate, it'll be tomorrow."

*****

An hour later, Eddie and his mother walked into the Intensive Care Unit. His father was lying in bed, propped up on a stack of pillows. His eyes were closed. Plastic tubes were taped to both of his arms. He was surrounded by machines.

Elaine Zittner touched her husband's arm. His eyes opened. "How'd the market do?" he asked.

"Lovey, forget the market for a few minutes." She smiled.

"The Dow was down six percent at lunchtime. The Nasdaq was even worse. The nurses won't tell me anything."

"How do you feel, Dad?" Eddie asked.

"Like a pin cushion." His father's eyes danced.

The smile on his face . . . All Eddie could manage was a weak: "I'll bet."

"So where's your brother?"

"He's on his way. He was in Hartford."

"Oh." He turned to his wife. "Ellie?"

"What, Lovey?"

"This is like the last time."

"How so?"

"I didn't make it to April fifteenth. Again. Remember?"

Elaine Zittner started to cry. Eddie remembered his father's first heart attack, in early April of 1983, or 1984. "Yeah, Dad," he said, "but you got closer this time."

His father grinned. "Yeah, Easy . . . closer."

His mother, drying her eyes, said that she was going to sit outside for a while. Eddie stayed by his father's bedside. He tried to make light conversation, tried to be a diversion, tried to keep positive thoughts, but he listened, mostly, as his father said things to him that he hadn't heard before.

Mark Zittner arrived at four. Then they sat together as a family; a father drifting in and out of consciousness, and a mother and her sons wondering what the next few hours would bring.

At seven, Eddie decided to go to the cafeteria. Fifteen minutes later, carrying a box of sandwiches and coffee, he stepped out of the elevator and started down the bleak hallway. The only sound was that of his own shoes, scuffling along the tiled floor. And, as he turned a corner, he saw his mother and brother, embracing, crying quietly, and he knew that his father was gone.

46

Working title: **I was a Fisherman**

An unpublished short story
by Eddie Zittner

    I was a fisherman. Sunday mornings, I was ready to fish. I would gather up our fishing gear and put it in the kitchen, near the back door. We had two fishing poles, both taller than me. They were fitted with old-style casting reels, the ones that would free-spool and tangle unless you kept your thumb on the fishing line. I also put out an old detergent bucket my mother had given me. We used it to carry packages of extra hooks and sinkers, and a couple of rags I had lifted from her stash in the laundry room. If we caught any fish that day, we would carry them home in the bucket.

    On weekend mornings, my father would lounge around the house dressed in a sweatshirt and jeans, in sharp contrast to the suits and ties he wore on weekdays. He was a CPA, he told me; a Certified Public Accountant. He said he worked with people on their finances, and, in the spring, helped them do their tax returns. I was probably five or six at the time and had no concept of financial planning.

    But I could relate to the suit and tie: that was something special, different than what other men wore to work. At breakfast, my father would be swathed in an old bed sheet so that errant scraps of food wouldn't stain his clothes. I would spoon cornflakes into my mouth and stare at him, transfixed, as if Batman or even Superman was sitting across the table, albeit in an off-white cape. Finished, he would stand, whisper something to my mother, and brush his lips against her cheek. Then he would put on his raincoat, pulling the belt tight across his waist. As he left the house, I would rush to the window and watch as he marched resolutely down the street, briefcase in hand, to the train station a few blocks away. He was off to face the world; to engage in battles I could not yet understand.

    But this was Sunday, and he was in his sweatshirt and jeans this morning, and we were going fishing. I found him in the living room, sitting with my mother, drinking coffee and reading the newspaper. Be patient, he said. I'm not quite ready to leave, he said. No, not just yet, he said. But what child would be patient when he's ready to fish? I would stand beside the sofa and tug at his sleeve, urging him to drink his coffee, to finish his reading. The fish are waiting for us, I would say. After numerous tugs and a couple of sideways glances from my mother, he would consent, tossing the paper onto the coffee table. "Come on, Eddie," he would say as he lifted himself from the sofa, and I would follow him, silently, into the kitchen.

    I would load the poles and bucket into the back seat of whatever car he was driving that year. I remember a slope-top Ford sedan, long and low and black, with navy blue seats made of sticky plastic. After a few tries, the car would start, and my father would drive through Brooklyn, down to Sheepshead Bay, as I grinned out the window, a Mets baseball cap planted firmly on my head.

My father would always park near the bait and tackle shop, a flat wooden building decorated with ropes and rusty anchors. I would unload the fishing gear while he bought a package of frozen shrimp. Then we would walk across the parking lot, opposite the docks where the big fishing boats were berthed. We could see men and boys on the boats; men and boys who were going out into the Atlantic, into deep water, in pursuit of fierce bluefish and speedy mackerel. But we couldn't fish from those boats, my father said: I was too small. So we would walk out onto the seawall and fish, standing on hard concrete with other men and their sons.

A couple of years later, after more badgering from me and occasional support from my mother, my father consented to take me on one of the big boats. I was up early that Sunday morning. Five minutes after breakfast our gear was ready to go. But as always, I needed to be patient. So I sat on the sofa and waited, fidgeting with my cap as my little brother tugged at my shoelaces. Finally my father folded the paper and gulped the last of his coffee. "Let's go, sport," I remember him saying that day as I jumped off the sofa.

We drove down to the harbor, parking in the usual place near the bait and tackle shop. We began walking toward the boats, carrying our poles like rifles on our shoulders. But I hesitated and then stopped. What about the shrimp, I asked. We don't need shrimp today, my father told me; they have live sardines on the boat.

I remember many things from that day. I remember catching a rockfish, hauling it out of the ocean with my own fishing pole. I remember men catching silvery fish and putting them into burlap sacks that bled beside them. I remember the smell of the diesel engines. I remember holding my father's hand, and his uncertain steps as we climbed up the rickety gangplank. Most of all, I remember him standing alone, wearing his big straw hat, eyes hidden behind dark sunglasses, watching me from his spot on the railing.

*****

My father was a mountain man. His idea of heaven was driving along a winding mountain road as soft music played on the radio.

My parents would plan our family vacations in rambling discussions over dinner. I remember hearing words like Poconos, and Catskills, words that had no meaning to me. After the dishes were cleared, they would sit back down at the dinner table and work out the details, surrounded by maps and brochures. My father always planned the driving, using a yellow felt-tipped marker to trace out a route on maps that had been folded and refolded perhaps a thousand times. My mother would calculate the mileage for each day of driving, and pick out the motels where we would stay.

On the road, my father did most of the driving, while my mother navigated and tried to keep my brother and me under control. My father loved to nosh, and always kept some kind of snack on the seat next to him, usually a tin of peanuts. Every so often I would reach over from the back seat and sneak a few; he didn't seem to mind. When it was warm enough he would hang his arm out the window. It didn't matter that his wife would nag him about putting on some tanning oil ("at least on your elbow, dear"), or that his children whined about being too hot, or too cold, or too windswept, or too bored. He was oblivious to it all.

I remember one summer drive through the Appalachians, along the Blue Ridge Parkway, down into exotic places like Tennessee and North Carolina. We had a Buick station wagon that year; it was white over tan with wood paneling along the sides. My father had rented one of those roof racks for the luggage; that way my brother and I could stretch out in the back among a bunch of worn out pillows and blankets.

My father insisted on stopping at every lookout point along the way. He would park the car, careful of the sloping pavement, setting the parking brake just in case. My brother and I would complain about yet another delay, and about being hungry, thirsty, and tired, but to no avail, our mother shushing us from the front seat.

He would get out of the car and walk to the guardrail, taking deep breaths as he went, his belly rising, savoring the aroma of maple and pine. He would gaze out over mountains blanketed with green, immersing himself in the view as if easing himself into a cool stream. The wind would blow through his hair as a gentle waterfall might wash over his face. After a few minutes he would come back to the car to get his camera, a 35 millimeter Petri that he'd had since he'd been a teenager. Then he would walk back to the guardrail and snap a few pictures, trying to capture on film whatever he was searching for out above the mountains.

My brother and I would watch from the car. We would sometimes see crows or buzzards circling, and imagine them to be eagles, or great hawks. We might hear riders on the trails below, horses snorting, the drumming of their hooves muffled by pine needles.

When it became too dark to see, my father would give up his search, a sense of incompleteness about him. Then we would drive on, looking for a place to eat, something "not too fancy" as my mother would say. Usually that meant a truck stop or a diner. When we stopped, my brother and I would tumble out of the car and run barefoot in the dirt, racing to catch up to our parents.

*****

In my early teens, our family moved to Saddle River, a small town in northern New Jersey. Both of my parents were doing well: my father had hired two people to help him with his CPA business, and had moved to bigger offices in Manhattan. My mother had become a successful real estate agent, and was eager to move to the "well-to-do" suburbs.

When I was fourteen, my father purchased a boat. It was for me and my brother, he said, but my brother, a bookworm, didn't have much interest in boating and fishing. The boat was a beat up Boston Whaler; a fourteen footer with a ten horse Evinrude outboard motor. I remember putting it up on blocks that first spring. I spent the best part of a month scraping it down and then painting it, a pale yellow with mahogany brown trim.

There was a fair-sized lake about a mile from our house—bike-riding distance, my father said. He had rented a slip from the old man who ran the marina, and we kept the boat there. That summer, and for the next few summers, I would putter around that lake in solitary pursuit of "game fish": the wily perch, the slithery fresh-water eel, and the occasional small-mouth bass.

My father rarely went fishing with me. On the few occasions when he did, he'd always wear his big straw hat and dark sunglasses. He'd clamber onto the boat, bending low so he wouldn't lose his balance. He'd settle himself on the middle bench, facing forward, and hang on to both gunwales as I guided the boat out to one of my secret fishing holes. Once anchored, he seemed to relax a little bit. It was as if he was determined to be with me, to spend time with me, to have some fun with me, and, by sheer force of will, overcome whatever demons he was feeling inside. We would fish for an hour, maybe two, before he declared that it was time to head home. He always looked relieved when he set foot back on dry land.

I'm a slow learner. I finally figured out that he was afraid of the water. He never told me as much; I think it just dawned on me, one of those summer afternoons out on the lake.

When I was eighteen, my father sold the boat. No use keeping it, he said, with me away at college.

*****

At Rutgers, I got my degree in journalism, and found the girl—the woman—who would become my wife. We got married and rented an apartment near the university. She got a job in advertising, and I worked in a bookstore. I was going to be a writer. We were happy. We had plans to move to the suburbs and raise a family. But things didn't work out. We argued. We disagreed about big things and little things. One day, she asked me to move out, and I moved in with my brother, who had an apartment in

Manhattan. A few weeks later, she filed for divorce, and I was treading water in a concrete jungle.

I was at work one day when my cell phone buzzed. It was my mother, and she could hardly speak. What happened, I asked, and alarms went off inside me. Your father had another heart attack, she said. An hour later, I was in a grey hospital, riding a cold elevator full of faceless people. I met my mother in the hallway, and we embraced. My father had been drifting in and out of consciousness, she said, but he wanted me to come in when I arrived. She sat back down and stared out the window.

I walked into the room and saw my father lying on a hospital bed, propped up with a few pillows. He was awake, but heavily sedated. He looked like he was a thousand years old. I embraced him, careful not to disturb the tubes taped to his arms.

"How are you feeling, Dad?" I asked.

"Like a pin-cushion," he whispered, and his eyes danced, and I smiled, remembering all the times I had seen his face light up like that.

I tried to engage him in light conversation, but he did most of the talking.

He told me about his first heart attack, when I was just a kid. He told me about the hell my mother had gone through, worrying if her husband would survive.

The collapse of my marriage had hit him hard, he said, but he still thought Alison was a good person, with a good heart, who still loved me.

He talked about how my brother and I were so different, and yet, so similar. He was glad that my brother and I had become "close" again.

He wondered if he shouldn't have pushed me harder, to make something more of myself. Then he said, no, that was wrong, strike that, that he shouldn't doubt me, and that I shouldn't doubt myself. I was doing all right, he said, and I would find my own way, eventually.

He told me how much he'd enjoyed our trips to the mountains, and the seashore, and yes, even fishing on the lake those few times.

When he stopped talking, I searched for something to say—something meaningful, something "profound." But my mind was a blank. All I could think of was "Stay positive, Dad. It's amazing what the doctors can do these days."

He raised his arm and touched his chest. "This?" he said. "This is nothing. I'll be out of here tomorrow."

And I saw it, just then: the look in his eyes. It was recognition of the darkness that lay ahead, and an understanding of it, and, perhaps, even a hint of acceptance. But at the same time, I saw his determination, and his desire, and his willingness to carry on, no matter how he was feeling inside. I had seen that look once before, as he and I had walked up a rickety gangplank, one Sunday morning, a long time ago.

My father never got out of the hospital. He died that evening, in a room overlooking New York harbor. He had lived and died near lakes and streams and rivers and deep oceans, but he had died dreaming, I am sure, of mountains blanketed with green.

47

Tuesday, April 18, 2000

Lois Lane Smith stared out the office window overlooking West 47th Street and contemplated her next move. *Go out and follow more story leads? Or finish the ones she'd already started?*

The last couple of weeks had been a blur. She'd ended an affair with one married man, started an affair with another, and ended that one, too. She'd kept herself occupied by churning out handfuls of human interest stories. In the last few days she'd had lunch with her mother, dinner with her girlfriends, wandered along Fifth Avenue in search of something new to wear, and, in desperation, had gone to the movies by herself.

April is the cruelest month . . . and it's not over yet.

Her cell phone buzzed. She glanced at the display. *Why the fuck is he calling me?*

"Hello."

"Lois, it's Phil. Don't hang up."

"What do you want, Phil?"

"You're still mad at me."

"Not mad, Phil. I've moved on. I just don't care anymore."

Silence. She assumed the message was finally sinking into Phil's thick skull.

He finally replied: "I didn't call you so we could get together again."

Moved on to someone else, have you? "Why'd you call then?"

"Something I saw in Sunday's *Newark Star-Ledger*."

"What?" She spat the word out.

"Wasn't your Steely Dan guy named Zittner?'

"Yeah, Eddie Zittner . . . why?"

"His father died last week . . . assuming it's the same family. I have the obituary right here."

Oh my god! "Read it to me."

"Harold W. Zittner, of Saddle River, died of heart failure on Thursday, April 14th . . ."

"Family members? Does it list family members?"

"Survived by loving wife Elaine and sons Edward and Mark. Funeral services were held—"

"Phil, thanks, I've gotta go." She disconnected, speed-dialed Eddie's cell phone, and got an immediate message: "The number you dialed is currently unavailable."

Where is he? She hurried to the pay phone that was just down the hall, opened the Manhattan White Pages, and quickly looked up the number of Borders on Second Avenue. She jotted it down in her day planner, and punched it into her cell phone as she walked back toward the window. It had started to rain, she noted. Someone answered on the third ring.

"Borders."

"Who am I speaking to?"

"This is the manager."

I'm in luck. "My name is Lois Lane Smith. I'm a friend of Eddie Zittner. Is he at work today?"

"Did you hear that—"

"Yes, I heard about his father."

"Sad . . . it hit Eddie very hard. I spoke to him yesterday."

"Is he in New Jersey? Do you know how to reach him?"

"He said he was coming back last night; said he'd be at work today. He should be here at eleven."

She glanced at her watch. *Just over an hour from now.* "Thank you very much," she said, and disconnected.

Fifteen minutes later, she climbed out of a taxi, hurried across a rain-slick sidewalk, and pushed through the entryway of the Café Indulge. She spotted him sitting in the corner, the same corner where they'd argued last week—a week ago today.

She walked toward him. He was sipping coffee, and she saw a pecan danish lying untouched on a plate. He looked up as she approached, did a double take, and set the cup down on the table, spilling a few drops. Then he stood, and for a few seconds they just stared at each other. Finally, she said, "Eddie, I heard about your father. I'm so sorry . . ." She stepped around the table and embraced him.

He hesitated at first, but then gave her a polite hug back. "Thank you," he mumbled as he disengaged. They stood, silent, staring at each other. "How'd you know I'd be here?" he asked.

"I called Borders. They said you were coming in at eleven. It was just a lucky guess."

"I guess I'm a creature of habit." A tiny smile wrinkled his face.

"Yeah," she replied, "I guess you are."

He gestured toward the empty chair. "Can you stay a while?"

"Sure." She sat down. A waitress glided over and, without a word, poured her a cup of coffee.

She looked at him. "I don't know what to say."

"You don't have to say anything."

"How's your mother doing?"

"She's doing okay, better than last time. Her sister came to stay with her for a while."

"Better than last time?"

"My father had his first heart attack, oh, fifteen years ago. No, longer than that, actually, almost twenty years ago. My mother kind of went crazy when it happened."

"Oh." *Better to leave that alone.* "How's your brother doing?"

"About as well as I am. He went back to work today, too. We came back last night."

It was quiet for a few seconds as they both sipped coffee.

She continued, "And how about you, Eddie? How are you?"

"Me? I'm fine. Eldest son, remember?" He forced a smile.

Putting up a good front, anyway. "What will you do now? I mean, with your life? *God, that sounds stupid.*

"Well, I got the divorce papers, finally, on Wednesday, the day before my father died."

And the day after we argued, Lois thought. *Argued about trust . . . right here at this very table.* "What will you do? I mean, will you stay with your brother? Keep working at Borders?"

"I don't know yet, exactly, but I know I need to get on with it, whatever 'it' turns out to be. I can't be a clerk in a bookstore forever."

"Where will you live?"

"I don't know."

"Will you stay in Manhattan?" *Are you interested, Lois, or is this just the reporter in you?*

He smiled again. "And continue my search for Steely Dan?"

She felt her face reddening. "That's not what I meant."

Raindrops were pelting the windows next to them. She watched as he turned and stared at luckless pedestrians caught in the downpour. Then he turned back to her. "I know that's not what you meant, Lois." He forced another smile. "I think I'm giving up my search for Steely Dan. There are more important things in life than getting someone's autograph."

She watched as his smile dissolved and his eyes began to fill. She watched as he picked up his napkin and wiped away the tears. And, at that very moment, Lois Lane Smith fell in love with Easy Eddie Zittner.

48

Wednesday, April 26, 2000

When Sheila had called him yesterday, she hadn't been very specific about why Bernard Sterling wanted to meet with him again. "He has some new information" was all that she would say.

After work, Eddie had taken a taxi directly to the *Rolling Stone* offices on Avenue of the Americas, arriving just before his four-thirty appointment. Sheila was waiting at reception, and, after a polite greeting, escorted him down a hallway and through gleaming black doors into an opulent conference room. Left alone, Eddie sat in one of the butter-soft leather chairs, and whistled softly as he ran a hand across the polished mahogany table. Then he wandered around the room, first admiring the view of Midtown, and then inspecting framed photos of various luminaries that lined the walls. Then back to the comfort of the leather chair. A moment later, Bernard Sterling burst into the room.

"Hello, dear boy!" Sterling extended his hand as he strode toward him. "How are you?"

He jumped to his feet. "Fine, Mr. Sterling." *John Denver . . . in designer jeans and a gold silk shirt.*

Sterling grabbed his hand and shook it vigorously. "Call me Nardo. We're old friends, aren't we?"

"I guess so . . . Nardo."

Sterling beamed at him and released his grip. "Have a seat, have a seat." Eddie eased himself back into his chair, and Sterling took the one next to him. "Can I have Sheila get you anything? A soft drink? Coffee? Jack Daniels?" Sterling rolled his eyes. "Just kidding about the whiskey, old boy, although, I must say, there were times today I could have used one . . . or two."

"No thanks. Sheila already offered."

"Great gal, isn't she? I don't know what I'd do without her."

Eddie wasn't sure that required an answer, but mumbled "she's very nice" to be on the safe side.

Sterling turned serious. "I spoke to Lois. She told me you've had a rough patch this month."

"Yes."

"I am sorry about your father, Eddie." Sterling looked solemn, and then sighed. "It's difficult to lose a loved one."

"Thank you," he whispered.

Sterling busied himself shuffling through a stack of papers, and then turned his attention back to Eddie. "Sheila tells me you and Lois have become something of an 'item.'"

Eddie didn't know how much Lois had told Sheila, much less how much Sheila might have passed on to Sterling. "I don't know if you could call us an 'item,' but we are seeing each other . . . again." He smiled.

"Good, good," Sterling replied. "And did you happen to see our article about the Dark Brothers?"

Eddie sat up in his chair. *The first feature article about The Dan in how many years?* "Yes, it was great . . . terrific . . . well written."

"They're finally getting their due," Sterling said. "People in high places are whispering about Grammys and Hall of Fame membership."

"It's about time," he replied, reflexively peeking at his watch. It was creeping up on five. He was still wondering why Sterling had wanted to see him.

Sterling picked up on Eddie's impatience. "I'll bet you're wondering why I wanted to meet with you."

"As a matter of fact, yes, I was," he replied.

"Well, here at the magazine, we're always developing all sorts of new ideas."

New ideas. He nodded.

Sterling swiveled his chair toward the window. "Need to keep the magazine 'fresh,' as they say."

Fresh. Yeah, I can relate to that.

"Follow all the newest trends."

All the newest trends . . . got it.

"On the other hand," Sterling swiveled back to face him, "We can't ignore our roots now, can we?"

"No," he replied, startled. "No, I guess not."

"And that's where you come in."

"How?" Eddie looked puzzled.

"How, indeed." Sterling leaned closer. "We need someone to write a series of articles about former celebrities who have fallen by the wayside—fallen on hard times, so to speak. Do you follow me?"

"Do you mean rock stars?"

"Not only rock stars," Sterling replied. "They can be former movie stars, directors . . . even worn-out sitcom hacks."

"People who've gone broke? Or just dropped out of sight?"

"Either," Sterling replied.

"Like, for example," he racked his brain, "Vanilla Ice?"

"Precisely! Good choice!"

Eddie felt himself getting excited, and reminded himself to remain cool and professional. He took a deep breath. "And what, exactly, are you looking for in the articles?"

"Where are they now?" Sterling boomed, raising his arms to the heavens. "What are they doing? How did they go bust? Or are they flush with cash, and hiding it under the mattress?"

Human interest! Eddie was dumbfounded.

Sterling rambled on: "And, most important: What about their fans? Do they yearn for a comeback? Do they still give a damn?"

Son-of-a-bitch! Human interest stories!

"It's back pages stuff, Eddie, but if it catches on, it could, as they say, work its way to the front of the magazine." Sterling looked pleased with himself.

Eddie took another deep breath. *Unless I'm totally wrong, he's offering me a job!* "Would I be a member of the magazine staff?"

"Not yet, not yet," Sterling cautioned. "Let's not get ahead of ourselves. You would start out as a free-lancer. Perhaps in time, if the series catches on . . . but it's regular work, Eddie. And it won't be a walk in the park. You'd have to produce an article for every issue. Deadlines, Eddie . . . they can be quite taxing."

Taxing . . . Shit! I've got to get with Alison and file our tax returns.

"Well, son, what do you think?"

Eddie leaned back in his chair. "All the interviews would be in the city?"

"Heavens, no! New York might be the center of the universe, but fallen celebrities are everywhere."

"So I'd be traveling?"

"Well," Sterling thought for a moment, "we do have a budget. Let's see . . . why not start out in the colonies, eh? Maine to Memphis! No, that's not right . . . how about Maine to Monterey? That would cover the entire forty-eight!"

Eddie smiled. "And who would I be working for?"

"Me, of course. I'd have a couple of working editors assigned to help you along." Now Sterling stole a peek at his watch, and glanced at the conference room door.

"I'm speechless, Mr. Sterling."

"Please, call me Nardo."

"Nardo . . . you've never even seen any of my writing."

"Actually, I have. Lois sent me a copy of something you wrote."

"No kidding." *What could Lois have given him?*

"Yes. It was the beginning of a short story; something about two men on the subway."

"Oh! And you thought it was good?"

"Good? Well, it showed promise, I'll say that." Sterling checked the door again.

"Well, Nardo, I'm still speechless."

"What do you say, dear boy? Will you do it?"

Eddie remembered something his father always said: before you take the job, find out what it pays. *Good advice.* "Nardo, one more question: what will I be making?"

"Money?" Sterling looked thoughtful. "Good point. We have a scale for free-lancers: a base rate plus expenses, as I recall. I'll get you a copy of the policy."

Eddie took a good look around the conference room, and then focused his attention back on Bernard Sterling. *He may be a bit eccentric . . . but I think I can trust him.* "You've got a deal, Mr. Sterling." He stood and extended his hand. Sterling, caught unaware, stood awkwardly, took Eddie's hand, and shook it.

"Good show!" Sterling said, disengaging and sitting back down.

Eddie returned to his seat. "When would I start?"

"Immediately. I'll have Sheila set up a meeting with our working editors." Sterling glanced at the door again. "Where the dickens *is* that girl?" He pulled a cell phone from his pocket, but before he could call, Sheila opened the door and popped her head in. She was grinning as she mouthed the words: "They're here."

Sterling looked relieved, and then immensely satisfied. "Let's wander into my office," he said as he pushed himself out of his chair. "There are a couple of fellows I'd like you to meet."

Epilogue

Tuesday, December 8, 2000, from the Newark Star-Ledger:

Friedman – Anitone

Alison Friedman of Somerset was married Sunday, December 6, to Jerome (Jerry) Anitone of New Brunswick. Alison is an account executive at Jacobs Advertising Agency. Jerry is the manager of Brunswick Books. The couple plans to honeymoon in Miami Beach.

****

Date: January 2, 2001

From: MarkZ@FastowHart.com

To: EZEddie32@nyc.rr.com

Subject: Happy New Year!

Greetings from Atlantis, on the sunny shores of Paradise Island! This hotel is, well, it's everything they say. Fantastic! Wish you were here!

Seriously, bro, next time, the four of us should do a vacation together. Yeah, I know you had to work on your articles (that's how many now? A dozen?), and Lois couldn't get enough time off, but think about it.

Marcie and I have had some serious talks about our future, and we've decided NOT to fuck it up by getting married, at least for the time being (according to her, living together in sin is just fine). So far she has made good on her promise to forget about "The Law" for one solid month. I'm guessing that she'll start studying for the bar exam at 12:01 AM on January 17th.

Guess what, bro? I'm a sailor! I sail! Yesterday I learned how, in a dinghy about the size of my bathtub. Tomorrow, Marcie wants to try water skiing again (the first time was a disaster!).

I called Mom yesterday to wish her a Happy New Year, and she said she was doing fine. She has more real estate deals going than ever, she says. She told me she had lunch with you and Lois a few days ago. She didn't want me to tell you, but she said she really likes Lois . . . high praise, indeed, coming from Ma!

Marcie says hi to you and Lois. She said to tell you she's been soaking up the vertical rays.

Seriously, bro, think about next summer. We could all go to Hawaii!
.....Mark

****

Date: January 2, 2001

From: EZEddie32@nyc.rr.com

To: MarkZ@FastowHart.com

Subject: re: Happy New Year!

  Mark, glad you and Marcie are "living it up" in the Bahamas. Lois and I (and millions of others) are freezing our asses off here in the city. We try to keep each other warm at night (and generally succeed)! Say hi to Marcie.
   …..EZ

PS: I've told you a hundred times to stop calling me "bro." It is NOT COOL!!!

****

February 21, 2001: Steely Dan wins three Grammys, including Album of the Year for *Two Against Nature.*

****

Wednesday, March 5, 2001, from the Northern New Jersey Real Estate News:

Elaine Zittner is Agent of the Year!

  At last night's annual dinner, Elaine Zittner was named Agent of the Year for 2000. Ellie, as she is known in NNJ real estate circles, looked absolutely stunned when her name was announced, but she quickly recovered her composure and made her way to the podium, accompanied by her sons Edward and Mark (who were told in advance that she had won the award).
  It was a tearful moment at the podium, following a very difficult year for Ellie. As many of you know, last April she lost her beloved husband, Harry. But she's a trooper, and a true professional in every sense of the word. She's had a remarkable career in real estate—a top producer for almost twenty years! May the next twenty be as productive as the last twenty! Congratulations, Ellie! We wish you luck and God-speed. (photos on page 3)

****

Wednesday, March 14, 2001: Steely Dan is inducted into the Rock and Roll Hall of Fame.

****

Date: Friday, April 11, 2001

From: JerryA45@nyc.rr.com

To: EZEddie32@nyc.rr.com

Subject: (no subject)

     Eddie, I guess you heard by now that Alison and I have split up. She's become a real social climber. She's trying to keep it quiet, but everyone at the agency knows she's running around with her boss. I guess I should have known.
     Brunswick Books is finally going under. We're having an "Everything Must Go" sale. I'm looking for another job.
     Not much else I can say, Eddie, except that I'm sorry for the way things worked out.
     ....Jerry

****

Sunday, May 12, 2001, from the New York Post:

Wedding of the Week
Smith, 28, and Zittner, 30

     May 5 – It's always special when one of your own gets hitched! Even more special is how they met! Lois Lane Smith, Feature Writer from our own City Desk, married free-lance writer Edward (Eddie) Zittner at Temple Emanuel in Queens.
     Last year, Eddie was marching the sidewalks of Manhattan, on a personal crusade to get the autographs of a couple of reclusive rock stars. Lois spotted him and wrote an article about his quest ("Searching for Steely Dan," March 12, 2000). "It wasn't anything close to love at first sight," Lois said. "As a matter of fact, I thought he was a flake." Eddie laughed when he heard this. "She's right," he said, "back then I was a little crazy."

A week later, Eddie was arrested while demonstrating, and Lois again covered the story ("Behind Steely Bars," March 19, 2000; note: the NYPD dropped the charges and released Eddie the same day.) Eddie was then featured in a third article, also written by Lois ("Steely Dan, Where Are You?" March 29, 2000).

"I guess I wore her down with my charm," Eddie said. "Something like that," Lois added. Eddie is now a staff writer at *Rolling Stone* magazine. The couple, currently living in the West Village, will honeymoon in Hawaii.

Essentials:

Her Dress: "Silver and White," by Oleg Cassini
Best Edible: Ron Ben-Israel red wedding cake with Grand Marnier filling.
Wedding Song: Tony Bennett's "For Once in My Life"

****

Friday, July 9, 2001, from the Maple Heights, New Jersey Town Crier:

Famous Writers On The Way!

It's not often that we have celebrities move into our quiet neighborhood, but it's happening next month!

Edward Zittner and his brand-new wife, Lois Lane Smith-Zittner, will be moving into a cozy two-bedroom just down the block from the community center. "The Mister," known for his "Where Are They Now?" series, is a staff writer at *Rolling Stone* magazine. "The Missus" is a featured writer for the *New York Post*.

And that second bedroom will come in handy! A third Zittner is expected just after the first of the year. How much do you want to bet that Baby Zittner will be writing before he (or she!) learns how to walk!

I hope you enjoyed **Searching for Steely Dan**.

My next book, **At the Mix Bar**, will be published when I finish writing it (hopefully, in early 2007.) Here's the first chapter . . .

. . . Rick

At the Mix Bar

1.

Food animals did not fare well in the early part of the 21st Century. New strains of bird flu, mad cow disease, swine syndrome, and red tide pretty much decimated anything that flew, bellowed, grunted, or swam.
The world came to depend on grains and legumes.
But most people, being creatures of habit, craved foods with familiar shapes and textures. So giant factories, used to inhaling cows and chickens and spitting out hamburgers and hot wings, were re-tooled to synthesize burgers and wings, and rib-eyes, drumsticks, cheeses, and sliced salami, out of wheat, rice, corn, soy, and kidney beans.
For those who wanted their food without pretense, "Mix" became a popular alternative. Mix Bars were eating establishments where grain and legume-based "food materials" were mixed with various chemicals, resulting in nutritious (if not visually satisfying) food. Mix Bars catered to teenagers, college students, and young professionals—people who were willing to try new things and were turned off by the deteriorating quality of manufactured food.
Soybeans—a better source of protein, by far, than any other legume, or any grain—became the world's most important crop.

Blackburn had never eaten mix before. He'd heard about it, but never had the urge to try it. When the Retro Mix had opened, just a week ago, there had been a lot of "buzz" around campus. Word was that the place was a throwback to the last century: comfortable chairs, magazines (real paper magazines!), board games (Yahtzee! Monopoly! Checkers!) and old time rock-and-roll. The Retro was just a few blocks south of the University of Texas campus, thus attracting lots of students, but it was also close enough to downtown Austin to attract the young professionals who worked there. Blackburn figured that even if he didn't like mix, he could groove to the oldies. And maybe pick up a girl.

As he approached the entrance to the Retro, he stopped and removed the earPods that were playing Pink Floyd—his own personal mix of their best music—softly in his ears. As he pushed through the double doors, his ears were assaulted with a new sound; slicker, and bouncier, and funkier: the first few bars of Earth, Wind, and Fire's "September." As he grooved to the music, he realized that it was, indeed, the 21st day of September—*just like in the song!* He looked around and noted there were no news screens, no sports screens, no showbiz screens, no interactive games—no electronic entertainment of any kind. No obvious sign of anything "high-tech." He got in line behind a teenager, a young man (it appeared) dressed completely in red, metallic red, his hair silver white, in the brush cut style currently popular. He looked like a giant fire hydrant Blackburn had seen in a very old movie. *Brazil? Was that the name of it?*

Blackburn scanned the seating area—overflowing with an odd mix of grungy students and people dressed in business suits—and then turned back to the serving area. Three lines, he noted, and three people behind the counter, taking orders and preparing mix at workstations right behind them.

The teenage fire hydrant had reached the head of the line, and handed the "mixer" a piece of paper with his order on it—handwritten, no less! The mixer, an old man in a beat up UT baseball cap, leaned over the counter and scowled. "You," the mixer said, voice trembling, "I remember you. You've been in here three straight days now, with a long list of shit you want, different each time. I ain't got time to put this together. Don't you know this takes a helluva long time, getting all this shit together?"

"So what," the teenager replied, standing his ground. "Three straight days; that makes me a regular customer. Anyway, I've got a right to order anything on the menu. Don't I?"

Grumbling, the old man glanced at the list again, turned around, and started measuring ingredients: a thick, gooey, molasses-like substance, then some rough white grainy material, then some brown pellets that looked like rabbit shit, and finally a number of finely-ground powders: yellow, dark green, and iridescent purple. He measured each ingredient precisely before dumping it into the mixing bowl. Blackburn watched as the old man closed the lid and turned the machine on. After perhaps thirty seconds, the machine stopped its churning, and the old man scooped the mix into a serving bowl. Then he turned, placed the bowl on a tray, and handed the teenager a printed receipt. The entire process had taken less than two minutes.

"I Can Help" poured from the jukebox. *The inimitable Billy Swan.* It was Blackburn's turn to order.

"What'll you have?" the old man asked.

"I've never been to a mix bar before. How do you order?"

The mixer stared right through Blackburn, unmoving, and then spoke: "The menu is right behind me…can't you read?"

"Yeah, I can read." Blackburn glanced over the old man's shoulder. The menu was written in swirling letters; multi-colored chalk on an old style slate black board. *Probably fake.*

"What's a thirty-thirty-thirty?" Blackburn asked.

"That's thirty percent protein, thirty percent carb, and thirty percent fat."

"Sounds like a lot of fat."

"To each his own . . ."

"Okay . . . and what else is in it?"

"That's it. Just what I told you." The old man looked perplexed.

"Thirty-thirty-thirty. That's only ninety percent."

"Oh." The old man thought for a few seconds. "The rest is fiber."

"Fiber." Blackburn chewed on the word. The old man just stared at him. "Uh, okay," Blackburn continued, finally making up his mind, "give me a forty-thirty-twenty."

"You're sure?"

"Yeah, that sounds good."

"Bingo," the old man said, writing the order on a pad of paper—with a real pencil! "Now, what additives do you want?"

"Additives . . . what are my choices?"

The old man gestured over his shoulder with his thumb.

"Uh, okay." Blackburn looked over the list of additives written on the board. Most of the names were Greek to him.

The old man said, "Hey, come on, the line is getting longer. Why don't I just give you the "booster" mix? That's what guys like you normally go for."

Guys like me? Blackburn's eyes narrowed. "What's in it?"

"It's a bunch of vitamins, minerals, other stuff . . . you know, guaranteed to make you smarter and stronger."

"Uh, okay."

The old man muttered "bingo" again, scribbled something on the pad of paper, and then asked, "What flavor?"

"Let me guess . . . they're on the menu board, right?"

"See, you're getting smarter already."

Blackburn scanned the flavors: Vanilla, Chocolate, Chicken Enchilada, Ironworks Barbeque (named after a once-famous restaurant in downtown Austin), Kentucky Bourbon, Pina Colada, and Hong Kong. And three specials, today only: Monkey, Fintastic, and Sweat.

"What's Hong Kong?" he asked.

"Think about it. What would Hong Kong taste like?"

A man standing behind him leaned over and said, "It's good, Cantonese style. Throw in some jalapeno, and it's almost like Kung Pau."

Blackburn turned and looked at the man. *Ponytail, well-trimmed beard, white shirt, tie, jeans, boots . . . a techie, for sure.*

"Hey," the old man said, regaining Blackburn's attention. "Don't listen to him. We don't have jalapeno today. That's only on Thursday."

"What's Monkey?" Blackburn asked.

"Monkey is jungle fruit."

"Oh. And Fintastic?"

"Fish. You won't like it." The old man looked doubtful.

I won't like it . . . "What about Sweat?"

"You won't like that, either. It's mainly for body builders."

Opinionated much? "Okay . . . I'll have the barbeque." He'd heard good things about the Ironworks, which had shut down years ago, but apparently still licensed its "secret blend" of spices.

"Excellent choice." The old man scribbled on the pad, and then asked, "And how about texture?"

"What do you mean, texture?"

"You can have it cereal style, or whipped, you know, like mousse?"

"I don't . . . what do you mean by 'cereal style'?"

"Let me make this real simple: smooth or lumpy?"

"Uh . . . smooth."

"Bingo." The old man scribbled on the pad of paper, and then punched a small display, which triggered a wireless transaction with Blackburn's money account, wherever it happened to be, *assuming*, of course, that he was carrying his wireless identification pod. Blackburn ran his hands over his pants pockets. *Did I bring the damned thing?* He breathed a sigh of relief as he felt the small bulge in his back pocket. No currency was accepted at this restaurant, or, for that matter, any other retail business establishment in the civilized world. After the currency crisis of 2021, most countries had banned the use of coins and paper money.

The display spit out a small piece of paper. "Here," the old man said, handing him the receipt. "I'll have it ready for you in two shakes."

Blackburn watched the old man measure ingredients and dump them into the mixing bowl. A minute later, he had his lunch. The old man mumbled "Next," and the techie moved forward, ready to place his order. The first few notes of "Honky Tonk Woman" blasted from the jukebox.

Blackburn walked over to the drink bar, wondering if Mick Jagger was still alive. He helped himself to an iced tea, turned, and scanned the restaurant, looking for a place to sit, preferably near an attractive co-ed eating alone. But the place was jammed. He spotted a few empty seats at a large community table on the patio. He strolled through the doorway and offered a friendly "Hey" as he placed his tray on the table. He got a couple of grunts and nods, and took them as signs of acceptance. He sat down and started to eat. *Not bad . . . kind of a barbequed beef pudding.* After a few spoonfuls, he looked up and spotted the UT Tower in the distance. He smiled and tried to remember the name of the guy who had climbed up there that day, with a rifle . . . . *What year was that?* He tried to remember the date, and the shooter's name, as he shoveled more mix into his mouth.

Seconds later, a man slid into the seat opposite him. Blackburn looked up and recognized the techie who had been in line behind him. The techie was eating a chunky concoction that was deep purple. *Must be Monkey.* The techie introduced himself as "Smith."

Blackburn nodded. "Nice to meet you. Bill Blackburn. Call me Blackie."

"Blackie." Smith swallowed a mouthful of mix, smiled and nodded. "You go to UT?"

"Yeah, I'm a senior," he lied. He had enough credits to call himself a junior, but he was taking two senior level courses. *Who keeps track of what class you're in, anyway?* "What about you?"

Smith swallowed more mix, leaned back, and balanced a bottle of Lone Star Soy on his belt buckle. "I work in that big software lab, you know, down in Oak Hill?"

"Yeah, I think I've seen it a couple of times." Another lie, he'd never been to Oak Hill. "What kind of software do you write?"

Smith ignored the question, and changed the subject. "So, you like the mix?"

Blackburn paused for a moment as he chewed and then swallowed. "It's not bad. First time I ever had it."

"You've never had mix before?"

"Nope. Never."

Smith smiled. "Great stuff. It's got everything you need."

Blackburn's curiosity was aroused. "Everything? What do you mean?"

"It's got all the right proteins, fats, vitamins . . . you name it."

Blackburn tried to recall what his mother had told him—maybe a hundred times—about eating a balanced diet. "So . . . how do they get all of that out of wheat and beans and . . . whatever else they use?"

Smith leaned back and took another swig of beer. "It's all soy, my friend, all soy."

My friend? Blackburn stared into his bowl. "I thought it was . . . "

"It's all soy." Smith wore a satisfied look, a smug look, but frowned when he saw confusion on Blackburn's face. "Didn't you know that?"

"No," Blackburn replied, shaking his head. "I guess I didn't."

"Yeah," Smith continued, "this is the first mix bar in Texas that's all soy."

"No shit?" Blackburn used his spoon to poke at his mix.

"No shit, but, hey, don't worry about it. It's genetically engineered. I eat it all the time. Look at me." Smith raised a fist in the air. "Strong and healthy."

Blackburn raised a tiny spoonful of mix to his lips, sniffed at it, and finally popped it into his mouth. He chewed it for a few seconds.

"Good, right?" Smith grinned.

"Well, yeah," Blackburn couldn't help but grin back. "It tastes okay. I just didn't realize it was all soy."

"Yup, all soy." The smug look was back on Smith's face.

"Hmm." He'd have to ask his mother about this "all soy" mix. *Wonder if she's ever heard about it?* Blackburn's mind wandered before finally landing back on software. "So," picking up the conversation where they'd left it a few minutes ago, "what kind of software do you write?"

Smith looked surprised, but answered quickly. "Oh, I don't actually write software."

"No?"

"No. I just do some of the systems design"

"Oh." Blackburn grimaced as "Muskrat Love" assaulted his ears. *Who in his right mind would want to hear The Captain and Tennille sing this shit?* He looked around the patio. No one hurling or spewing or anything like that; no one seemed to be paying any attention to the music. He turned back to Smith. "What kind of systems?"

"Uh . . . financial systems."

Blackburn watched Smith stuff another heaping spoonful of mix into his mouth. *Looks like he's in a hurry.* "Financial systems . . . that doesn't tell me much."

Smith swallowed and took another gulp of beer. "Systems that look at trends in financial transactions. Does that tell you enough?"

"Trends. Is that a market research kind of thing?" Blackburn was always on the lookout for interesting new fields of study.

"Something like that."

"So, what brings you up here?" Blackburn blushed. He knew he had a tendency to ask way too many questions. "Sorry. I didn't mean to pry. It's just that we're a long way from Oak Hill." *What, eight miles? Ten?*

Smith swallowed more mix. "My sister. She's a student at UT. I'm meeting her in twenty minutes." Smith flicked his wrist and his cuff dropped an inch, exposing an implanted display. He glanced at it. "Fifteen minutes."

Blackburn's eyes lit up. "Nice. Can I take a look?"

Smith unbuttoned his cuff, pushed the sleeve up to his elbow, and extended his arm, palm facing up. Blackburn whistled softly. The flexible display extended from Smith's wrist almost to his elbow. The time, date, GPS locator, and an array of icons shone softly through a thin layer of skin.

"Wireless?" he blurted, not thinking. Then, recovering, he corrected himself, "Sorry, obviously it's wireless." Running wires through the human body had gone out of style years ago. He looked closely at Smith, looking for telltales of the other implants.

"You can't see them," Smith said, scraping remnants of purple mix from the sides of his bowl. "The implants, I mean."

"Sorry. I didn't mean to . . ."

"It's okay. Natural curiosity. The main transceiver is behind my ponytail."

"Mmm," Blackburn nodded. That was the most common location for the transceiver; shielding material and skull protected the brain, and drugs bonded to the transceiver's surface took care of any reactions to the RF. Blackburn had wanted an implanted computer since before puberty. But good implants were a privilege of the rich and famous. "What about voice and sound?"

Smith tapped his jawbone just beneath his ear, then drained his Lone Star Soy and stood up. "I've got to go."

Wow. Three implants. Top of the line. Blackburn thought he might ask Smith if he had a video eye implant, but thought better of it. He looked up at Smith. "If you don't mind my asking, how'd you pay for it?"

"The lab sprung for it. I need it for my work. Hey, see you around."

"Yeah." Blackburn watched as Smith walked through the patio and turned left, heading north toward the university. Sinatra was singing "Come Fly with Me."